Assassins

Nicholas Mosley was born in 1923. He is the
author of twelve novels, including *Accident* and
Impossible Object, and the five volumes of the
Catastrophe Practice series, *Catastrophe Practice,*
Imago Bird, *Serpent,* *Judith* and *Hopeful
Monsters.* He has also written two biographies,
a travel book and a book about religion.
Nicholas Mosley is married, has five children,
and lives in London.

GW00708106

NICHOLAS MOSLEY

Assassins

Minerva

*The characters in this book are entirely imaginary
and bear no relation to any living person*

A Minerva Paperback
ASSASSINS

First published in Great Britain 1966
by Hodder & Stoughton Ltd
This revised Minerva edition published 1993
by Mandarin Paperbacks
an imprint of Reed Consumer Books Ltd
Michelin House, 81 Fulham Road, London SW3 6RB
and Auckland, Melbourne, Singapore and Toronto

Reprinted 1993 (twice)

Copyright © Nicholas Mosley 1966
Revised edition copyright © Nicholas Mosley 1993

A CIP catalogue record for this title
is available from the British Library

ISBN 0 7493 9856 6

Printed and bound in Great Britain
by Cox & Wyman Ltd, Reading, Berks

Phototypeset by Intype, London

This book is sold subject to the condition
that it shall not, by way of trade or otherwise,
be lent, resold, hired out, or otherwise circulated
without the publisher's prior consent in any form
of binding or cover other than that in which
it is published and without a similar condition
including this condition being imposed
on the subsequent purchaser.

From the roof of a long stone house with battlements a man in a brown mackintosh looked down at a yard with stables; a girl in riding clothes walking across it. The roof of the house had sham turrets and a clock tower. The girl went through a stable door and its rectangle split into diagonals of darkness and light. She re-emerged pushing a white horse backwards, a tail and hooves slipping on the cobbles. The man on the roof faced sideways across a park and a small valley. At the bottom was a dark lake and a boathouse. The girl threw a saddle over the horse and leaned against it: she wore a brown cap with her hair scraped beneath it which made her face look big-boned and masculine. Across the valley were columns of dark and pale trees. The sun was behind the trees and the air misty. The man on the roof was a silhouette with a small thin head. The girl jumped on the horse and lay across it with one knee raised as it walked forwards over the cobbles.

The girl straightened and felt for the stirrups and sat stiff-backed like a guardsman. The drive went past laurels and rhododendrons and over grassland. The horse trotted and the girl bounced softly; her face pale and curiously concave. As the drive went down hill she leaned forward and put her mouth by the horse's ear.

There were lodge gates at the end of the drive with a wall going away on either side and beyond it a road. Two policemen stood in front of the gates. The girl pulled the horse up and it stood pawing the ground and blowing. The girl shouted 'Oh Silver!' She said to the policemen 'Can you open the gate please?' The horse went in a circle with its hooves flicking the gravel. A policeman turned to the gate and opened it. The girl shouted 'Oh do get up!' She kicked the horse and it shot through on to the road. She pulled at it again. She jerked to and fro like a metronome.

At the far side of the road were two young men holding a banner. The banner said *Freedom For* and then sagged, so that the last words were illegible. Under the banner, between the men, was a young girl wearing jeans and with long dark hair. They were like caryatids beneath a roof collapsing.

The policeman walked to the middle of the road and peered to right and left; he held his hand out. The girl said 'Oh thank you!' She kicked the horse and it cantered over the road and up a farm track opposite. Its hooves were silver in the flying mud. She stood in the stirrups with her body horizontal. The policeman walked back and closed the gates.

The track went up past a beech wood and a field of pigs which were yellow and black like small boats. There was a gamekeeper's cottage with a chimney of red and brown criss-crossed bricks. The girl turned off into the wood across a ditch and beneath branches. The ground was soft and the air suddenly hushed like a cathedral. The horse walked. She stroked its neck and kissed it and said 'Sorry.'

At the far side of the wood behind a beech tree in a hollow of brambles a young man knelt holding a rifle. He saw the girl approaching on the white horse; her face beneath the riding cap big-boned and somehow as if deathly. She was a young girl, not more than fourteen or fifteen. Bars of light from the trees ran up her like fire, and disappeared.

The girl came to the end of the beech trees where there was a ditch and the road again and beyond it the continuation of woods. She kicked the horse and it slithered over the ditch. Up the road, at about a hundred yards, was a car parked with policemen round it; a man with a blue overcoat and a walking stick. When he saw the horse he raised his arm and stood in silhouette like a scarecrow. The horse had turned its head back in the direction of the lodge gates; the girl pulled at it. The man with the overcoat began striding up the road and slashing with his stick horizontally. The girl got the horse's head round, kicked, and it slithered into the woods the way it had come. The man began to run awkwardly; he reached the place where the girl had been and looked into the woods after her. He was a tall red-faced man with a slight hair-lip. The girl and horse had gone some distance and were standing beneath a beech tree. The bars of light made them look camouflaged.

To one side, out of sight of the road, the young man with the rifle knelt with his head down and the rifle flat on the ground. Ants crawled towards the dark barrel and made a detour, bumping into one another busily.

There was the sound of motorcycles on the road. The man with the stick looked away from the girl towards the parked car and policemen. The policemen formed a line and stood to attention. The girl in the wood dragged at the horse which was eating bracken. The man with the rifle looked up and saw the girl's face hurt and angry. On the road there was first one motorcycle with a policeman in a white helmet who slowed, spoke to the man with the walking stick, roared the engine, shot away again; then six motorcyclists in formation wearing white gauntlets and white helmets and immediately behind, like pulled barges, two closed cars. The girl on the horse was jerked as the horse ate bracken. The man with the rifle looked towards the road. Within the second car there was a glimpse of men two at the front and two at the back and two in the middle facing backwards. The men in the front and middle were big, round-faced men; the two at the back smaller, a white blur. It was as if the men in the middle were facing nothing.

The man with the rifle, watching, did not move.

The girl on the horse put her cheek against its neck and breathed against it.

When the cars had gone, the man with the stick turned to the wood and called – 'Mary!' The girl on the horse did not answer. The police car came slowly along the road from where it had been parked. It stopped by the man with the

3

stick and after a time he turned and climbed in. It went on up the road after the other cars, in the direction of the lodge gates.

The girl pulled at the horse's head and shouted 'Oh I'm so bored of you!'

The man with the rifle saw the horse's startled face with bracken sticking out each side of its mouth.

The girl kicked the horse which cantered and slithered over the ditch and on to the road and across: broke into the woods on the far side.

The girl thought – A man kneeling behind a beech tree.

The man waited till the sound of the horse had gone: then picked up his rifle and began moving towards the road.

2

The man with the overcoat and walking-stick stood in the stable yard beneath the clock tower which had gold letters in Roman numerals against a black face. The man in a brown mackintosh appeared on the roof. The man in the yard called 'Jackson!' and the man on the roof answered 'Colonel Wedderburn sir!' He stood as if to attention leaning over the battlements.

Colonel Wedderburn said 'Did or did not anyone leave the house this morning!'

Jackson said 'Only Miss Mary sir.'

Colonel Wedderburn said 'Did I or did I not give orders that no one was to leave the house this morning?'

'No sir.'

'What do you mean, No sir?'

'I didn't get those orders sir.'

Colonel Wedderburn tapped his stick against his leg. His shadow was shortened underneath as if he were hammering it into the ground.

A man in a cloth cap and gumboots came out of the

4

stables pushing a wheelbarrow. Colonel Wedderburn shouted 'Watson!' The man lowered the wheelbarrow and took off his cap.

'Did you get orders that no one was to leave the house this morning?'

Watson scratched his head; bent down to see into the stable door which was divided in diagonals of darkness and light.

Colonel Wedderburn said 'Then why has Miss Mary gone out on her horse?'

Watson looked at the inside of his cap.

Colonel Wedderburn shouted 'God Almighty!'

A soldier in uniform came through an archway marching. He stopped in front of Colonel Wedderburn and stamped and stood to attention; he said 'Sir!' Watson picked up the wheelbarrow trudged forwards again. Colonel Wedderburn shouted 'Put that thing down!' The man on the roof began walking slowly along the battlements.

Colonel Wedderburn said 'Did you or did you not have orders that no one was to leave the house this morning?'

The soldier said 'Only official personnel, sir.'

Colonel Wedderburn said 'What do you mean official personnel?'

'Not members of the family, sir.'

'So you let Miss Mary out?'

'Yes sir.'

Watson had sat on the end of his wheelbarrow and was lighting a cigarette. His face in his cupped hands seemed to be burning.

Colonel Wedderburn shouted 'Jackson!' The man on the roof stopped. They waited. Colonel Wedderburn slashed at the cobbles as if they were nettles.

He suddenly turned and walked into the house. The others moved again as if the sun had come out.

In the house there was a corridor with a stone floor and white-washed walls and pipes like those on a ship; then a green baize door through which was another corridor, carpeted and panelled, with small tables and bowls of roses and bronze ornaments. There were people standing in groups, talking and holding papers. Colonel Wedderburn walked with his stick horizontal under his arm, the curved end forwards. Someone murmured 'Morning Charles' and he answered 'Mor-ning' in two notes with the second one higher. The corridor opened into a central hall with a staircase and a glass dome. Beyond it, where the corridor continued, were two soldiers in uniform. Colonel Wedderburn turned left in the hall and went into an office.

He put his stick on a desk and crossed to a window and looked out on to a terrace with urns and a balustrade. Two men in brown suits were on the terrace in the direction where the corridor continued inside the house. They leaned on the balustrade and looked out across the valley to the pale and dark columns of oak trees. The sun was on the lake and the water black. Colonel Wedderburn moved to the side of the window where he could see farther along the terrace. There was the wire netting of a tennis court and a conservatory.

In the other direction, in the stable yard where he had left the soldier and the man with a wheelbarrow, there was a swish of tires and one of the big black cars came in through the archway. A man in chauffeur's uniform got out and stretched. The policeman watched him. The car was empty. Watson dug a fork into his wheelbarrow. There was a whirr of pigeons overhead as they fluttered and landed at a dovecote. The man on the roof held a pair of field-glasses to his eyes; he looked out towards the boathouse, the distant valley.

3

The young man limped through beech trees stiffly as if with a wooden leg. He had dark curly hair brushed down on his forehead above a thin, rather delicate face. He stopped and listened. The trees made a green surface far above. He undid his jacket and pulled the rifle out of his trousers and the butt came up round his ear. He wore grey trousers and a tweed jacket with a belt at the back.

He went on through the wood carrying the rifle. He came to a fence and a field with bales of straw, walked round the edge holding the rifle upright against his body and then stopped again and sat and rubbed his ankles. He screwed his face up theatrically; acted as if demonstrating cramp.

The bales of straw lay on the field like fallen pillars. Beyond were the gold curve of the hill and the blue sky.

He walked on again carrying his rifle with his jacket draped over it. He came to a fir plantation and climbed the fence and went through branches with a hand in front of his face. The branches were dry and sticky. Beyond the fir trees was open ground and then more dark woods and bracken. He stuffed the rifle back into his trousers struggling with the butt like a crutch. He went across the open ground rolling exaggeratedly. On his right was a ride out through a slope of trees and in the distance above the bracken the chimneys of a large house. In the further wood he began dragging his rifle once more out of his trousers; baring his teeth and hopping. The trigger guard got stuck against his belt: a small curved mouth like that of a fish. He was moving over leaves with sticks making a cracking noise. On his right was a ridge of ground and beyond it the blue sky through branches. There was an oak tree in front just before the ground fell away. He leaned against it; got the muzzle of the rifle clear. He was at the back of the tree out of sight of the sky. The foresight of the rifle had scratched him as if he might have been gutted.

The tree against which he was leaning had large nails knocked into the trunk for climbing. Around the bottom of the tree was an area of trampled bracken and horse-droppings. The branches came low to the ground at the back. Up the tree, where the nails led, was a large wooden platform built with planks. The platform was on the branches looking to the front. He put a hand on a nail, testing it. The bark had pale green powder.

Climbing with the rifle held in one hand he came with his head above the platform and looked along the boards. There was a slight wind which moved the leaves against the blue sky. The boards were roughly nailed between branches; at the back near the trunk was a covered shelter with seats of packing-cases and a wooden playbox. He crawled and sat on a seat and looked out past the leaves: they blew like the sea. He put a hand down and opened the playbox: there was a mug, a teapot, a jar of sugar, a paraffin lamp and a box of matches. The lamp was rusty with blackened glass. The sugar was in a jam-jar and had gone into a lump like a specimen in a museum.

He laid the rifle on the planks and took from his jacket a telescopic sight which he slotted on to the rifle and adjusted with a small screw. The platform went out across two branches to where there were the sky and smoke and mist across the valley. When the branches moved they creaked like a ship. He picked up the rifle and crawled along the platform; went out on to a branch with his legs on either side and his hands on the rifle at a right angle. He came to a fork and leaned his elbows on it and lay stretched out; there was a screen of green leaves in front and to one side an open patch of sky. He crossed to another branch with the rifle making a bridge; lay there where he could see the smoke and mist of the house through the opening. There was the roof with battlements and the terrace with a balustrade and urns. At one end was a tennis court, at the other a yard with a clock tower. The branch swayed; he clung with claws like a cat.

He got his elbows resting on two branches and held them so that the rifle was aimed through the gap in the leaves. He looked through the sight and there was a circle with a cross and numbers calibrated; the cross floated up and down in blue sky. He moved his arms and the cross swung quickly past the front of the house and the terrace to a long green slope of grassland; then swayed up again, on a wave, past a chimney to the blue sky. He moved his legs and tried to hold his arms steady but it was the branch itself moving, making a hissing noise, a bowsprit above the sea. The sight of the rifle banged against his eye; the circle rushed past the front of the house and was lost in the grass and the misted leaves. He held his breath and lifted his elbows and pressed hard: there was a pain in his body and legs as if he were on spikes. The hairline wandered: the house seemed to have been removed as if by magic.

He let his breath out and rested his head on his arms. The wind made a tinny noise. There was the clink of metal and the sound of creaking again.

When he looked up without the telescope he saw the house quite clearly, the french windows opening and in front of them figures coming out on to the terrace. The distance was about six hundred yards. The air was steady. There were men in dark suits turning and looking back toward the windows; people coming out beyond them and moving hidden by their backs. The whole group was walking slowly along the terrace; the people in the centre surrounded, white and indistinct. There was a glimpse of a fair head, silver, and something lower, skin, someone bald. He put the telescope to his eye again and for a moment saw the men in blue and brown suits with the backs of their jackets jutting; then the branch swayed again and the telescope was jerking away across urns, the clock tower. The group on the terrace separated slightly and he saw, without the telescope, the tall man with silver hair and the shorter man who was bald. They stood with their hands on the balustrade and looked out across the lake and valley. There was a dip where the valley went down into the mist. Through the telescope again he swung past a spray of leaves; he gripped with his knees; the two figures were like flying fish; he felt sick. He pushed the safety catch of the rifle and worked the bolt. The metal was cold; it was as if it might freeze the skin off his face, body. The group on the terrace flashed past like mirages in a storm. He put the rifle down and rested. He was panting, as if in tears.

There was a noise on the platform behind him.

Swinging round and grasping with one hand at the rifle

he found himself collapsing between the two branches. With his other hand he lost contact with the tree, he was scraping down through leaves and nothingness. Above him, on the platform, was a young girl with fair hair. She was on one knee and was staring at him. He was on his back with the rifle jammed between branches. The girl had a strong-boned pink and white face. A spike of wood tore at him. The girl turned and began to climb down the trunk of the tree with her arms and legs like a bear. He moved the rifle and began falling again; his head was going down; at the bottom of the tree was a white horse tethered. He saw it upside down; its face looked up at him, eating grass. He landed on the ground with one wrist twisted underneath him. He turned and saw the girl just reaching the bottom; she wore a brown jersey and riding breeches and had hair like screens down the sides of her face. The horse was standing with its reins over a branch. He was on one elbow and was pointing the rifle at her. His wrist was numb. The girl was brushing her hair back. She watched him. His jacket was torn and his shirt had come out of his trousers. He had a pale face with hair down the sides. His nose was long and thin; he had a small, rather curly mouth. The end of the barrel of the gun was silver with notches where the sun shone on it: small shadows round the darkness of the hole.

4

On the desk in Colonel Wedderburn's office was a small piece of cardboard in the shape of a tent with *Lt. Col. Wedderburn* on it in black letters. Colonel Wedderburn had taken off his coat and was wearing a cardigan open down the front and a regimental tie. He sat at the desk and wrote diagonally across a large sheet of paper. There was a knock on the door and he shouted 'Come in,' and a woman appeared carrying an armful of files. She was about thirty-five with neat brown hair and a grey skirt and a cardigan open down the front. She raised one knee and rested the files on it to shut the door, putting her chin down on the files like a shot-putter. When she had finished this Colonel Wedderburn jumped up and said 'Connie!' and came round the edge of the desk and put out a hand which did not quite touch her. She moved into the middle of the room with her chin still on the files. Colonel Wedderburn put his hand just above the back of a chair and Connie sat in it.

She put the files down, crossed her legs, pulled at her skirt which rose above her knees again.

Colonel Wedderburn said 'Connie no one was to go out of the house this morning that was quite clear, wasn't it?'

Connie picked up a file, sorted a loose piece of paper, fitted it into the file. She had a pretty, sunburned face and a mouth that pressed into a pout.

Colonel Wedderburn buttoned up his cardigan.

Connie said 'No one was to go out of the house?'

Colonel Wedderburn tapped with a pencil; said 'Mary.'

'Oh dear, where has she gone?'

Colonel Wedderburn said 'She went out at half past nine. I saw her on the road at ten. It was just before they arrived.'

Connie said in a flat voice 'How dreadful!'

'Connie this won't do.'

'Shall I go out and look?'

Colonel Wedderburn flicked his pencil round in his fingers. He said 'Connie this isn't the point. I haven't got authority in this house. I'm not given authority. I haven't got a job here. I've got a non-job.'

Connie put up a hand and stroked the side of her mouth. She said 'But where has she gone?'

Colonel Wedderburn said 'And there's another thing. Apparently Watson doesn't think he comes under my authority. The position is impossible.'

Connie looked up at him with blue eyes. She said 'But shouldn't we be doing something?'

'What do you suggest?'

'Well, look.'

'She's gone into the woods.'

'Then I'd better go after her.'

'She's gone on her horse.'

'Oh, you didn't tell me she'd gone on her horse.'

'I told you Watson. Why d'you think I told you Watson?'

Connie said 'I can't think.' She pressed her lips out.

Colonel Wedderburn leaned across his desk; said 'Cut it. Stuff it, Connie.'

Connie looked at her outstretched fingernails.

Colonel Wedderburn said 'What I want you to do is put it to him that I can't run the show without authority. Tell him that. For the next three days.'

Connie said 'What was she doing on the road?'

'Crossing it.'

'I mean, what was she doing after she crossed it?'

Colonel Wedderburn said 'Anyway what's the point? I haven't got the men to look.'

Connie said 'I thought you meant it was serious.' She smiled.

Colonel Wedderburn said 'What's funny?'

Connie said 'I thought you were going to say – What's the point of bolting the stable door after the horse has gone.' She spoke in a mocking voice.

Colonel Wedderburn said 'I can do this too, Connie.'

A bell rang outside. Colonel Wedderburn stood, began putting on his jacket. He said 'You don't care anything about that child.'

Connie sat with her file on her lap.

He said 'Poor bloody child.'

Connie said 'Is there anything else you want me to do? Can't you do it yourself then?'

Colonel Wedderburn said 'That's all, Connie, thank you.'

He went to the door. He turned leaning on his stick. Her legs were crossed; she had thin ankles on which the stockings were like loose skin. Colonel Wedderburn waved as if saluting, or blowing a kiss to her.

5

In the corridor of the large country house there was a movement like a current among the standing groups; a putting-down of tea cups, a folding of newspapers, a turning to high wooden doors beyond the hall on either side of which men stood in uniform; the doors opening slightly not enough for anything to be visible but with an air of a curtain going up on a dark stage; a smell of the cold, of backyards; a man's arm in a white cuff and a dark jacket coming through for the handle on the outside and somewhere a bell ringing. The men in uniform stood to attention. The doors opened farther and a murmur of voices came out and a man with dark hair and spectacles appeared. He moved past the soldiers and the groups and bowls of flowers and in the central hall of light met Colonel Wedderburn. He said – 'The tricoteuses?'

Colonel Wedderburn said 'Out at the back.'

The man with spectacles said 'They've got two minutes.'

He turned under the stairs and went into a porchway to an outer door at the side of the house opposite to the terrace. He put his head into the sun. On an oval sweep of the drive was a crowd of men carrying cameras, laughing and smoking. They were behind a rope which was looped on sticks with men in uniform at either end. One of the crowd raised a hand and called 'Mr. Seymour sir!' The man with spectacles looked round, smiled, his head cut off in the doorway.

'Nice weather we're having Mr. Seymour!'

Seymour looked up, screwed his eyes, his glasses flashing silver.

The men behind the ropes began moving into a line, flicked their cigarettes out, pulled at the straps of their cameras. Someone threw a fircone; a head ducked, feet slithered on the gravel.

Seymour's head disappeared.

In the corridor the high wooden doors were opening again showing jambs lined with velvet; beyond were two lines of men like bearers at a funeral, big men in brown and blue suits coming through stiffly and herding into the passage and behind them, or in the middle, two men, one tall and grey and stooping, the other bald and with a beard. The tall man leaned as if waiting for the small man to speak; which he did not, facing in the opposite direction as if acknowledging cheering. They were emerging from a large formal room with eighteenth century portraits and long mirrors; an oval table in the middle, chairs, papers, glasses, blotters; at the back french windows on to the terrace. The tall man paused by the high doors to make way for the other, the top of his head in black-and-white lines like a comb, the small man bowing to make way for him, they were like two comic Chinamen. They gave up and came through the door together. The men in brown and blue suits moved ahead down the corridor. In the hall Seymour was standing with Colonel Wedderburn watching the two approaching and laughing. The tall man leaned slightly sideways as if on a ship; the small man held his hands across his front like a monk. As the tall man went past Seymour stepped forwards and said quietly 'Does the people need a pee?'

The tall man put his hand on Seymour's arm; altered the angle of his head. The small man had stopped in the hall under the dome of light.

Seymour said 'We said two minutes.'

The tall man bent down to the small man and said 'Can you spare two minutes?'

The small man put his head sideways. A man in a striped suit, just behind, came up and spoke in his ear.

The tall man looked up at the dome of light.

The small man nodded. The man in the striped suit said 'Two minutes.'

Seymour had gone ahead to the porchway door to the drive. He held it open. They went through, the tall silver-haired man ducking, their backs like elephants. In the sunlight they blinked. Men in brown and blue suits had gone ahead of them into the drive; stood in a curve facing outwards.

The line of men behind the ropes raised their cameras and clicked. They pressed together, jostled and worked their elbows. The men who had been playing with the fircone ran and joined the line. Someone called 'Sir, can you give an indication – '

The tall man looked into the sun, put a hand up, shaded his eyes. In the distance parkland went in rolling slopes to the lodge gates. Trees were dotted in small clear groups.

'Mr. Foreign Secretary sir, have you taken into account the very strong feeling in this country – '

Seymour, by the door, held a hand up.

The tall man had stuck his chin out and was smiling. He touched the small man on the arm. The small man looked up, smiled, held his hand out. They shook hands, in profile, like cardboard cut-outs. The cameras clicked.

'Sir Simon, are you discussing with Mr. Korin the question of political prisoners?'

A slight wind had appeared. The tall man, Sir Simon, put a hand to the side of his hair. He turned back towards the house. The small man, Korin, stayed in profile against the stones. The man in the striped suit spoke in his ear.

Seymour, a hand on the door, murmured 'Workies!'

Korin, listening to the man in the striped suit, nodded, frowned, took a step forwards and began orating in a foreign language. He cut at the air with his hand sideways like a sickle. Sir Simon came and stood stiffly by his side. The men in brown and blue suits moved inwards.

A voice from the crowd shouted 'Can we have a translation of that please?' There was a roar of laughter.

Sir Simon smiled, his top lip like a visor; then dropped his jaw as if he were amazed, patted his stomach and said 'I want my cuppa!'

There was another roar. The crowd jostled, clicked, turned with their backs and made adjustments to their cameras.

Korin leaned to the man in the striped suit who whispered in his ear.

Korin laughed; gripped Sir Simon by the elbow.

The photographers seemed to be climbing on one another's shoulders.

Korin and Sir Simon moved towards the house. The men in brown and blue suits followed, their backs crowding as if they were going into a tunnel. The photographers split up and began moving towards the parkland. They wandered a certain distance with coats, elbows, straps flapping; then suddenly ran, as if in response to an alarm, struggling up a slope to a line of cars on the horizon. The cars shimmered with heat off metal; the men bending towards them hung with equipment.

6

Mary walked through woods slightly behind the boy with the rifle stepping over brambles, creepers, keeping to his tracks, falling behind; then he would turn and wait for her and she would come up dragging her legs and elbows through the bracken. He had said 'Follow.' He had a belt at the back of his jacket with two leather buttons. His hair came over his collar. Mary's clothes were sticky and her blouse came out of the top of her breeches. When the boy stopped he put both hands on the rifle and watched her. He had a long thin face and a straight nose. Mary had said 'Where are we going?'

They were on the edge of the fir plantation. There was wire netting along the ground to prevent the pheasants running. The gamekeeper sometimes came here and hung jays and stoats from a stick. They were going along the wire towards the beech woods. She had left her horse Silver beneath the tree. It would pull at the bridle which would come off over its eyes and ears. It eyes were soft like water.

The boy was peering on either side through the beech trees. Mary said 'I can't go on.'

There was a buzzing as soon as they stopped. Flies landed on the bracken like ash.

When he had fallen through the tree and had pointed the rifle at her she could have walked away towards the house. She could stumble and pretend to twist her ankle; her face in pain. He walked slightly ahead of her and when he turned and watched her she pushed her hair back. It was hot. She could run through the beechwoods with her hair and arms flying; be set on by black dogs, as in a painting.

Her ankle hurt. There were gaps between the bottom of her jodhpurs and her shoes. The brambles tore at her.

The beech trees had smooth trunks. Running, she would trip and he would put the rifle against the back of her neck. She would lie with her face on the ground and her hands clasped behind her. The point of the rifle would be sharp and cold. He would shoot and she would throw her arms out, sinking down in the leaves and the light that was like a cathedral.

The boy stopped by barbed wire. He said 'Wait'. He had a slight foreign accent. She could not think what to say. She stood on one foot and rubbed her ankle.

He had walked some distance away and was looking down a ride towards the road. He was quite old, about twenty-three or four.

He said 'Come on'.

The sun was on the back of her head like a mist. Her feet crushed insects in the bracken. She was a giant treading on crowds in cities, running with their arms up.

Sometimes she and a friend went for walks like this at school. On Sundays, with the trees golden. The girl in front with brown legs and scratches.

She said 'I'm hot'.

His jacket with the belt was ugly. It drooped upwards as if he were on a hook.

She said 'I won't tell anyone. I mean, that you were here.'

They were coming down towards the road. He was trying to put the muzzle of the rifle down his trousers.

She thought – On the road I'll start running.

There was a peculiar smell about him, dry and dusty. She took a deep breath and felt tightness in her nose and lungs. Her heart thumped.

She had felt fear, and a violent cold. She was aware of this as if she were wide awake for the first time. She was unbearably lonely.

The grass was in thick tufts so that she had to fling her arms out to prevent herself from falling.

He was climbing over the fence. He pointed the rifle at her and she pushed her hair back.

She lifted one leg over the fence and the wire cut her. She hopped on one foot and pushed the wire down and screwed her face up.

He came back to her. She put her hand on his shoulder and the cloth was sticky. His hair was like feathers.

They were going down through the beechwoods again. They came to the ditch in front of the road. Her heart was just behind her eyes, at the top of her brain. She had to stretch her mouth to breathe. He was groping for something in the ditch. She looked up the road; there was the stone arch of a culvert. He was digging; he had buried something. He might bury her in the ditch.

She moved towards the road.

He had put the rifle down and was pulling at something under the culvert covered with bracken and dead branches. Along the road was nothing; she was on her own in the sunlight. She was about a mile from the lodge gates. He was pulling from the bracken the handlebars of a motor-scooter. She was on the road clenching and unclenching her hands; the road was crumbling at the edges, pale grey gravel above tarmac. The gravel slipped. He called to her. She was sure she was going to die. She looked at the brown and grey stones. They had been chipped off rock by men hitting them: there was a pain in her head, lungs, stomach. The bright air was a wall. She heard him running behind her and she began to run, her legs swinging sideways as if over waves. He hit her on the side of the head. She went to the side of the road and fell, putting her hands over her face. Her head seemed broken. She slid to the ditch and sat waiting for the pain. He had hit her with the rifle. She took a hand away and there was cold white flesh. The pain came in and she drew in her breath and chewed. She dabbed at the side of her face and looked at her hand again. Her ear was broken. The boy was standing over her with the rifle. She kept one eye closed and the pain came in and she rolled sideways. The stones were sharp. She took her hand away; at last there was blood. It was soft and hot above her ear. The boy squatted and rested his fingers on the ground. He said 'I told you!' His voice trembled. His eyes were empty. There was the sound of a tractor on the road. She was lying on her face near the ditch, underneath the level of the road. The noise of the tractor was closer, in small puffs like explosions. He was trying to lift her by the elbow. She remained limp so that his hands dragged up as if undressing her. He knelt with his head close and said 'I'll kill you!' He had black eyes and slight hairs at the edge of his mouth and the inside pink. His nose touched her cheek. The tractor went past with a man with fair hair and a red face, an exhaust pipe blowing. The boy's face was pressing down on her. She looked at her fingernails which were bitten. His face was brown with moles under the skin. There was the smell of dust and of burning paper. The tractor had gone past. He pressed with one hand on her knee and when she looked up she saw again that he was afraid. She thought – I could defeat him.

He was pulling at her by the elbow. She stood up. They walked back in the woods below the road towards the culvert. He had an arm around her. The trees were misty. They came to the motor-scooter where it lay on its side in the ditch. It was like a dead animal. He let go of her and lifted the scooter and the rifle knocked it and got in the way. She licked the blood on her hand which tasted of metal. He pushed the scooter till it faced up an incline to the road; he propped it against his knee and beckoned to her. She lifted her shoulder to her ear and blood went on her jersey. He dropped the scooter and came towards her; she put her hands in front of her face. The scooter twisted like something gutted. He took her by the arm and she went with him to the scooter and he propped it again and she put a leg over and sat. He picked up the rifle. Her jodhpurs were in a tight line across the seat. The seat was like a zebra. He was putting the rifle into a canvas case which had a long strap along the back; he raised this above her head and she put her hands up as if he would hit her. He was trying to get the strap of the rifle-case over her head. He pushed it down as if her arms were being tied: she shook her hair; she lifted one elbow so that the rifle case was slanted across her back like a guitar. He sat on the seat in front and pulled at the scooter and kicked it. The seat bounced and she had to put her arms forward to steady herself. He kicked and the scooter started. He took her arms and pulled them to his front. Her hands were limp. He hit at them and she put them together and clasped him. She tossed her hair back. The top of the rifle case was against the back of her neck. The scooter jerked up the incline to the road. She clung, as if to a stake. They were swerving over bumps and the saddle hurt her. She pressed her cheek against the back of his neck. His hair was like the feathers of a bird. She pressed her legs against the sides of the scooter. They were on the road suddenly and were travelling smoothly and accelerating. The air was rushing past and over the world, and they were alive.

7

In the large formal room with eighteenth century portraits and long mirrors there were men seated around the oval table with their arms resting beside papers, glasses, blotters; at the back, along the walls, were other men in brown and blue suits standing; beyond them were the sun and the french windows and the distant line of oak trees. At the centre of the table on one side was the tall man with silver hair, Sir Simon; on the other, the small man with the beard, Korin. At the end of the table a man was reading from a sheet of paper holding it like a mirror. He was saying 'Phase one to include items one to six in the schedule apart from the provisos of paragraphs (a) and (b) and to be completed in such time as – ' he waited while the man in the striped suit whispered into Korin's ear. Sir Simon suddenly glanced high and to his back: Seymour, standing by the wall behind him, stepped forward. The man at the end of the table said ' – to be decided. The figure of two hundred and fifty thousand to include members of the regular armed forces – ' he put down one sheet of paper, picked up another ' – and those designated. In the original schedule. Phase one.' He looked up quickly.

Seymour had put his face down to Sir Simon's, who whispered in his ear.

Opposite, Korin turned away from the man in the striped suit.

Sir Simon nodded.

Korin spoke in the foreign language.

The man in the striped suit said 'The schedule?'

The man at the end of the table said 'The figure of two hundred and fifty thousand.' He ran his hands down the edge of his sheets of paper.

Seymour, behind Sir Simon, began making faint gestures with his hand no higher than his waist to a man in a blue suit on the far side by the window. The man peered round; gazed along the terrace. There was a man in uniform by the balustrade. The man in the blue suit looked back to Seymour and raised his eyebrows. Seymour pursed his lips and gently blew.

The man at the end of the table said 'The question of designation.'

Seymour made small pushing movements with his hands.

Sir Simon said 'There's no precedent.'

The man by the window sucked his lips in; drew his eyebrows together; quietly put a hand on the latch of the window.

The man in the striped suit leaned towards Korin's ear. Korin gazed at one of the eighteenth century portraits of a lady in a gold dress and a wig. The man by the window pressed the latch, went down on his haunches, and with one arm stretched above him groped for a bolt. His neck was slightly purple.

Sir Simon said 'The status.'

Korin, his hands on the table, his eyes towards the portraits, began orating in the foreign language. The man by the window unscrewed a knob on a brass bar: pushed the window which opened with a bang. A man beside Sir Simon drew his chair closer; watched Korin; when Korin stopped he said quietly 'As Chairman of the Central Committee of the People's Democratic Republic I have made it plain in public statement and utterance – ' Sir Simon gazed across the room at the light blowing in through the curtains; dust hung like insects; Korin's voice came and went. The man beside Sir Simon said 'The settlement by negotiation of all outstanding – '

The man by the window screwed tight the brass knob, rose to his feet, trod on the foot of someone next to him, lurched, looked carefully round the room. Seymour nodded.

Sir Simon scribbled on a piece of paper *It is not my intention now. Will surely understand not only my own position but that of nevertheless a qualified optimism that a breakthrough.* He spun the pencil round and crossed out the last word and put two exclamation marks after it. He looked up. At the top of a black-dusted mirror was a scroll and a bunch of grapes. The dust was like a black cloud. Korin spoke, stopped, stretched his lips sideways as if he were cleaning his teeth. The man beside Sir Simon said 'On numerous occasions during the last five years – ' Sir Simon whirled his pencil and drew a picture of a fir tree; a cloud of locusts coming in. The edges of the tree were like saws. A cold white slope with wavy lines. Underneath he wrote *the sheen of their spears like snow on the sea.*

The man beside him said 'The efforts of the People's Democratic Republic since nineteen fifty-seven – '

Korin finished speaking. He looked round sharply to the window where the curtains blew. A man in a brown suit had stepped to one side of the window. He was looking out, with his hands behind his back, as if he were expecting someone from outside.

Seymour stood on tip-toe trying to see the terrace.

The man at the end of the table smoothed his papers and banged them.

The door opposite the window opened and Connie came in. She carried a pile of files, leaning back like a water-skier.

Sir Simon tapped on the table and said 'The definition?'

The man beside Korin spoke. Korin spoke. The man beside Sir Simon said 'Let us get on then.'

Sir Simon said 'By all means.'

Seymour had raised an eyebrow at the man in the blue suit by the window.

Korin held up a hand. Sir Simon put on a pair of spectacles, looked over the top of them at Korin; Korin smiled. The man by the window bent and began unscrewing the brass knob again. Korin spoke. The man beside Sir Simon spoke into Sir Simon's ear. He said 'That's what we're here for.'

Sir Simon said 'It has always been our position that from the point of view of the schedule this item is unnecessary.'

The man by the window was closing it again.

Connie moved round the wall till she was standing next to Seymour. She put a hand on his arm and pulled his face down to hers: she was pressed close to him as if they were sharing an umbrella. She pursed her lips and whispered 'Trotsky?' Seymour looked round smiling. He shook his head.

23

Sir Simon said 'We've dealt with this. There is some urgency.'

Korin was standing up at the other side of the table. Men in brown suits were behind him watching. They had their hands in their pockets like gangsters. Korin spoke.

Sir Simon had pulled towards him the piece of paper with the drawing of the fir tree. He made the line blacker down the jagged edges. Korin's voice got lower and more emotional. The bottom of his eyelids rose till they appeared convex. Sir Simon wrote *They burn themselves*.

Connie had let go of Seymour and they were standing side by side looking out across the terrace. Beyond the balustrade and line of urns and silhouetted against the distant trees a white horse had appeared moving with its saddle empty and the reins pulled down around a leg. It limped with its head jerking and the stirrups kicking it. A policeman was following running a few steps behind and when the horse stopped, slowing and holding his hand out. The horse tried to kick and the reins tripped it. It went down on its knees like a ship sinking.

Connie and Seymour watched. Connie's mouth pressed into a pout. Seymour's spectacles, reflecting light from the bright windows, became bright with distortions of the terrace and oak trees. He turned to Connie and raised his eyebrows, his hands folded like a priest. Connie began moving towards the door.

8

Colonel Wedderburn sat in a Land Rover facing the lodge gates and looking through to where at the far side of the road a tall young man with crew-cut hair carried a banner of white lettering on a black background saying *Free the Students*. Beside him was a girl with long dark hair wearing jeans. A few yards away, separated by the farm track, were two cars parked against which men leaned carrying cameras. They laughed and smoked occasionally kicking stones on the gravel. The two groups took no notice of each other.

A policeman was standing by Colonel Wedderburn, who said 'Is that the same lot as this morning?'

The policeman said 'No. They change the guard.'

Colonel Wedderburn said 'Those girls all look alike.'

The cameramen turned to the Land Rover and held their cameras in front of them and watched.

Colonel Wedderburn said 'You didn't see a horse?'

The policeman looked along the wall at the edge of the park.

Colonel Wedderburn said 'Come this way. Some time ago.'

The policeman said 'No.'

Colonel Wedderburn nodded towards the men with cameras: 'They didn't?'

The policeman looked back over the parkland, to the distant house.

Colonel Wedderburn said 'Open the gates then.'

While the policeman walked forward the young man holding the banner shifted it to his other hand and moved his feet and looked at the sky. The girl with long hair moved close to him. Colonel Wedderburn thought – Like prisoners about to be shot.

The gates opened and Colonel Wedderburn drove through. The cameramen held their cameras up. He went past turning right along the road and accelerated. In the driving mirror he saw some of the men climb into a car and follow him.

He drove a mile till he came to the place where he had seen Mary come on her horse from the woods. He stopped, remaining seated. It was a bright day. She had been coming from the left, had turned back, might have continued across the road after he had gone. The car with the cameramen had stopped some distance behind.

In front of him was a culvert. There was an incline by it on the right down which he could get the Land Rover.

The bracken had been trampled. There was a ride up through the woods.

One of the cameramen had got out of the car and was walking towards him, made miniature in the driving mirror.

He would need dogs. They could start from the house, or perhaps from here.

The cameraman called 'Colonel Wedderburn sir!'

Colonel Wedderburn, facing his front, chanted 'Morning!' in two notes, the second one higher.

'Nice weather we're having!'

Colonel Wedderburn started the engine; sat with his eyes screwed up and a hand on the steering wheel as if he were already travelling.

'And what brings you out this morning sir?'

Colonel Wedderburn chanted 'Rou-tine!' in a high pitched voice, the second note falling.

The cameraman looked back along the road. He was beside Colonel Wedderburn. He said 'A nice bit of routine by the gates! Wouldn't mind a bit of it myself!'

Colonel Wedderburn said 'Where do they go when they change the guard?'

The cameraman said in a sad voice 'Colonel Wedderburn sir! Where do flies go in winter?'

Colonel Wedderburn wrinkled the corners of his eyes. The cameraman was leaning on the Land Rover. Colonel Wedderburn put it into gear and moved off fast. The tires kicked a few stones back. He sang out 'Thank you!' like a bird-song.

The Land-Rover slid off down the incline past the culvert. It crashed through bracken and sticks and disappeared into the wood.

The cameraman brushed at his clothes. The car that had been following came up to him.

Colonel Wedderburn bounced up the ride with beech trees on one side and the fir plantation on the other, still driving fast, so that he was jerked about as if being beaten up, one hand on the wheel and the other on a bar by the windscreen. The wheels skidded over tufts; span sideways like a bull's back legs. He came to the top of the ride where it opened above the valley. Beyond was the view of the house, its mist and battlements.

He stopped and switched off the engine; listened.

He hooted the horn. He said in a voice quiet so it would not carry – 'Mary?'

He climbed out of the Land Rover and walked along a fence at the top of the ridge. There was a gap before the beginning of oak trees.

The sun steamed. Flies were on the bracken like dead bodies.

There was an oak tree in a clearing with long horizontal branches. Beneath it was bracken that had been trampled and horse droppings. He leaned with a hand on the trunk of the tree. The trunk had nails in it.

Looking up, he saw the platform of the treehouse. There was no wind. The treehouse was like the nest of some enormous bird: a fortress into which a ladder could be pulled up so that it would be safe from any animals and from enemies.

9

The scooter drew up in a country lane by honeysuckle and a broken gatepost past which a path went down to a cottage of which only the roof showed above grass. Mary had her arms round the boy in front; her chin underneath his shoulder. The lane was beneath tall hedgerows. The boy revved the engine and it died: in the quietness there was the sound of a tractor on a distant hill. The boy took her hands and unclasped them and got off the scooter and leaned against it. Mary stretched her shoulders and scratched her leg. The boy touched her shoulder. She got off the scooter and he pushed it to the gate to the path towards the cottage. He turned and watched her. She still had the rifle case across her back; was pulling it over her head. When it was clear she went ahead of him down the path. He followed with the scooter. The cottage was in a hollow of unkempt grass and weeds. Beyond it were willow trees and a slope towards a valley; a small wood and corn-fields on the far side. The upstairs windows of the cottage were boarded. A path went round to the back to a garden of nettles and old fruit trees. There was an outhouse that looked like a lavatory. A path went on towards the willows and valley. The boy wheeled the scooter to the back and propped it against a wall. He looked in through a window. The back door was padlocked. He took a key and pressed it in the rusty slot. He stood aside for Mary; put a hand out for the rifle.

Inside was a passage from the back door to the front, a staircase going up on the left. The walls peeled with the underneath of wallpaper yellow. A door led into a kitchen on the right with a table and plates and cutlery and a teapot. There was a jam-jar of sugar in a lump like a geological specimen; a paraffin lamp with cracked and blackened glass. Mary stared at them. The boy was putting the rifle into a cupboard behind the door. There were benches along each side of the table. Mary sat with her hands between her knees, her hair tossed back.

They were in a room of grey wallpaper with pink roses; a patch where a picture had once hung. The sun came in from the window at the back and warmed her. There was dust in bars.

The boy had taken from the cupboard a transistor radio in black and white plastic. He put it on the table; pulled an aerial up one side like grass. He sat on the bench opposite. He switched on the radio and there was the sound of a pop-group singing falsetto. Mary put her hands over her ears. The boy fiddled with a knob and noise flicked past like bullets. Mary screwed her face up.

The boy switched off the radio. He said 'Who are you?'

Mary, her hands on her ears, shouted 'What?'

He said 'What's your name?'

'Diana.'

'Diana what?'

'Perry.'

She had put her hands down. He switched on the radio again. He moved his jaw as if in time to the music.

Mary shouted 'I can't hear!'

He switched off the radio. The silence was like a light coming and going.

He said 'Where do you come from?'

'Hassington.'

'What's that?'

'A village,'

He looked beyond her out of the back window into the garden. He held the radio in two hands as if he were aiming it at her.

Mary clasped her stomach and rolled her head as if she were ill.

He said 'What were you doing?'

'Where?'

'In those woods.'

'Riding.'

'Why?'

Mary shouted 'God, what d'you mean why?' Her hair had fallen in front of her face so that it was as if she were breathing through a narrow gap like a goldfish.

He stood up and went to the kitchen range which was old and rusty with a kettle and a saucepan on it; he stuffed some newspapers and sticks in the grate.

Mary said 'I've said I won't tell.'

He said 'Tell what?'

'Are you one of those people?'

'Who?'

He was lighting paper and smoke blew into the room.

Mary said 'They were at the gate this morning.' When she spoke her voice jerked out of control, like a difficult horse.

He blew at the paper. Dust flew up and a flame appeared.

He said 'What gate?'

Mary went red in the face. She looked round the room and blinked.

There was the grey wallpaper; the pink roses like slugs. The place where the picture had hung watched her. Blood seemed to be rushing to the top of her head, to make her unconscious.

She shouted 'I'm on your side!'

He said 'How old are you?'

'Fifteen.'

'You look more than fifteen.'

'Oh everybody says that!'

He put more sticks on the fire, opened the kettle, looked in, moved it over the fire, took the lid off the teapot. There was milk in a carton.

He said 'Do you like tea?'

'Yes.'

'Sugar?'

'Please.'

She held her hands squeezed between her thighs. The pain in her stomach had lessened, like cold water warming around her. Her head throbbed and made her feel sleepy. The boy moved about the room quietly with his long sad face. He had thin fingers. When he put the lid on the teapot he turned it as if it screwed. The sun came in; the room seemed to sway slightly like her treehouse, with the jam-jar and the teapot and kettle.

He put two mugs on the table and butter and a loaf. He cut some bread, squeezing it with dirty fingers. The knife crumbled it. His fingers seemed to taste in her mouth. He went back to the grate and poured from the kettle. She said 'Thanks.'

Tears came into her eyes.

He switched on the radio again and a voice said 'Today talks began between . . .' He switched it off.

She was in the quiet room with the sun outside and the smell of cooking. He had taken his jacket off and was in a white shirt open at the neck. The sleeves were baggy like a dancer.

She said 'Why do you want me?'

He said 'I don't.'

'Then why do you keep me here?'

'I'm waiting.'

'What for?'

'Someone.'

He was making tea, pouring into her mug. The end of the teapot was chipped. She couldn't remember who he was, or what she was doing.

She said 'Let me go.'

'It's too far.'

'I can walk.'

He looked startled. 'No.'

'I could say I fell off my horse.'

He touched the bottom of the teapot; sucked his finger. The wood of the table was grooved like railway lines.

She shouted 'Why did you take me then?'

He said quickly 'So you couldn't go back.'

'But I didn't see you.' Then – 'You don't believe me do you?'

'No.'

She shouted 'Oh honestly!'

She sat with her hands round her mug. The china burned. Lifting it, she held it in front of her face so that steam drifted up past her nose, eyes. Like this she was guarded. He sat opposite her across the table. The two of them seemed not to exist: to be in her imagination.

She sipped the tea by stretching her top lip over the mug and sucking. She blew on it and the surface folded back like the Red Sea. She rubbed her lips along the top. She pressed her legs together. She was imitating a bee.

When she looked up again he was watching her and smiling. He had white teeth which were long and narrow. He said 'Go on.'

She said 'Go on what?' She pushed her hair back from her face and it fell forwards again.

He nodded towards the door. He said 'Try it!'

She moved restlessly. She said 'I don't want to!'

He was acting something different: rubbing his hands along his thighs, as if listening to music, the bottom of his face falling in.

She said 'I think you're mad!'

His face lengthened. He said 'Little girl!'

Mary stood up and climbed over the bench. She began to move slowly towards the door. He waited till she had her hand on the handle then he got up and stood beside her. She remained still. He leaned towards her, his narrow trousers like paper. Mary turned the handle of the door. He took her by the shoulder and pulled her and put her head under his arm and squeezed. She said 'Ouch!' Her hands moved on his arm like spiders. They walked back like this towards the table, her body horizontal, her face down by his belt. She put her hands out behind her. He did not squeeze hard. She could feel him breathing. They stood there. Then he suddenly let go; it was as if she were falling; which was not what she had expected.

10

In the large country house Connie put her head round the door of Mary's room and saw it neat and impersonal with frilled dressing-table, a bed smoothed with coloured pillows in a star, chairs facing an empty carpet, things put away, hidden, behind coloured panels. Connie closed the door and crossed the room. On the dressing-table was a photograph of a woman with short fair hair and pearls; a three-piece mirror on legs like those of a tortoise. Connie opened a drawer and saw powder, hairgrips, letters, nametapes, a broken pen, a comb, reels of cotton, lipstick, foreign coins and a tube of veganin. She thought – Things you could cut yourself with? In another drawer was a diary with an elastic band round it lying amongst stockings and white silk. Connie took the diary. She crossed to a built-in cupboard of grey-green paint and a panel of flowers; pulled the door and on to the floor fell coat-hangers, a tennis racket, gramophone records, cardboard boxes, a riding whip. Connie pushed at the pile with her toe. The records had bright shiny covers. On two or three were pictures of boys with brown jaws and long white teeth; their hair coming over their eyes like feathers.

Connie went to the bed and sat holding the diary. She closed her eyes. She imagined Mary's large flat face and full mouth; Mary sitting on the floor with her blouse coming out; Mary a child with no mother. Connie pulled at the elastic band round the diary: Mary climbing into bed with elastic round her waist; her skin mottled.

Connie opened the diary. There was thick, rather neat handwriting.

April 13th. He has not spoken to me for two days. Oh God why does this happen? Today I was in the dining room when he came in. He stood with his back to me. I DID NOT EXIST. I never, never knew there was such pain.

Connie looked up at the photograph on the dressing-table. The fair-haired woman fingered her pearls. At the bottom was written 'To darling Mary from her father June 1957'.

She had gone off with some man to Rhodesia: had died there.

Connie turned a page. *I went with Silver today on the ride through the beech trees. There is an outlet by the lake where if he trod unwarily a horse might get sucked in. Silver knows this. He is a good horse. He knows where to put his feet.*

Connie thought – I wonder if there is anything about me.

A folded letter fell out. In spidery handwriting was *Dearest Woman What a long time no h* - and then the drawing of an ear. *I am speckled at the news of p.t.d. Did you get Fanshaw? Such nose of douce*

Connie turned the letter this way and that. The word speckled might have been speeched.

She remembered her own schooldays. There had been a dormitory under a sloping roof, noises from a green and white tennis court. The air seemed to burn. She had been ill one summer. A girl had come in and had lain on her bed. The stretched tendons of knees, thighs.

Connie flipped the pages. She read *I suppose I will never forget the moment of shame. But life must go on, and I only don't know how to manage it. I shall always be alone. What aeons in prospect!*

Connie turned back a page. *What am I to say? Is it never to be mentioned? It is not only that I feel ill. I DON'T FEEL ANYTHING.*

Connie turned back a page. *Yesterday at this time when it happened.*

Connie turned back a page. *What am I to do when I see him? It is not just that he was drunk*

Connie said 'Oh no!' She closed the diary.

She began, in her imagination, to have a conversation with herself. She said 'Girls always imagine this'. Then – 'But this doesn't stop it being true.'

There were footsteps along the passage. Connie's heart jumped.

The door opened and Seymour's head came in. His body followed in a shiny black suit like that of a woman.

Connie said 'Andrew!'

She put the diary behind her back. He shut the door and came over. He said 'You look as guilty as Mary!'

She said 'But what's the news?'

He said 'Nothing.'

'But what do you think?'

'Well, she fell off.'

He went to the dressing-table and peered at the photograph of the woman with fair hair. He said 'They're looking now.'

'Who is?'

'All the king's horses and one or two of Charles Wedderburn's men.' He picked up the photograph.

She said 'But she might be hurt.'

'Indeed.'

'But have you told him?'

34

He came to the bed and stood close to her. When he looked down his spectacles had rings in them like a target. He said 'Connie. No.'

Connie smoothed a finger down the side of her lips.

He said 'Once Charles Wedderburn lost a railway train and they couldn't find it.'

Connie put a hand gently on his arm. She said 'You don't think – '

He said 'Possibly.'

'Really?' Connie looked amazed.

'But the official line is – No.'

Connie still had one hand behind her back with the diary. She said 'Why did you come here?'

'To see what I could find.'

'So did I.'

'And did you?' He went to the dressing-table and stared at the photograph again. The woman had a long neck like a dancer.

Connie said 'I feel so dreadfully – '

Andrew Seymour said 'How old was Mary when Celia went off? Did she ever stay with Celia and Johnny?'

'I don't know.' Connie brought the diary round from her back and held it in her lap.

Andrew Seymour said 'I did think Johnny the most frightful shit, didn't you?' He came back and stood by the bed. He had his hands in his pockets. His dark jacket flapped widely. He said 'There's nothing we can do.'

Connie said 'Then what can we?'

He said 'You do look nice on that bed Connie. What a big girl for such a small bed!'

Connie said 'I found her diary.'

'I know.'

'How do you know?'

Andrew Seymour said 'I always wanted to see a young girl's diary!'

Connie opened the diary. She said 'They were all round the gate this morning.'

Andrew Seymour said 'Come on let's have a look. Has she got any boy friends? Does she have any fantasy life?'

Connie said 'How extraordinary you should say that!'

He walked round the room. He said 'What is the novel in which two people have read a young girl's diary?'

Connie said 'She may be lying there out in the woods, helpless.'

Andrew Seymour said 'Charles is looking. Dear Charles in the end is competent.'

Connie said 'Andrew, she doesn't just fall off her horse!'

Andrew Seymour stood still. His spectacles glittered at her. He said 'I'm not going to tell Simon. He's got too much on.'

Connie said 'He is her father.'

'And I'm going to tell Charles Wedderburn not to.' He spoke like a schoolmaster, his hands behind his back. 'Now, what's in the diary?'

'I thought you'd read it.'

'Children always make up their diaries. Girls write them especially to be read.'

'You know who it's about?'

'It isn't true. You can tell by the style.'

She said 'Simon?'

'If it was true it wouldn't have been said.'

She said 'Don't you say anything that's true then?'

He said 'Like the Cretan who said all men are liars? No, psychologically.'

She said 'Andrew, I don't see how you can!'

'Have read her diary?'

She said 'You protect Simon so much!'

He came and stood close to her. He said 'You know, on that bed you're almost virginal.'

Connie put her hand on her face; said 'Do stop!'

He put his hand on her head and twisted it from side to side. He said 'I do love the back of your neck. It's like the first peel of a mango. Do you know that smell?'

Connie said 'You don't want me to say anything?'

'Not at the moment.'

Connie suddenly sat upright and straightened her skirt. She said 'I do think it's fascinating, don't you, how they have a private language of their own?'

Andrew Seymour said 'Come on we've got a lot to do.' He went to the door.

Connie followed and put a hand on his arm. Standing close, looking up with her mouth slightly pouted, she said 'She's so terribly lonely. Can't we find her some friends?'

Andrew Seymour smiled. He said 'I'm her friend.'

She took her hand away. She said 'Anyway I'm going to do something.'

Andrew Seymour said 'Have you tidied the bed?'

Connie said 'We haven't untidied it.'

She crossed the room and put the diary back in the drawer.

Andrew Seymour looked out carefully into the passage.

II

There was a movement like a current again in the corridor of the country house; Sir Simon appearing round a corner followed at a few paces by a man in a blue suit, moving down the corridor with his head lowered and his movements slightly jerky as if in a gale. Colonel Wedderburn stepped forwards in the hall and said 'Sir, can I have a word?' Sir Simon said 'What is it?' With no change of momentum they went on past a stained glass window and bowls of roses and a statuette of a horseman with a lance through a dragon's mouth. Colonel Wedderburn said 'Your daughter Mary went out riding this morning and her horse has come back but no rider.' Sir Simon said 'I thought there were orders that no one was to go out.' Colonel Wedderburn said 'I know sir, but unfortunately they were disobeyed.' Sir Simon said 'What do you mean unfortunately?' He reached a door at the side of the corridor; waited with his hand on the doorknob. Colonel Wedderburn said 'My authority didn't extend to a member of the house.' Sir Simon said 'Don't waste my time.' He opened the door and went into a small room lined with books and black curtains and an armchair and a table on which there was a decanter of whisky and a jug of water. Colonel Wedderburn followed; the man in the blue suit stayed outside. Colonel Wedderburn said 'We've got men looking for her sir.' Sir Simon sat and unfolded a rug that had been lying on a footrest. He said 'When did she go, what time, when did the horse get back?' Colonel Wedderburn said 'About nine thirty sir, the horse got back soon after eleven. I didn't want to disturb you sir.' Sir Simon said 'Who knows about this?' His feet stuck up beyond the rug; elastic boots came above his ankles. Colonel Wedderburn said 'I've got men sir – ' Sir Simon said 'Who knows, who knows, that's English.' He drew his lower lip in, puffed his cheeks out. Colonel Wedderburn said 'Only one or two members of the household.' Sir Simon said 'See they don't talk. See no one else knows it.' Colonel Wedderburn said 'Yes sir.' Sir Simon was taking out of his pocket a small bottle of pills; he unscrewed the top. He said 'You think she's fallen?' He reached behind him; said 'Get me some water will you?' Colonel Wedderburn went to the table; said 'I'm sure it's just a toss.' He handed a glass. Sir Simon said 'They'll be through those woods like a pack of wolves.' He swallowed the pills and held a hand on his stomach; lay back with his eyes closed. There was a rustle of soot falling down the chimney. He said 'Find her. And let me know.' Colonel Wedderburn said 'Right sir.' He went out.

In the corridor he turned right and came to an opening where there was a small spiral staircase. He went up, climbing two steps at a time in darkness lit by embrasures like arrow-slits. The steps were of stone. He came to light at the top and stepped out on the roof with wide lead guttering and battlements. Taking deep breaths and forcing his shoulders back he looked out on the landscape as if it was a battlefield. In front was the valley going down to the lake and the boathouse and the dark line of oak trees; to the left and right the clocktower and stables and conservatory and tennis court and long grey roofs jumbled like a village; behind, parkland dotted with elms and puffs of cloud. The battlements seemed close to the clouds as if a ladder had been drawn up and they were floating. There was an impression of the desert; of flags on poles and bugles.

The man in the brown mackintosh came along the battlements. Colonel Wedderburn said 'Did Harris go with the dogs?'

'Yes sir.'

'And how many men?'

'Six.'

'Don't let anyone else then.'

He rocked with his hands behind his back: frowned at the sun, at its angle against his eyes.

Crossing the terrace, and beginning to hurry down the slope of grass towards the lake, was the figure of a woman in a brown skirt and cardigan clasping her arms in front of her.

Colonel Wedderburn leaned over and opened his mouth; was silent as if he would not be able to make himself heard; then ran to the staircase.

The man on the battlement leaned over; heard Colonel Wedderburn clattering like a stone down a well, saw him reappear on the terrace viewed from above like a shortening shadow. The shadow moved quickly after the woman past the balustrade and urns, catching up with what was ahead of it. The woman went down a path hidden by fir trees.

The man on the roof stepped back; patrolled behind the battlements.

Colonel Wedderburn saw Connie in front of him and trod off the path on to a grass verge. He walked on his toes with long steps like a camel. Connie was moving through bars and zig-zags of light made by fir trees. Colonel Wedderburn came up close behind her and clapped his hands and said 'Bo!'

Connie jumped with her hand on her heart; her eyes wide.

Colonel Wedderburn said 'The big bad wolf!'

Connie was beneath a fir tree like a squirrel.

Colonel Wedderburn said 'You're not to go wandering around.'

Connie said 'You did frighten me!'

She took deep breaths; smoothed her skirt down; said 'I've got to look!'

'I've got men looking.'

'I know. Oh Charles, what d'you think has happened?'

She peered behind her as if for a chance to escape.

He said 'Now Connie, is there any reason, or anyone you can think of who might know, why she might have gone off on her own?'

They stood on a slope beneath fir trees as if on a mountain.

She said 'On her own?'

'Or is there any indication about who she might have gone off with?'

'But surely she's fallen?'

The sun was behind Colonel Wedderburn which made his eyebrows and his mouth seem misty.

He said 'She had a tree house in the woods.'

'I know.'

'In it there was a teapot, a jar of sugar, and a loaf of bread.'

'She adored that horse!'

He looked round. His face became dark red against his collar and his pale brown jacket.

He said 'Will you go up to her room and see what you can find?'

'I've done that.'

'Did she have any friends? Is there a letter or something?'

'Charles, who could have?'

Colonel Wedderburn said 'You don't just fall.'

Connie sat down on the bank by the path and put her head in her hands. She said 'I feel so dreadfully – '

Colonel Wedderburn said 'There are enough of those monkeys by the gates.'

Connie looked up with her mouth open; held her stomach as if she were ill.

Colonel Wedderburn said 'Did she have a boy friend?'

'She's only fourteen!'

He tapped his leg: said 'They start young.'

Connie stood up and brushed at her skirt where pine-needles had stuck to it. She said 'Who's going to tell him then?'

He said 'I've told him.'

'But Andrew Seymour said – '

'I don't give a – ' he made a farting noise ' – what Andrew Seymour said.'

Connie stood at some distance looking at the ground. She said 'If she's fallen they'll find her.'

He said 'But we're not allowed to make it public.'

She blinked.

Colonel Wedderburn said 'This is the serious stuff you see. None of your pen-pushing.'

Connie said 'We know she wasn't happy.'

12

Amongst a row of cars parked along the side of a street in West London in one, a red Mini, a man in a dark grey mackintosh sat reading a newspaper. He turned a page every few minutes and looked at the advertisements for jobs in universities abroad and vacancies for engineers. The street was a crescent with porticos and pillars slightly crumbling. At the bottom of the newspaper he held a notebook open in which there was writing in a foreign language. He twisted a pencil up and down. Out of one door with grey pillars appeared a young woman pushing a pram. The man in the car looked at his watch. The woman lowered the pram down the steps pulling at it like a horse. She had long dark hair and a green coat. The man in the car wrote in his notebook.

When the woman had gone round a corner the man in the car climbed out and locked the car and followed her round the corner. There was a busier street with a notice HADDON ROAD. Stalls were out on the pavement with cans of fruit and vegetables. The woman had stopped some way up by a milk machine. She put in a coin and waited and pulled out the drawer. The man in the grey mackintosh walked past and stood by a notice-board: there was a double divan room on the third floor to let; removals by van; part time work in the evenings. The woman had gone into a grocer's shop; had left her pram inside the doorway. The man went to the window and saw his reflection in the glass – a round face and dark grey hat and behind him in the street vans and bicycles. The woman was beyond the barriers of cans; the bicycles in a white light moving in the window. The name of the shop, in gold letters, was EDWARDS. There was a black woman behind the cash register knitting. He tried to see into the pram; a blue coverlet hid a round object – a loaf of bread or a baby. A man in a tweed coat had come up and was standing by the noticeboard beside him. The man in the mackintosh moved away; after a time turned and found the man in the tweed coat following him. He walked past him back again to the noticeboard. Accommodation for gentlemen only: a club for companionship after 6 p.m. The man in the tweed coat had followed and was standing beside him. The first man turned suddenly and smiled. The man in the tweed coat looked round quickly. The first man said 'You're not very good at this are you?' He spoke in a slight foreign accent. The man in the tweed coat said 'No.' His hands were shaking. The first man walked into the grocer's shop and looked at the pram. Inside was the top of a gas cylinder wrapped like a baby. The woman was talking to an assistant behind a pyramid of cans with pictures of alligators. The man in the tweed coat had followed him. He went out again, still with the man in the tweed coat who said 'Couldn't we have coffee?' The first man was walking up the street the way he had come. A policeman in uniform suddenly appeared round a corner. The man in the tweed coat went quickly back towards the grocer's. The first man looked round. There was a wall just in front of him with a door marked GENTS. He went through into an area of rust and concrete; a row of doors like cells. He locked himself in. He could hear the footsteps of the policeman outside; a shadow on a frosted pane of glass. He took his hat off; stood as if to attention. The footsteps went past. In the darkness, and the sound of rushing water, he made out on the walls drawings and faded writing as if in a cave. He sat down, ran a hand over his hair, took out a packet of cigarettes. To one side on the wall on a level with his face was a drawing of a woman and in her lower middle, suitably placed, a peep-hole. He put a finger over it; looked round, startled; tried to light a cigarette with one hand like a conjuror.

13

Mary lay on a bed in a bare room with a wooden floor and whitewashed walls. The window had two pieces of wood nailed across it behind which there were flies and a bee trying to get out. She lay on a striped mattress sewn with small circles of leather curling at the edges. She held one between finger and thumb and pulled and it was like a bit of skin coming off. On top of her was a piece of rug with rough canvas backing. She had taken her shoes off and had put them neatly under the bed; beside the bed was a chair with an empty plate. The noise of the radio came through the floorboards from downstairs. She pressed her hands against her stomach and wrinkled her nose; gasped and rolled her head from side to side. On the radio the music stopped and there was the sound of a man talking. Mary raised her knees and listened. The bee trapped between the boards and the panes of glass in the window buzzed loudly. The walls of the room had big brown stains like continents. The piece of leather on the mattress had come away in her hand; she felt cold; she groaned and bit her lip. She swung her legs over the edge of the bed and sat up and felt for her shoes. They scraped on the floorboards. The radio downstairs was giving out the weather report. The wind and the sea was in rocks and caves; black clouds moving. She hobbled across to the door with her fists pressed into her stomach; she knelt and put her cheek against the boards where there was a gap at the bottom of the door. A draught blew against her eye. She put up a hand and pulled at the door which was locked. She clenched a fist and banged; waited. The voice downstairs softened and retreated like a wave. Mary raised herself and crept to the bed. The voice on the radio appeared to be coming up with footsteps, on the stairs. She sat and held her hands between her legs. The radio came along the landing towards the door. The door was at an angle with the jambs as if someone had heaved at it. A key was put in the lock and a woman's voice on the radio said 'Later this afternoon housewives' theatre presents – ' The door opened. The boy looked taller in the doorway; his thin clothes and long sad face. The radio got loud and soft as it twisted where he carried it. Mary said 'I've got to go out.' The voice on the radio said 'Hughie is the son of Lou and Annie is his girl friend.' Mary pressed her fists into her groin: said 'I won't be a minute.' The boy looked back on to the landing. The voice on the radio said 'Who is engaged to Anthea.' Mary crossed the room and went past him on to the landing where there was a window and the narrow wooden stairs. The boy said 'You'll have to go out.' Mary said 'I know.' She began going downstairs, the smell of dust and mushrooms. The boy followed her. On the radio there were pips and a man's voice – 'Here is the news.' Mary reached the bottom. The man's voice said 'This morning Dr. Korin, Chairman of the People's Democratic Republic, drove to Hassington Grove, the Foreign Secretary's house in Sussex. He is to have talks with Sir Simon Mann over the weekend. Twenty-five schoolchildren were hurt when a bus – ' Mary was standing in the short passageway at the bottom of the stairs. On her left was the door to the kitchen with the table and bench and teapot and jam-jar; beyond, the door to the garden. The boy sat on the bottom step of the stairs; he said 'Wait.' There was a place in the wall where the plaster had crumbled and slats were showing. The wireless had an aerial sticking up like a sword. The voice said 'Talks began today at Hassington Grove in Sussex between the Foreign Secretary Sir Simon Mann and Dr. Korin, Chairman of the People's Democratic Republic. Dr. Korin drove from the embassy in Portman Square in London with a strong police escort and roads and woods leading to Hassington Grove were guarded. There have been no serious demonstrations against Dr. Korin since the incident in Portman Square earlier this week: but pickets carrying banners hostile to Dr. Korin were at the gates of Hassington Grove yesterday and this morning. The talks at Hassington Grove are unofficial, but the subjects expected to be covered are the strengthening of diplomatic relations between the two countries, the expansion of trade, and the question of reduction of armed forces in Europe. It is not expected that there will be any discussion about the political prisoners still in detention after the Students' Revolt of two years ago. It was in protest against these detentions that the demonstrations against Dr. Korin have taken place.' There was a pause: Mary had the heel of one foot on the toe of the other; was pressing hard. The voice said 'At Malden in Essex a party of schoolchildren – ' The boy switched the radio off. In the silence there were bees flying between wood and the windows. The sun came in through bars of light. Mary moved towards the back door. The boy stood up and followed her. Outside there was heat as of a greenhouse; air proliferating. The cinder path went down through nettles towards willows. The boy leaned against the back door. Mary said 'I won't do anything.' She went down the path holding her arms up above the nettles. The nettles had collapsed in patches like whirlpools. She came to a fork in the path where one branch went to the outhouse; the other to the willows at the bottom. The outhouse leaned like a spoon in a jam-jar; there was a buzzing from it as of bees, of a black crust rotting. She put her hands to her head; her hair felt like salt. She looked back at the boy who was leaning against the doorpost of the cottage. She lifted her arms high and walked off the path among the nettles. She came to a hollow of rubble of bricks and stones; stopped; squatted with the tops of the nettles covering her. The nettles had thick stems like fir trees. There was the sky without clouds coming close and hurting her. She took hold of a stone; hit against a brick which broke. Bits of dust came off on her fingers. There was the heaviness of insects dragging at the bells of blue flowers. She closed her eyes; she shivered and felt warm. She put a hand back to steady herself. When she opened her eyes there were silver and gold specks floating. She edged forwards on her knees among thick weeds like spears, their blades behind her waiting.

When she stood up the boy was some way down the path, watching her. She pulled down her jersey; went through the nettles and up the path looking at the cinders. There was a rain-tub at the back door propped on bricks. She passed the boy and went into the cottage. There was the door into the kitchen with the fire and the teapot and the jam-jar. She said 'Can I go in?' and added 'I won't go away.' She sat and took hold of the teapot and peered down the spout. She said 'I promise.'

He sat opposite her and folded his hands on the table. He nodded, as if humming.

She said 'The insects are terrible.'

He said 'Not for this time of year.'

She pushed her hair back. She put a finger into the spout of the teapot and turned it.

She said 'Ants can eat anything. They can strip a horse in a matter of minutes.'

He said 'They'll be taking over soon.'

She wrinkled her forehead as if listening to something

behind her. She said 'I don't know. They can't go out of their dimension.'

He smiled; a hollow look as if he were being strangled.

She said 'Oh don't look at me!'

He said 'Why not?'

She said 'I don't like being looked at.'

She turned back to the teapot. She put the spout to her mouth and blew.

He said 'Ants can digest concrete.'

Mary did a quick high-pitched giggle. She pressed her hand over her mouth.

He said 'They've a very advanced social structure. They use their children for gum, when there's a hole in their nest.'

Mary frowned; shouted 'Are you mad?'

He said 'They squeeze them. Do you know how they feed?'

'No.'

'They lick each other till they're sick. Then they eat it.'

Mary did a small scream: looked at him with hot eyes; drew back with her mouth open.

He said 'They keep cows. They put them out on grass-land and eat what they produce.'

She said 'What do they produce?'

He smiled.

She shouted 'Oh come on!'

He held his head to one side; pulled his mouth straight; closed his eyes and seemed to press. Then he exploded through his nose and giggled.

Mary had gone red in the face. She shook her shoulders, leaned forwards and bit her fingers.

He said 'They tickle their sides – '

He turned sideways and flipped under his arms as if he were a fish.

Mary rocked; put her forehead against the table.

He stood up and groped his way forwards as if in the dark: then in the corner held his stomach and bent his knees and groaned.

Mary made a crying noise: said 'Do stop!'

He came back to the table and sat down opposite her.

She pulled out a handkerchief and wiped her eyes; held it to her nose.

There were bluebottles banging against the walls. He took the teapot and peered down the spout. She ran her finger along the grooves in the table which were like pencil-marks.

He said 'What did you think I was doing?'

'When?'

'In the woods.'

'Nothing.'

'But I must have been doing something.'

She said 'I thought you were just in the woods.'

She frowned and pushed her hair back.

He said 'It's trespassing.'

She said 'Not if you don't damage anything.'

'But I was. I might have.'

'That's the law. I know it.'

He took the lid off the teapot and held it to his eye so that he looked at her through the tiny hole for steam like an optician.

He said 'You know that house through the trees?'

'What house?'

'Who is it lives there?'

She said 'Some important person or other I should think.'

She thought – This is like games we play. I've been playing these games all my life.

He said 'Do you know how far it is to that house?'

She looked behind out of the window: pretended to look behind out of the window.

He said 'A thousand yards.'

'It's a thousand yards from here to the house?'

He shouted 'Not from here stupid!'

She said 'Oh.'

'Would I say it's a thousand yards from here to the house?'

She looked back at him. He had taken the lid down from his eye. His face seemed in different pieces, patches of red and brown on an oval.

She said 'I don't know.'

'What I meant was – ' He shook his head.

He was pushing at the top of the table as if driving splinters underneath his nails.

She said again 'I didn't see you.'

'I was after rabbits.'

'Yes. They're coming back again. After having been almost wiped out.'

He said 'I thought you were someone else. I still think you are.'

'Well I'm not.'

She put her cheek down on the table. There were breadcrumbs like boulders.

He said 'We'll need some food.'

'Yes.'

'Can you cook?'

'Of course.'

By focusing and unfocusing an eye she could flick distances backwards and forwards like a tennis ball.

She said 'Where do you come from?'

'London.'

'No I mean originally.'

He said 'Oh. Guess.'

'Somewhere in Europe.'

'Yes.'

'Oh I know!'

'Where?'

'No.'

Her hair got into her eyes and she blew at it. It was like strands of honey. She said 'I think England's finished.'

He said 'Why?' Then – 'You shouldn't say that.'

His face was both ugly and beautiful, like a dog's.

She said 'Oh, I don't know. They're so stuffy. Talking all the time. Blah blah blah. They don't mean what they say.'

He watched her. She was like a surface about to boil; a sea in a thunderstorm.

She said 'They think they're serious, but they never are. It's all a game.'

14

In the evening the sky grew dark for a storm. Sir Simon sat in the small room with the table with the jug of water and the pills and the decanter of whisky. The leather arm-chair had a writing board propped in front of him. The trees outside were swept with the glisten of rain. An electric fire was on. Walls were lined with books. By the window Andrew Seymour held an evening paper to catch the light. Sir Simon said 'The figure of thirteen million.'

Andrew Seymour said 'Of our share.'

'How was that got?'

'They did an estimate; a question.'

Sir Simon wrote on a piece of paper propped in front of him.

He said 'I'll try this for the telly.'

Andrew Seymour went to the table, poured whisky, splashed soda, some of which went on his sleeve, pulled out a handkerchief, dabbed, saw that the soda had gone on the hand holding the handkerchief, looked round, the sky outside dark as metal.

Sir Simon read 'I do not think it right at the present time to go beyond my statement of the whatever it was, twenty-eighth. I said then it was the policy of the government to explore all possibilities of decreasing tension in Eastern Europe and contributing to world peace. The visit to this country of the Chairman of the People's Democratic Republic is at the invitation of Her Majesty's Government and with this end in view. Next. Although talks with Dr. Korin have been interrupted by the indisposition of the

Prime Minister – ' He broke off. He said 'There's a story I'll tell you later.'

Andrew Seymour said 'Good.'

Sir Simon went on ' – topics dealt with have been those in the forefront of all our minds, and I think it fair to say that no awkward questions have been shirked. There is no question of such talks being aimed at establishing agreements that will affect in any way this country's present commitments in Europe or elsewhere. Our Allies have naturally been informed. And so on. That's one they'll jump on.'

Seymour said 'Yes.' He read the evening paper behind Sir Simon's back.

Sir Simon said 'Next. There are many matters beyond the question of defence, our previous commitments, and doubtless the scope of the imagination of some members of the opposition, which have been touched on by Dr. Korin and myself. Yes. As I understand it, their argument is, that we make contact with the people of Eastern Europe by censuring them, a position ambivalent even for ostriches.'

Andrew Seymour said 'Equivocal.'

Sir Simon said 'Equivocal.' He wrote.

Andrew Seymour said in an actor's voice – 'Have you discussed, sir, with Mr. Korin the question of the many hundreds of students imprisoned for two years without trial and reported to be in conditions of grave hardship; of Dr. Korin's personal responsibility for this both at the time and now; and do you not think that before any negotiations the question ought to be raised as to their release?'

Sir Simon said 'While I have every sympathy for this point of view, no, it cannot be part of government policy to dictate to other governments about internal affairs.'

Andrew Seymour said 'Swindlesod'll be on to you.'

Sir Simon said 'The opinions of the government on this and other such matters are however well known.'

Andrew Seymour said 'Turn it back on him.'

Sir Simon said 'I have.'

Andrew Seymour said 'He's just back from West Africa.'

Sir Simon wrote; then read – 'The occasions on which the government feels it right to comment on the internal affairs of other countries are necessarily limited, as you yourself Mr. Swinnerton will agree.'

Andrew Seymour said 'Do you know what Malcolm said about the telly boys? The gentleman's dilemma – such pricks as you can't even kick against.'

Sir Simon, writing, said 'Oh where would we be without them, they let us go to the country, the only sane thing, instead of having to rely on the stupidity of our peers.' He timed the last word like a comic.

Andrew Seymour said – 'In view of the dangers of public hostility, demonstrations, sir, do you not think that this visit has been ill-timed?' He took a sip of whisky; said in his ordinary voice 'Also the question of Korin's security and so on.'

Sir Simon said 'Security can be left to the proper authority.'

'In view of past experience.'

Sir Simon said 'Good old security.'

Andrew Seymour, standing under a lamp to read the evening paper, said 'There's been a crowd round at the embassy again. Who's doing it?'

Sir Simon said 'Thirty per cent Peace Front, thirty per cent universities, and thirty per cent fascists of one sort or another. The usual indistinguishable mixture.'

Andrew Seymour said 'Not communists.'

Sir Simon said 'Communists'll play the double game. Back him in public and kick him in private. They're not fools.'

Andrew Seymour said 'The people most to lose from Korin are the diehards.'

Sir Simon pushed the writing rest forwards; lay back in his chair. He said 'Korin's more vulnerable than any of us. He's hated by the left because of the students and by the right because of us. Yet what do left and right mean nowadays? Korin's a pragmatist; a Talleyrand. One of the great equivocators, Talleyrand. Agent-general for the clergy, friend of Mirabeau, exiled by the Girondins.' His voice took on a hypnotic lilt. 'Engineered the coup d'etat of Bonaparte, the abdication of Bonaparte, the reconciliation of Europe – ah – a great idea, still the only real one, never popular.'

Andrew Seymour said 'No.'

Sir Simon said 'Do you know what Napoleon said to Talleyrand? – "You would sell your own father if you could establish proof of ownership." ' He chuckled.

Andrew Seymour said 'A modern advice.'

Sir Simon said 'What good to they think they do?'

Andrew Seymour folded the paper; walked round the room. 'The demonstrators?'

Sir Simon said 'You're in touch with young people Andrew. Can you explain why they don't enjoy themselves more? Why there seems to be this appalling lack of pleasure?'

Andrew Seymour said 'Oh they've got nothing to rebel against.'

Sir Simon said 'We don't give them anything to?'

Andrew Seymour said 'Not unless something extraordinary happens.' When he walked he rolled slightly as if the floor were lurching. 'That's why we need it.'

There was a knock on the door. Andrew Seymour went to open it.

Connie was in the passage. They whispered. Connie came in holding her hands clasped in front of her. She said in a slow voice 'I'm so sorry but Mary's still not back. And they haven't found her.'

Sir Simon said 'Where's Wedderburn?'

'He's gone to London.'

Sir Simon said 'I told him to search those woods. Has he or has he not done that?'

'Yes.'

'Which?'

'He has.'

'Then will he personally give me a report as to his findings, and will he supervise what is to be done next and inform me of it; and will he personally report to me why the instructions he gave out at the beginning were not kept?'

Connie said 'Yes.'

Sir Simon shouted 'Well what is it?'

'Can I ring up Mary's friends and see if she's gone – '

Sir Simon said 'Are you suggesting that in the middle of these three days when I am engaged in a certain amount of complex work, that in the middle of a security check of a certain degree of seriousness, she has been allowed to go off without announcement to some friends?' He spoke like an orator.

Connie said 'I knew you didn't want it known.'

'Who are these people?'

'The Perrys.'

'Who are the Perrys?'

'Her friends.'

Sir Simon said 'And Wedderburn's got all the police out like an army through those woods – '

Connie looked at the ceiling.

Sir Simon said ' – and we're going to be held up to ridicule, the whole business of government held up to contempt, for a child, for those incapable of looking after a child, the whole of security diverted from a head of state for a girl who has gone out to tea with her neighbours. Is that the story?'

Connie said 'She might have broken her neck.'

Sir Simon said 'I thought you'd said she'd gone to tea with the Perrys.'

Connie said 'I only said that because it's so odd they haven't found her. I wanted to ring up and find out.'

Sir Simon said 'This is what you will do. First, you will enquire of all the staff of this house if they know anything. If you've already done it, do it again. Second, you will telephone the Perrys. But do not, I repeat not, let them know anything is unusual. Third, you will find Wedderburn and tell him to report back here. Fourth, you will report to me yourself in one hour. Is that clear?'

Connie said 'Yes.'

Sir Simon said 'Do it then.'

Connie said 'She might have been kidnapped.'

Sir Simon said 'Will you get out.'

Connie went to the door and closed it quietly behind her.

Andrew Seymour was by the standard lamp with the evening paper. Sir Simon held his hands to the electric fire and rubbed them. He said 'Ten-thirty tomorrow is what, Iran?'

Andrew Seymour said 'Yes. Do you want the stuff?'

Sir Simon said 'In the morning?'

Andrew Seymour took a notebook from his pocket and wrote. He walked to where Sir Simon had put his glass of whisky on the floor, picked it up, took it to the table.

Sir Simon lay back in the chair and said 'What Connie was suggesting was that I'm not a good father so Mary has to run away at a time when it will cause maximum inconvenience to myself, thus fulfilling all predictions of juvenile behaviour, which is all my fault, and she just has to be brought back and given a treat for supper.'

Andrew Seymour was studying a print of Queen Victoria and the Duke of Wellington riding in Windsor Park.

Sir Simon said 'Can you explain if in the Freudian system it is possible to blame a child for anything? And at what age does the sad change occur?'

Andrew Seymour said 'I don't think anyone ever gets blamed.'

Sir Simon said 'It's a marvellous world.'

Andrew Seymour said 'That's why they get so little pleasure.' He came over to the chair. 'People like being blamed. So they won't have guilt.'

Sir Simon said 'Ah. Get me that stuff now will you Andrew?'

Andrew Seymour said 'The Iran stuff?'

'Yes.'

Andrew Seymour went to a drawer in a desk and pulled papers out. He said 'You were going to tell me that story about Malcolm.'

Sir Simon said 'Yes. You know he's seeing this psychiatrist?'

Andrew Seymour said 'Yes.'

'Well, the psychiatrist said to him – Do you know the origin of shingles? And Malcolm said – The action of water, the symbol of the unconscious, on the perpetually exposed rock-face.' He chuckled.

Andrew Seymour placed the papers on the writing desk. He said 'That's very good.'

15

Colonel Wedderburn was shown into a room with dark green walls and white mouldings and a large mahogany desk. Behind it was a tall red-faced man with almost invisible red hair. He said 'Charles.' Colonel Wedderburn sat at the side of the desk and took out a gunmetal cigarette case; tapped a cigarette and leaned forwards to get the case back in his hip pocket. The man with the red face said 'A noggin.' Colonel Wedderburn nodded and felt in his waistcoat with a finger and thumb like an arrow. The man with the red face said 'Here': he pushed across a box of matches. A woman appeared at the door: Colonel Wedderburn held up a lighter and flicked it. The man nodded to the woman who went out. Colonel Wedderburn lit his cigarette; arched his back to get the lighter back in his waistcoat. The woman came back carrying a tray with two glasses and two bottles. Colonel Wedderburn bent to a briefcase on the floor; pulled and pushed a strap through the metal of a buckle. The man said 'Yours.' Colonel Wedderburn raised one finger. The woman went out, leaving the glasses and bottles.

The man said 'What time did she go?'

'About ten. We've been out since lunch. But the point – '
he leaned forwards, tapped his cigarette on an ashtray ' – is
that we're not allowed to look. We're covering six square
miles of wood and it's not to be known.'

The red-faced man said 'How many men?'

After a pause Colonel Wedderburn said 'Twelve.'

The man with the red face leaned forwards and altered
the position of the ashtray.

Colonel Wedderburn said 'What we need is half the
county and the army. But they're round the gates like a
pack of vultures.'

The red-faced man felt in the roof of his mouth with a
finger.

Colonel Wedderburn said 'But this isn't the point
anyway. I found her riding-hat in some sort of treehouse.
She must have left it there. And there were no other signs.'

'You mean she isn't hurt?'

'Oh of course officially.' Colonel Wedderburn leaned forwards and tapped.

'You haven't told them?'

'I don't want alarm and despondency.'

'So what do you want from me?'

Colonel Wedderburn brushed at his clothes where ash
had fallen. He said 'She may just have fallen and be hurt.
She may just have gone off with her boy friend.'

'Has she got a boy friend?'

'I don't know.'

Colonel Wedderburn looked at the end of his cigarette;
twisted it.

The red-faced man leaned across the desk and pulled
some papers towards him. He said 'Well well well, who've
we got. League for Freedom, Students' Union, Socialist – '
He opened the file 'Boys and Girls come out to play – '

Colonel Wedderburn said 'Who was it today?'

'O.D.L. . . . Offices in Victoria Street.'

Colonel Wedderburn said 'That lot!'

'But it could be students' rag week.'

'I don't buy that.'

The man said 'Not Miss Freedom Nineteen-eighty-four?'

Colonel Wedderburn leaned forward and tapped. 'They haven't got the organisation.'

The man changed 'Not the organ, not the organise –. It couldn't be just chance?'

'Where'd they take her?'

'What sort of girl is she?'

'Fourteen. Looks older. They all do nowadays.'

'And a boy friend?' He looked angry. 'They'll be getting a slot on the telly.'

Colonel Wedderburn picked some tobacco off his lip; looked at the tip of his finger. He said 'Who're the serious ones?'

The man said 'Well well well.' He turned some pages. 'The Natolin lot.'

'You're keeping an eye on them?'

'Surely. And so are they.'

'Korin?'

'And then the pre-war lot.' The red-faced man pushed the files away. He said 'Go and see Grigoriev.'

Colonel Wedderburn squeezed his cigarette.

The man said 'They know their own people. Better than us. And they won't want it public.'

Colonel Wedderburn said 'All right I like the student idea. What would they have done? Have you got any addresses?'

The man smiled. 'Do you want me to check?'

'Please.' He leaned forwards and tapped.

The red-faced man wrote on a piece of paper.

Colonel Wedderburn said 'Tomorrow?'

'After she's come back from boy friend and been met by angry father on doorstep?'

Colonel Wedderburn said 'One thing an English girl doesn't do is leave her horse.'

The man said 'Of course it could always be a nut.'

'There's always a nut.' Colonel Wedderburn jabbed his cigarette out.

The man said 'Who was supposed to be looking after her?'

After a pause – 'Connie Johnson.'

'What's she now?'

'His secretary.'

The red-faced man said 'Well well well.'

Colonel Wedderburn said 'And how have things been with you?'

'Oh we've had a fire. Had the roof half off.'

'Bad?'

'Only a few thousand gallons of water.'

Colonel Wedderburn said 'Can I use your phone?'

The man pushed it across. He said 'One of the children with a stove.'

Colonel Wedderburn dialled and held the receiver to his ear. He said into the mouthpiece 'Anything? No. No. Right.' He put the receiver down. He said 'Was it a Benedict?'

After a pause the man said 'No.'

'They're the best.'

The man said 'Anything?'

Colonel Wedderburn said 'He's doing his nut.'

The man said 'I know what I'd do with her.'

Colonel Wedderburn stood. He picked up his briefcase. He said 'Now now. You'd end in the law courts!'

The man stood. They went towards the door. Colonel Wedderburn put his stick beneath his arm. The man said 'Officially, then, it's just that she's fallen: and we're still going through the woods.'

Colonel Wedderburn said 'Yes. And you're not even supposed to know that.'

16

Connie walked in the back corridor of the country house beyond the green baize door where there were pipes like the boiler room of a ship, holding her arms crossed in front of her in an X, her hands on her shoulders. At the end of the corridor towards the courtyard and the stables there was a room with the door open and inside neon lights making the walls yellow and men standing around in gumboots drinking tea. There were maps spread on a central table; a low ceiling and the windows covered with black blinds. Connie went in: the men, whom she did not know, turned: they offered her a mug which she took and held with both hands with the steam rising up past her eyes and mind. She was reminded of the war; of men standing around in a shelter or a command-post, happily waiting to go out to fight or die.

Walking round she looked at the maps which had circles and lines drawn on them in areas shaded like a wood; made out the house and the valley and the far line of oak trees all in diagram, as if for a game about who would arrive 'home' first without being prevented by the enemy. She blew on her tea and felt nostalgia for what she only just remembered; a warmth, companionship, engendered by danger. She thought – Who is the enemy? Men were pointing at the map and talking; one said 'Here; they're still on the road; by the gates; go round this way.' Connie thought – We are always retreating.

She sat in a corner and watched as two men in gumboots came in and others went out. They carried torches and small haversacks; she thought – For first aid. She tried to think of Mary. She had a picture of a girl that flickered as if half on fire. Then it went. Her mind couldn't control it.

When she looked round again Andrew Seymour was in the room talking by the table. Men were saying 'Found her hat. No. Nothing.' Connie went and touched Andrew Seymour's arm and stood close to him. She was always doing this: he didn't like it: with power, she felt safe.

She said 'Andrew, I've got such a feeling of evil.' She drew him to one side; the men with gumboots had gone into the passage. 'All the time on the surface we act and do our thousands of little things and underneath there's chaos, this inability to think about anyone else, let alone the whole. Why is it that only when something awful happens are we brought up against it, then all the rest of the time has meant nothing, has been like a dream?'

Andrew Seymour said 'Yes I like that.' He was looking towards the door.

Connie said 'I can't imagine Mary. Where is she, what is she doing? Can anyone imagine the terror a young girl like that, lying out there alone in the cold and dark or perhaps unconscious or even worse, or with someone – ' she shook her head ' – it doesn't bear thinking about!'

Andrew Seymour said 'You always were a pessimist Connie.'

Connie said 'I just can't bear the inability to feel.'

Andrew Seymour said 'We like that.'

Connie said 'Here we all are doing our best and staying up all night but we don't even know why, what's really happened. We're so much in the dark. We scratch at the surface and out comes terror, and this actually makes us happier, it makes us feel what we're here for! But we're not really touching it.'

Andrew Seymour said 'Everyone has a built-in protection against terror, Connie.'

Connie said 'How can you say that?'

Andrew Seymour said 'You said it.'

Connie said 'I'm thinking about Mary.'

Andrew Seymour said 'You're thinking of yourself.'

Connie moved away. She went round the table and looked at the maps. Two circles had been drawn and a line connecting them. They looked like spectacles over a nose. There had been drawings like this peering over walls in the war.

Up against a wall of the room was an old harmonium. Above it was a large painting of a dog with a dead bird in its mouth. The room was lit by a bare bulb with a shade green above and white underneath.

In the corner was a telephone switchboard. Plugs stood

upright in slots like defence works. Above them were holes which sometimes blinked with numbers, like eyes.

17

Mary lay in the upstairs room of the cottage in the dark. The boy sat on the floor in an opposite corner. Between them were plates and a frying-pan and knives and forks. The boy was saying –

'I see it as a sort of sphere, on the inside with radiuses to a central point and round the outside lines, I don't know, meeting at poles. The outside is what we see and everything can be measured. But on the inside which we don't see there's just one going to the centre. There's nothing else like it.' He seemed to be drawing on the ground with his finger.

Mary said 'Yes I think I see.'

'There all these forces to this central point. It's a field of energy.'

'Like magnetism.'

'Yes.'

Mary said 'I believe in reincarnation.'

The boy said 'If I want to influence somewhere in a different part of the globe I can, but not directly. The impression we make on things works through a sort of stored-up memory. They have proof of this now. I read a book in which everything was explained in harmonies between the energy waves of matter and the electrical impulses of the brain. They can record these by placing terminals at various points under the skin and the impulses are recorded on a graph. These graphs have likenesses with other graphs which they take of earth tremors or of the weather. The charts go up and down in the same sort of ratios.'

Mary said 'I don't think anything ever gets destroyed.'

The boy said 'They carry out experiments about what

sort of impulses affect the brain and in what way. They can make you do things like work your muscles or bring pictures into the brain but they can't yet do it at a distance. But they will, and then it will be the same as matter, matter and brain.'

Mary said 'Oh do you think that?'

She could just make out his shape, in the corner, like someone in prison.

Mary said 'I sometimes feel that I don't exist, that it is always other people working through me. I feel that there are other people outside and they have some sort of control, like knobs, and they can make me do what they want. I think there's some sort of conspiracy and everybody else knows about it except me. Do you ever feel that?'

He seemed to be digging at the floor with his fingernails.

She said 'I think that somewhere there is a real me, but that this has to be guarded or else I shall lose it. If I let it be seen too much then they will know, and they will get me. I think if I ever show myself too much I will disappear.'

She found herself trembling; shaking as if the air were alive.

The boy said 'Oh there's a lot of corruption!'

Mary whispered 'I must be careful!'

The boy said 'Look.' He was kneeling; scraping lines on the ground as if with a brush. 'there are only two forces in the world: a plus and a minus. A plus and a plus are all right: but every plus and minus results in a minus and the minus wins. And there are two pluses and minuses for every one plus and a plus. So that the minus spreads throughout the world; it's taking over. And the minus is evil. Unless – ' He jabbed at the floor.

Mary said 'What?'

'The minus is countered by the minus. Then there's a plus.'

'Yes I know.'

'Then things are held in check. That's the only way.'

'You believe that?'

He seemed to have moved over the floor slightly closer; stretching as if against chains on his hands and knees.

Mary said 'I've never talked to anyone like this before.'

'Haven't you?'

She said 'What's your name?'

'Peter.'

'That's an English name.'

'My mother was English.'

She sat up with her back against the iron of the bed. She pulled the rug up to her waist. She said 'I feel all right, I really do.'

He said 'My father had quite a big estate. He had horses and servants. He went about in a private train.'

Mary said 'I don't see very much of my father. He's busy. Some families are always fussing, you know, but mine's not. Though he is fond of me.' She laughed.

He was squatting in the middle of the floor with his arms between his knees. He said 'My mother – '

She said 'It's very hard for him I think. He was left alone when my mother went. And with a daughter! So of course he can't spend much time. But I think he should marry again. He has one person but he doesn't seem to like her very much. He's getting terribly round-shouldered. He talks to me sometimes, honestly, like a child. Connie – that's the person – gets bored with him too. She's his secretary. At least they call her that. She's quite pretty. He has a proper secretary too, who's a man. I don't like him. I think he must be homosexual.'

The boy had sat cross-legged; had not come any closer.

Mary said 'My mother ran away to Rhodesia when I was small and I wasn't allowed to see her. Then she died. I think sometimes my father doesn't remember that she'd gone away before. This must be quite a common thing when you're unhappy. My bedroom is at the top of the house on the second floor. The walls are pale green and grey. It's got a lot of cushions in it. My father hardly ever comes up to say goodnight. He can't even climb up the stairs! Once he did when he was drunk, and the smell was

64

disgusting. I can't think why anyone drinks. The Perrys, they're my friends, have a terrible time. Their father is a sex-maniac.'

He had hopped, like a rabbit, to the side of the bed.

She said 'What are you doing?'

'Nothing.'

'You must be doing something.'

He had settled down with his head just above the mattress.

He said 'Servants. Horses. A room at the top of the house!'

She moved to the edge of the bed by the wall.

He said 'I'm not going to hurt you.' He had kneeled upright; reared over the edge of the bed in the dark like a diagram.

He said 'Lie on your front.'

She kept close to the wall.

He said 'Go on talking.' His voice sounded muffled.

She said 'What about? Where I go to school it's disgusting. There's a woman with big blue blisters on her arm. Honestly. They drip into the soup. I think it must be a disease.'

He seemed to lean over her and breathe hard, like someone counting money.

She said 'They never talk about anything. It's always clothes and gossip. There aren't any locks on the doors. Always about sex.'

She was on her front with her mouth against a pillow of a dirty brown material. It felt sour. She licked her lips without touching it. Her hands were at the side of her head, just touching iron.

She said 'I'm going to leave as soon as I can. Live in London. I know some girls who do.'

The bed seemed to rock. He was pushing it like a boat.

She stretched her feet; raised her hands and took hold of the bars at the head of the bed.

She said 'What are you doing?'

'Nothing.'

She said 'You must be doing something.'

She turned her head and tried to see him. His face was stretched over her halfway down like something diving or feeding from a trough. He seemed to have no arms. His hands were gripping the edge of the bed at his waist.

She said 'What's the matter?'

She couldn't turn her body without bumping his face; a shock like touching wires.

She tightened her leg muscles.

His nose was like a bee-sting.

She suddenly jerked and sat with her back against the wall. She put her hands across her front to her shoulders in an X. She pulled her feet up and tried to get them under her. She took a deep breath and held it and rolled her head from side to side.

The room, and her position on the bed, seemed to be held in some tension as if there were a thin surface between; a membrane from her mind and body to the outside air which pulsed. Upon this surface images flitted with the speed of light – a lion's paw on a deer's belly, the feet of insects scudding on water, eyes from which she was trying to squeeze blood. The surface was thin and slightly convex at the edges: a fly struggled in milk before the skin broke and it drowned. She let her breath out with a gasp then in again quick: the air hummed: she held on so tight that there was a sort of fire suspended by will. The trembling was all over her chest, groin, brain; then outside in the bed that shook. The boy had his head down pressed against the mattress, gripped between his hands as if he were praying. When she let her breath out he did the same; and in; so that they strained alternately like pistons. At the top of their strokes nothing happened; there were small sparks in damp air. Then, in the dark, she seemed to see the top of his head exploding; a mist flying out at the back like a sunspot which might have only been the pressure of her own lids against her eyes. She had been trying to blink back tears. The boy seemed almost crying. His head had settled again in a quiet sun. She breathed easier; let the

66

tension go as if into a drain. Tentatively, because she was tired, she put out a hand and touched the boy on the shoulder. She said 'What is it?' He flung himself away and lay face down on the floor. She stretched over him on the bed, on her hands and knees, as if they had had some battle and he were dying. She pushed her hair back; looked maternal; tried to stop a yawn.

18

Connie sat up in bed in a panelled room with flowered curtains. She had a shawl round her shoulders and wore spectacles. Footsteps came along the passage quietly. There was a knock on the door and she took her spectacles off. Sir Simon put his head round the door; he made a face with his jaw dropped and his mouth in an O. He said 'Woof!' He wore an old tartan dressing-gown. He came in and shut the door. He said in a hoarse voice 'In the doghouse!'

Connie put an envelope in the book she had been reading.

Sir Simon said 'Bread and water!' Connie put the book to one side; smoothed the sheet.

Sir Simon sat on the edge of the bed and fingered a place on his dressing-gown where a button had come off.

Connie put on her spectacles and looked at the dressing-gown.

Sir Simon said, quoting. 'Alas so young and beautiful, so lonely, loving, helpless!'

Connie said 'Have you got the button?'

Sir Simon said 'I'm only beastly for my alibi! So they won't think I'm interested – ' He put a hand to the back of her neck.

Connie pulled at the loose ends of cotton. She had a few grey hairs in her golden curls.

He said 'They're staying out all night. If she's in the wood they'll find her.'

Connie said 'Take your hand away.'

Sir Simon said 'Better?'

Connie reached in a drawer at the side of her bed. The shawl fell away from her shoulders showing brown skin and freckles.

Sir Simon said 'I'll go out with them. Spend the night in the woods.'

Connie sat up with a needle and reel of cotton. Sir Simon handed her a button from his dressing-gown pocket.

Connie took the button and began stitching. She said 'I just want you to be polite.'

He watched the top of her bowed head.

She said 'In front of others. You can do what you like on our own.'

He said as if quoting – 'I'm interested only in the higher things, the eternal verities.'

She said 'What's happening?'

He said 'Wedderburn's an idle brute! The weariness of saying everything three times.'

She said 'You don't give him authority.'

'He should take authority. That's his job.'

Connie bent down and bit at the cotton and broke it and put the needle in her mouth.

Sir Simon said 'Sometimes, you know, you're my worst enemy.'

Connie said 'There was something she was upset about, you know.'

He stuck his jaw out and said 'What did I do wrong?'

Connie took the needle out of her mouth, stuck it in the reel of cotton, patted the dressing-gown. 'Can't you treat her seriously? Talk with her.'

'Children are a job for experts. It needs a good deal of care, a good deal of time. As Plato knew.'

Connie put a hand on his arm: said 'What can we do?'

'She's probably with a boy friend.'

'She hasn't got a boy friend.' Connie closed her eyes.

Sir Simon said 'Well I'm staying up.'

Connie said 'No don't be stupid.'

'No, it's the least I can do.'

'I'll go out again.'

'No don't you go out.'

Connie drew her legs up. She held her head sideways and spoke hesitantly with a slight lisp.

'She adores you. You must give her confidence. If you don't she'll just remain a child. you've got to love her. She's got no one else to love.' She put up a hand and pressed her forehead.

Sir Simon pushed out his lower lip and frowned.

Connie said 'Honestly!' She drew a finger down her forehead.

Sir Simon said 'Headache?'

Connie said 'Yes.'

'I'll get some aspirins.'

'No don't bother.'

He crossed the floor to a door which led into a bathroom; switched on a light where his shadow appeared dark against white walls.

Connie heard footsteps coming along the passage. She jumped out of bed and went to the passage door. In the bathroom there was a crash of breaking glass. Sir Simon said in a deep voice 'Bloody hell.'

Connie leaned on the door to the passage. She called – 'Have you cut yourself?'

There was a faint tapping on a level with her shoulder. Sir Simon said 'Yes.'

Connie said 'Wait a minute.'

She opened the door to the passage slightly. Colonel Wedderburn was outside. He began making faces as if talking; Connie pointed towards the bathroom. Colonel Wedderburn raised his eyebrows. Connie shook her head and pushed at the door. Colonel Wedderburn put his hand round and took the key out of the keyhole on the inside. Connie grabbed his hand.

Sir Simon, from the bathroom, said 'What do they want these caps for?'

Connie let go of Colonel Wedderburn's hand and closed the door. She pressed her fingers against her temples.

She went into the bathroom and found Sir Simon by a basin in which there was a broken bottle and yellow liquid and blood. He lifted his hand and shook it and some liquid sprayed on to the walls. He sucked his finger and spat and bubbles appeared at his mouth.

Connie said 'Wait.'

Sir Simon said 'Cheap glass.'

Connie held his hand under the tap. She was dressed in blue pyjamas which ended in frills at the wrists and below the knees.

Sir Simon said 'Is this stuff poison?'

Connie sat on the edge of the bath and rested her head against his side and laughed.

Sir Simon sucked his finger.

Connie took some sticking plaster and wrapped it round his hand. He put his other hand down and patted her behind. He said 'Faithful collie.'

They began walking with their arms round each other's waists into the bedroom.

Sir Simon said 'Might not be up to it tonight. The old feller. Cracking up. How's my collie? How are you feeling?'

Connie said 'You are so sweet!'

There was a stamping sound in the passage as if someone outside was pretending to walk along towards the bedroom and stop there.

Connie looked at the bed; the bathroom; took her arm from Sir Simon's waist. She said 'Who is it?'

Colonel Wedderburn's voice said 'Connie can I talk to you?'

Connie said 'No.' Then – 'Tomorrow.'

Colonel Wedderburn said 'It's urgent.' Then – 'I was instructed.'

Connie looked at Sir Simon: Sir Simon stood in the middle of the room and nodded. Connie went to the door

and opened it. Colonel Wedderburn came in and stood as
if to attention. He said 'Sorry to disturb you, sir, I was
told to report at once when I got back.'

Sir Simon shouted 'What is it?'

Colonel Wedderburn said 'I've seen Harrison sir and
finalised arrangements. He's checking all contacts his end;
Freedom Group, students, O. D. L. and so on. He's not
to make it known, the enquiry's general. All this is pre-
cautionary sir; I want to have the ground covered. I've got
the men in the woods again taking it in strips; if nothing's
found by morning I want permission to use the army sir.
I've got one or two dogs now but I can't do much with the
press around.In the morning I'll keep the roads clear.' He
gazed past Sir Simon at the curtains.

Sir Simon said 'What have they found?'

'There's a line, sir, from the treehouse through the plan-
tations to the road; some of the undergrowth is disturbed.
This isn't indicative. She could have walked along the road.
There've been cars on the road so the dogs can't follow.
She could have gone in a car on the road.'

Sir Simon said 'God Almighty!'

Colonel Wedderburn said 'I wanted to report sir that
everything conceivable is being done. The chances are of
course that she is perfectly – ' he stood to attention; licked
his lip; stretched the muscles of his neck as Sir Simon
sometimes did ' – that is, has just had a fall, sir, or is with
some friend or other.' He seemed to blush.

Sir Simon said 'Thank you Wedderburn.'

'Apologies sir.'

'Not at all.'

Colonel Wedderburn backed towards the door: turned
and said 'Don't worry sir' then went out.

Sir Simon sat on Connie's bed. He hung his arms
between his knees. Connie sat beside him and put her head
on his shoulder.

He said 'I don't find it easy to love.'

Connie put her head lower; hugged him.

He said 'There is some antithesis between love and

power, though I sometimes believe that you can't have one without the other.'

Connie said 'You do love Mary.'

He said 'I loved my wife. Before she went to Africa I drove with her down to Southampton. You know? I think she had some presentiment she was going to die. She wouldn't let me go on the gangplank. They were all ready to sail. I remember standing on the quay and seeing her crying. It was a difficult life for her. She liked the country-side. She was always brought up with dogs and horses.'

Connie said 'Mary will be all right.'

He put a hand on her thigh. The room was golden with dark shadows. He said 'But this is very good, my collie.'

19

In the woods at night there was a man being pulled along by a dog through leaves and branches. He was crouched with an arm in front of his face and a small feather in his hat like a hunter. He came to an opening where moonlight fell between trees in tinsel: he pulled at the dog and the dog made a gasping noise as if it were being murdered. In a corner of the clearing beneath an oak tree were two shapes wrapped like babies. The man with the dog shone a torch on damp leaves and lights reflected in the branches. The shapes were sleeping bags. He walked forwards with the dog pulling and groaning. He said 'Sit up, let's see you.'

There was a cold wind. One of the sleeping-bags stirred, a cocoon's skin moving, a slit at the end and a bearded head coming out. The head blinked, hurt by the torch. Beside it on the ground was a placard on the end of a stick with writing – *Free the* – then cut off by shadow. The man with the dog turned the torch to the other sleeping bag; saw long hair at the end, pulled the dog back, said 'Come along Miss.' The bearded head said 'Don't!' The man with the dog bent down and took hold of the foot of the sleeping-bag, tugged; the hair disappeared. The stuff of the sleeping-bag was cold and wet. The bearded man said 'By what right – ' The figure in the other bag kicked and curled up into a ball. The man with the dog pulled at the end sharply. He hit the dog on its hindquarters and shouted 'Sit!' The dog had a soft tongue flopping over teeth. The man took the bottom of the sleeping-bag and lifted it; the bag went limp and the body bulged at the top end. The man with the beard said 'Have you the right to assault us?' The dog jumped and put its feet on the bag: the body in the bag screamed. The man with the torch hit at the dog and the dog closed its eyes. The man with the beard climbed out into the night; he was thin and white like a ghost. The man with the dog said 'Come on out then!' The top of the other sleeping bag opened and a girl came out naked. She looked like water. She had long dark hair. She moved over the damp leaves towards a tree. The dog pulled forwards rattling in its throat. The girl seemed luminous. A flashbulb went off like an explosion. They ducked. Behind closed eyes the world settled again; moonlight cleared.

A man came into the hollow carrying a camera and flash-bulb equipment. He was adjusting a box at his waist. He said quietly 'You've got the dog on her?' He put a hand out to the dog and said 'Goody.' He raised his camera and took another flash of the girl. The girl was down on one knee, a thigh making a line along her stomach and breast. Her arm tried to enclose herself. Her hair was against her face like wet paint.

The dog was straining at its collar. The man holding it said 'I'll kill you.'

The man with the camera said 'Galatea.' He knelt and there was another flash. They were like bombs going off. The man said 'And Acis wasn't it?' He turned to the bearded man in his underclothes. He said 'Brother.' Splinters of light were like arrows. They blinked.

The man with the dog said 'That's enough.'

The man with the camera kneeled, facing the dog. He

waited till the dog jumped at him with its teeth bared; then took a picture.

The man with the dog said 'I'll let him go.'

The man with the camera adjusted his equipment. He said 'Who are they, Adam and Eve?' He pulled out a packet of cigarettes. He stepped out of the way of the dog.

The man with the dog said 'Hand it over.'

The man with the camera said 'You should keep that under control.'

'Come on.'

The girl had gone to her sleeping-bag and was pulling clothes out.

The man with the dog put the torch on her.

The man with the camera said 'There's money in this.' The torch went out. He said 'Oh be a sport!'

In the darkness the young man and the girl were dressing on the damp leaves.

The man with the camera said 'You haven't seen me. I'll leave the dog out. Midnight orgy in Sussex Woods. Witches sabbath.' He lit a cigarette: a small round face with wrinkles like a genie. He said 'What are you doing with the dog? Hunting 'em? If you can't join 'em beat 'em. I could do with a bit of that myself on a Friday night.' He called to the girl 'What's your name dear?'

The man with the dog hit it and it sat. The dog's tongue hung out.

'Have one.' the man with the camera offered his cigarettes. 'That's right – them!' He laughed.

The man with the dog took a cigarette.

'Does old Bonzo smoke? The cameraman leaned down.

In the darkness the boy and girl were rolling up their sleeping bags.

The man with the torch waved it and said 'Come over here.'

The boy and girl trod on the leaves; acorns and rotting fungus.

The man with the dog swung the torch up and down the

girl. She wore jeans and a dark cardigan. He said 'What's your name?'

The man with the beard said 'Did you get a picture of that dog?'

The man with the camera said 'Yes I got a picture dear.'

He began walking away. He went stooping towards the trees.

The man with the dog said 'Stay where you are!' He put his hand on the collar of the dog.

The man with the camera stopped.

They stood in a triangle, as if fastened to each other by chains.

The man with the camera said 'What do we do now? All strip off? Brr. Cold night for a mudlark. Gawd, nude bodies in wood. They won't believe it. What's going on? Do her if you're interested. Or do you do it with dogs? Justine. Oh what have we come to! Defending the realm.'

The man with the dog had the torch on the man by the tree. The man with the beard said 'I want to know your name for having assaulted us.'

The man with the dog let the dog jerk forward.

The man with the camera came out from behind a tree.

The bearded man and the girl had sat down on their sleeping-bags. They sat with their arms round each other's shoulders, their knees drawn up, hair over their eyes like animals in a lair.

The cameraman said 'Come one, come on now, break it up. It's a fine night and we were all out for a walk. We were dreaming. The black dog. Christ.' He put his hand on the policeman's shoulder. 'You stick with me. Don't they look pretty? Let's see them get into the bags. Go on, get in the bags. If you zip some of those bags you can make a nice double one. D'you know that? Soft, isn't it?

The policeman switched his torch off. The cameraman looked round the circle of trees, the cold wind in the dark. He said 'At our time of life. Aren't we lucky!'

20

In the morning Sir Simon sat up in bed wearing blue pyjamas with white piping, spectacles halfway down his nose, a tray in front of him with a cup of tea and a plate of biscuits. There was a despatch box by his side containing papers. He held sheets of foolscap; sipped his tea. The back of the bed on a level with his head was shaped like a sea-shell. He read –

After the collapse of the students' rebellion two years ago Korin's position seemed assured over both the party machinery and the army: his last serious rival, Palanek, disappeared about this time and is reported to be living in retirement: the old Borolev group had withdrawn their advocation of acting as a go-between in a realignment with the Soviet Union and the West, and the army was shaken by both the force and the aftermath of rebellion. The retention of Stanevski as Party President did not weaken the true reins of power. This tactic has often been observable in communist *realpolitik* – the use of the passive front-man in times of crisis or change.

Recently however there have been signs of the old Right re-exerting influence: not in the aim of the People's Democratic Republic at non-alignment, but rather in the carrying-through of the *détente* while still committed to the old party line. This is another symptom of communist ideology – the scapegoat essential for a policy-reversal to be achieved without loss of face.

On the other side are the survivors of the pre–1962 Praesidium loyal to Leninist orthodoxy and the concept of enemy by definition. In the recent *volte-faces* there have even been some rapproachements between Stanevski and the Stalinists: it was noticeable that at the Winter Congress Balack sat with the delegates from the Hanara region – known to be Stanevski sympathisers. The question remains what steps are practicable against Korin for whatever reason; and this reduces itself to possibilities of *coup d'etat*. The ODS are, as always, the unknown quantity. Without the rule of law power lies with the secret police.

Sir Simon felt by the side of his bed, found a pencil, turned the paper sideways, wrote in the margin – *Tabulate. Omit observations. Clarify.*

He read –

The Détente with the West. Whereas Korin's main reasons for this are probably self-preservatory it is also part of his idealistic policy of realignment in Europe. Perhaps also he remembers 1945 when supplies were dropped by allied planes and the Russians delayed their advance till his force was nearly wiped out. Korin depends for survival on a break with the East yet he has to appear more militant at the moment than his own Left. In this his obvious allies would be the Chinese, but they . . .

Sir Simon threw the paper away. On the bed there was the button of a bell, which he pressed. A maid came in. She approached the bed to take the tray. Sir Simon held on to it. When she had stretched across him he said softly 'Get Mr Seymour.'

The maid blushed. She walked back to the door with her hands bumping against her thighs.

Sir Simon picked up another piece of paper, lifted the cup, balanced the cup and paper and sent his eyes running to and fro along the lines as if he were changing gear.

DRAFT PROPOSAL. DISINSTALLATION OF M.I.F. AT ARDEVIL.

He read fast, his eyes running down the slopes, working up speed towards the bottom of the page and then slowing for the corners. He changed into third past a white fence and fir trees; his eyes, mind, on pedals, wheel; speeding up on the straights of the dark lines and white verges; the page skidding away beneath him in print as he lapped, passing the field, the engine behind his skull running smoothly.

Andrew Seymour came in.

Sir Simon said quietly 'Andrew get that stuff for me on to one page will you?'

Andrew Seymour bent and picked up papers from the floor.

Sir Simon said 'Who is it writes that?'

Andrew Seymour looked at the papers. He was dressed in a tartan dressing-gown.

Sir Simon said 'Is the girl back?'

'No.'

Sir Simon turned a piece of paper sideways, wrote in the margin.

Andrew Seymour said 'Wedderburn's gone to London. To see Grigoriev I think.'

Sir Simon said 'Get the Ankara stuff. Why?'

Andrew Seymour stood beside the bed; put his hand in the despatch box.

Sir Simon said 'So we've got to let the whole emotionalism, sensationalism, sobsisters – '

Andrew Seymour said 'I think that's why Grigoriev – '

Sir Simon said 'Get me the minutes of yesterday. Did he agree the sentence about – ' He shuffled in the despatch box.

Andrew Seymour said 'Intention.'

Sir Simon said 'Intention. Not the figures. We want, one, an admission he is willing to consider at a future date: two, the outline for Paris.'

Andrew Seymour said 'He won't do it without the point being China.'

'We'll give him that. And go along with the Americans on the other.'

Andrew Seymour said 'Yes.'

Sir Simon said 'Poor little girl, I am so dreadfully sorry.'

Andrew Seymour said 'I'll find out more.'

'Let me get on then.'

Sir Simon read –

At the time of the students' rebellion Korin was head of the KOP, or internal security. It was his quick reaction to the rising and the cordoning off of the university town of Lov that probably prevented the spread of the revolt to the factory workers and farmers as was intended. And by his use of retributory force exclusively against the students or groups of intellectuals and artisans obviously allied to them he effectively split the opposition in a classic example of communist *realpolitik* (Sir Simon frowned: made a cross in the margin). In Lov alone during the three days of fighting there were few prisoners taken by the security forces and it is estimated that the number of students and their co-fighters killed was 5–600. Many of these were boys and girls armed with no more than shotguns and home-made bombs; sometimes unarmed. When the resistance ceased through lack of ammunition and semi-starvation those remaining were transported to the old camp at Kara-Oraly (scene of the Tabitch murders of 1944) where they were and still are subjected to torture. They were joined by prisoners taken in the capital and in the six or seven major towns where the rising had also been effective for three days.

The difference between this revolt and the others in Eastern Europe since the War can be tabulated. 1. The nature of the rising itself. This was not in essence nationalistic for the reasons of the slogans used and the propaganda printed; these were pointed to a demand for international feeling and good will: they opposed the government's policy of national alignment and the vituperation against its enemies.

2. What the revolt was against. Previous risings have seemed to be in opposition to the *rigorousness* of foreign-imposed governments: in the students' revolt it was more the *corruption* of government. For the first time in post-war signs of dissatisfaction there was complaint not only of the repression, bigotry, cruelty, and so on, but also of the deception, grossness, venality of those in government. The printed tracts had a tone of the socio-anarchist tracts of the nineteenth century – a tone adopted traditionally by those protesting against old-fashioned capitalism and not against communism. The objection seemed to be a world of total lies and betrayal: a world

79

which men like Korin represented *in common* with the 'decadent' West.

3. The nature of the retribution. Reports indicate that the use of torture on prisoners has been prolonged. This has had no practical function (the gaining of information) nor symbolic function (the effect of public confession) because there is nothing more about the rising to be learned and the processes in the Kara-Oraly camp are anyway kept secret. In this there are parallels with the Nazi type of torture – for no practical purpose, but in character with the way in which those who feel guilty have to make victims of the innocent. Reports of the methods used indicate parallels also with the French in Algeria and with the American-sponsored governments of South and Central America – torture that does not leave outward traces so that it can be denied even when the fact of it is well known. In the present climate of opinion, appearances only are recognised. This torture includes near-suffocation by drowning, the application of electric shock to the genitals, and also tortures of a more specifically sexual nature – such as the insertion of hot liquid into the anus. It is reports of these tortures, pointless and obscene, and appearing to be inflicted specifically by the old upon the young, that have precipitated the strong feelings against Dr. Korin in this country as well as the recurrence of them in his own.

There is little evidence to connect Korin with these processes personally though he must be held responsible for the policy and the system. It is unfortunate that the necessities of the time –

Sir Simon put the paper to one side. He said 'There's no news of the girl?'

Andrew Seymour said 'No sir.'

'They were out all night?'

'Yes.'

'I want to see Wedderburn as soon as he gets back. Connie's telephoned all her friends.'

Sir Simon's face was long and grey. Two pinkish falls of

flesh drooped beneath his eyes like slugs. He pushed the tea-tray to one side, swung his legs to the floor, walked to the bathroom.

He said 'We've got to keep going.' There was a clanking noise, and water. He said 'There's nothing else to do.'

He came back into the bedroom. He said 'We've got to put it over why we're dealing with Korin. To the press: these students. Take this down for a statement; and for wider -. For Korin some personal appearance.'

Andrew Seymour took out a notebook.

Sir Simon said 'This is not a matter of joining forces with the best available man to prevent aggression: this was in the old days: you used the lesser evil, the lesser man, to fight the big. Times have changed. This is more important. Deeper. This is a joining of forces, to some extent, with one of the enemy, to help destroy what, formerly, the enemy himself stood for. This is a more subtle battle than the old. It is more subtle by necessity now. The naive and innocent think that you can beat the devil by fighting him. You can't. You can beat the devil by using him. You can beat him by his not becoming a devil. By his becoming – split. Ordinary. Illustrate this from political examples in the past. Fanatics are maintained by their enemies' treating them as fanatics. The exception to this is of course Hitler: but who knows if we had gone further while we had time. Gone further with accepting: not panicking, but being responsible. Which of course we were not. But responsibility is complexity. The recognition of it. Evolution rather than revolution. This occurs when evil is assimilated. This is not appeasement. The battle now, on world scale, is nemesis. Now – give a few metaphysical instances. Or biological. The swallowing up of evil rather than the rejection of it. As before – for the purposes of good. We are now at a time – ' Sir Simon's voice had gone husky ' – when we have to live with ever greater complexities not only in science, economics, daily living; but in principles and morals. Is it too much to ask – ' he began to put on the voice of an orator ' – that the younger generation may be aware of this, who are the generation of the future? Is it to be left to us, the generation of the past, to see the new patterns, the new pressures, the new subtleties, of the future?'

He said to Andrew Seymour 'Make something of that.'

Andrew Seymour said 'Who d'you want to do it?'

Sir Simon said 'Andrew find out more about the girl. This really is bloody. I don't know what to do. One does have to pay for it, doesn't one.'

He went back to bed. He tipped two white pills into his teacup: sat and picked up more papers. He said 'I'll have another hour before breakfast.'

21

Colonel Wedderburn was shown into a room with cream walls and bowls of red flowers and a large brown desk. There was a round-faced man with small pale eyes wearing a brown suit and a white shirt and white tie. He said 'Colonel.' Colonel Wedderburn said 'Sorry to be so early Colonel.' They shook hands. Colonel Wedderburn sat at the side of the desk and took out his gunmetal cigarette case and tapped and leaned forwards to get it back in his hip pocket. The man behind the desk said 'Coffee?' He spoke in a foreign accent. Colonel Wedderburn felt in his pocket with one finger and thumb like an arrow. The man looked towards the door where a woman came in carrying a tray. The man behind the desk said 'Sugar?' Colonel Wedderburn flicked his lighter and lit his cigarette. His face flared like a thing on stone, a cave-drawing.

When the woman had gone he said 'A tricky one this time.'

The man behind the desk pushed over an ashtray.

Colonel Wedderburn said 'I've come from Hassington.' He took a heave of smoke. 'They send you their compliments.'

The man behind the desk took a cigarette from a box; lit it. Colonel Wedderburn said 'Sorry!' He leaned forward and offered his cigarettes. The man behind the desk blew smoke. Colonel Wedderburn arched his back to get the lighter into his pocket.

'Yesterday morning, about nine-thirty, Sir Simon's daughter, Mary, about fifteen, went out riding.' He twisted the ashtray; watched it as if it were a roulette wheel. 'She was not supposed to. The horse came back a few hours later, but not the girl.' He lifted his coffee.

The man swung in his chair in profile: looked at the end of his cigarette.

Colonel Wedderburn said 'She's still not back. It's now twenty-four hours. We've been through the woods, the country. Of course she might have fallen and be hurt. If so we'll find her. But for reasons, we don't want it public.'

He tapped; switched his cigarette from finger and thumb to between the third and fourth fingers.

'It might be domestic. Staying away from home. In which case also we'll find her. But she wouldn't have let the horse go. Unless she wanted to give the impression.'

He put his head back and felt in the roof of his mouth with a finger.

'On the other hand she might have bumped into someone. Or someone bumped into her. We're checking on our own people.' He squeezed the tip of his finger with his thumb. 'They might have known where she went riding. There were one or two down yesterday as you know.'

The man behind the desk was still in profile. He had short hair above the ears: a vein showing like a bone. Colonel Wedderburn thought – He is too silent. His face had a line round it dark against the cream walls. The vein above his ear did not beat. The air around his profile was still.

Colonel Wedderburn said 'You might have some ideas. You'll have some of your own people. I don't pretend – ' he smiled ' – we know as much as you about your own.'

He tried to remember – He had come in at the door?

Grigoriev had been standing behind the desk. He had put his hand out. Grigoriev had said 'Colonel.' He had said 'Sorry I'm so early.' He had asked for coffee. Grigoriev had not looked at him: he had not seen the offered cigarette. Or had that been later? When the woman had brought the coffee he had been watching her.

Colonel Wedderburn said 'If you've been keeping an eye on any of your people – '

He thought – He knows.

Grigoriev swung round with one elbow on the desk.

Colonel Wedderburn said 'Of course it's unlikely.'

Grigoriev said 'You think it's one of your students?'

His voice was flat. His face was like something against a brick wall.

Colonel Wedderburn said 'Students' Union. League of Freedom.' He knocked at the ashtray. 'Possible.'

Their hands almost met at the ashtray. Grigoriev had blunt fingers with a ring.

Grigoriev said 'Yesterday morning?'

Colonel Wedderburn said 'She's five foot eight, fair hair, medium-to-big build I should say.' He suddenly felt in his pocket. 'Wearing riding breeches and a brown cardigan. No signs on the horse.' He rattled in his pocket and looked at Grigoriev quickly.

Grigoriev said 'Did she have usual rides in the woods?'

After a pause Colonel Wedderburn said 'No.' He brought his hand out and patted his stomach.

'Nothing found in the woods?'

'No.'

Colonel Wedderburn thought – Woods. He registered the word on a soft slate in his brain.

Grigoriev said – 'If one of your students – ' He smiled and shrugged.

Colonel Wedderburn said 'Can I leave it with you then Colonel?'

Grigoriev picked up a pencil and paper. He said 'They were round here again yesterday.'

'I know.'

'His Excellency had to leave by the back gate.'

'I'm sorry.'

Grigoriev was writing nothing with the pencil and paper. He should be writing – Mary, five foot eight, fair hair, medium build.

Colonel Wedderburn said 'If anything happens to the girl there'll he trouble.' He opened his hand, looked at it; it was full of pennies. He said 'Bad for all of us.'

Grigoriev said 'She's a young girl?'

Colonel Wedderburn said 'What?'

He could see Grigoriev thinking, sliding all over the road in front of him.

Grigoriev said 'Is she known. The public – '

Colonel Wedderburn said quickly 'We're keeping it quiet.'

'How many know it then?'

He had his head down. He had been looking towards the door through which the woman had come carrying coffee. Colonel Wedderburn registered – How many know it then?'

Colonel Wedderburn said 'Have you got any ideas?'

Grigoriev had said 'If some of your students – ' He faced Colonel Wedderburn. 'She will be in good hands with your experts.' He smiled.

Colonel Wedderburn frowned; a rattle of stones in his face.

Grigoriev said 'Haddon Road.'

Colonel Wedderburn registered – Haddon Road.

Grigoriev said 'You'll be getting your own men locked up!' He went on smiling, blowing through slightly pursed lips.

Colonel Wedderburn leaned quickly forwards and felt in his back pocket for his cigarettes. He did not know what was happening.

Grigoriev put his hands on the arms of his chair and stood up. He said 'Any other information Colonel?'

Colonel Wedderburn said 'No. I'll keep in touch.' He began chewing his lips.

Grigoriev walked towards the door. The back of his head seemed to be watching; as if there was a mirror in front of him.

Colonel Wedderburn held out his hand. He thought – Grigoriev is frightened.

Out in the passage Colonel Wedderburn arranged his face, his tie; swung his stick carefully.

Grigoriev, back in the room, picked up a telephone and spoke in the foreign language; went out of a small door disguised as panelling, down some stairs to a hall where he put on a mackintosh and hat and let himself out into a garden. He crossed the garden to a wall with another small door which he opened with a key from a ring; went out into a street of Victorian houses in red and white criss-crossed bricks. He glanced up the rows of parked cars and saw a red Mini with a man in it reading a newspaper. He went to a black saloon and sat in it and started the engine; pulling out, his hands on the wheel, his head watching the driving mirror, he saw the red Mini move out behind him. He drove towards a main road. He squared his shoulders and narrowed his eyes; slowed. There was a vein beating above his ear. An engine began racing efficiently inside his mind, where no one could catch or pass him.

22

Mary was dreaming of riding through the woods with the sun making bars through the branches. There were blue-bells and a stream under pine needles. A cold ran round her feet, her legs. Had the eiderdown fallen off? she pulled her knees up. At school she went down to the bottom of the bed and curled up in a ball there. She was in a diving-bell under water, protected from cold and fishes. There were pale blue blankets on the dormitory beds and wooden lockers with doors that did not fit. At home, her father had come into her room with his medals on and smelling of

whisky; had sat on the edge of her bed and the mattress
had tilted so that she was rolling towards him. Earlier, he
had been sitting in his room with the tasselled curtains and
the dark chair with the reading board in front of him and
his spectacles halfway down his nose. She had had to knock
on the door and go in and ask him: her heart had curled
up into a ball. He had looked up and said 'What is it?
There was the table with his pills on it and a white kidney-
bowl and whisky. She had said 'Connie told me she'd asked
you if I – ' Her nails bit into her palm, she stood on one
leg, it wasn't her speaking. He had said 'Couldn't you ask
yourself?' She had blushed like flames; had burned and
disappeared. She had said ' – if I can go to the zoo with
the Perrys.' He had said 'You're going to the zoo?' When
he looked over his spectacles he had X-ray eyes: he saw
what she was thinking. She had said 'Yes.' She had tried
to pretend she was all right; she held her mouth open and
pushed her hair back. He had said 'Where do they want
to put you then?' She had said 'What?' It was her own
voice breaking through; something from far away which
terrified her. She had stuck one hip out and pressed a hand
against her waist. He had said 'In the monkey house, what?'
She had shouted 'Oh Dad!' Her voice had panicked. She
had blinked and turned, her hair coming down past her
ears and eyes. She had smoothed down her skirt like Connie
did, behind.

Under the blankets you were safe, you could breathe
under water. At school they came round in the morning
and shook you. You went out into the cold which was like
a bell. Floors were polished and smelled of cooking fat.

Her father had come into her room in his medals and
white tie and whisky. He had said 'Fee fi fo fum.' She had
turned with her face to the wall. He had sat on the edge
of her bed and she had rolled towards him. He had put his
arm around her. He had said 'So they didn't keep you?'
She had jerked away and pulled the sheet up over her face.
He had laughed with his clicking sound. He had tried to
pull her round; had got one finger under her chin. She had

resisted. He had said 'The big bad wolf!' He had put a hand under the bedclothes; then suddenly let go; was just sitting on her bed in the darkness. She had turned to look. He was in profile with the light coming in from the passage; an old man with his outline like a spaniel. She had thought – I am part of him. He had suddenly opened his arms and she had flung herself into them and had cried. She had watched herself crying with her eyes against his waistcoat. It was her unreal self that was crying: crying really. Her real self was far away.

She thought – I wonder if anyone has read my diary. In the top drawer of my dressing-table.

She was shaking with cold. She was not in her room at home. At school there were cold white sheets and a bed like a tube. Here there was rough material over her knees. She had been riding in the beech woods. There had been the boy with the gun. The cold came all over her making her violent, existing, in body, person, mind.

She became awake. There was the rough brown rug in front of her eyes. The light came through small holes like a blocked sieve. There were the bare boards of the room. He had been sitting in the corner. The door was opposite, and a window with boards across it.

He had knelt and he had touched her: she had touched him.

She was lying awake in her riding-breeches, socks, blouse, curled up in a ball. They would get the police and come to find her. The army with horses and dogs.

She had felt fear; his head like the sun, coming down on her.

He might be looking out of the boarded window with his gun and a fur cap with a squirrel tail.

She had said – It's not really oneself, it's something that is pretending I'm not really me. Everyone is always acting. Do you know what I mean?

He had said – Yes.

He had sat on the floor in the corner. He had come over to her bed: had leaned in the darkness. She had rolled on her stomach. There was the princess in the story and the man who was a beast.

He might still be in the corner.

When you pretended to be asleep you had the blankets over your face and if you wanted to see out you had to get the blankets down by a movement as if still sleeping. You groaned; if he was in the room he would move. She rolled on to her back and pulled at the rug; pushed down her legs and sighed. There was a light on her eyelids. The muscles of her legs tightened.

She was all in one piece. Body.

She opened one eye. The light was cold: the ceiling of the room withdrew from her.

She turned her head suddenly and the room was empty.

He had been sitting with his dark hair, skin, in the corner.

She moved very carefully with the top half of her body making the springs of the bed creak and an ache in the muscles at her waist. She swung her legs to the floor, a rough feeling in the roof of her mouth, the pain again making her screw her face up. She would go out into the garden by the willow trees. The floor creaked: there was no other sound. They had come up the lane at the front where there was a gatepost: he had said – I don't want to hurt you. She began to tip-toe across the floor. People did this in a haunted house with eyes at the back of them watching. He had wanted to shoot the man called Korin. Or her father. Or her. Should she die for her father then. He would take her head on his knee and would stroke and would comfort her. She reached the door and put her ear against it. Or she would be on the terrace in the sun with the cheering crowds. She bent at the door like a woman in a nightmare; looked through the keyhole.

The key was in the lock on the far side. She brushed her hair back. She turned the handle and pulled; the door was locked. There was the gap between the bottom of the door and the floorboards. Behind her was the bed with mattress and the rug; the boarded window with the light in bars. She tip-toed back to the bed and picked up the rug: it felt like paper. She tried to tear it. she screwed her face up and raised one leg. Looking out of the window, she could run past the willows at the end of the garden and over the stream. They would soon be coming up to the cottage with dogs and helmets. They would hunt her, dodging and shouting in the prairie grass. She hopped on one leg. The mattress was striped blue and grey with stars of brown leather. Underneath were sheets of yellow newspaper. She took one. There were lists of prices of stocks and shares like knitting. She went back to the door and knelt and pushed the paper underneath. A draught from the outside lifted it. She put her face on the boards and felt the wind from the landing like a knife in her eye. She raised herself and felt for a hairgrip. You did this at school. You opened the ends and bent them slightly and pushed them through the keyhole. The ends had protuberances that might grip. The house was quiet. You got the ends past the end of the key and twisted; felt with one end for the lock-piece of the key. You held the grip like pincers. Then you turned and pushed and the key fell out. The key would make a loud clattering noise. But she did not want to do this. In the room she was safe against the outside, the enemy.

She sat back on her heels. He had been with a gun. He had been going to shoot rabbits: at a thousand yards? Colonel Wedderburn had seen her on the road. She had seen Peter with the gun in the oak tree. The cars had gone past with the men in a white blur.

She thought – Even if I get the key I can keep it and can stay here.

Her heart thumped. She was head, body, mind. She probed into the keyhole. She could touch the end of the key with one end of the hairgrip. The key did not turn. It should fall on the paper and you pulled the paper back. The wind blew the paper up. The key was coming round so that the locking part was visible. You scraped at it, not believing; then it worked. She watched herself doing this.

She sat back on her heels. The thing was so fragile; if you pushed, the world might fall apart. In would rush wind, cold, devils. She looked round the room; there were torn bits of wallpaper where she had lain and held herself. If she opened the door she could stand with her back against the wall and they would rush past her. She would run down the path through the nettles towards the willows.

She thought – He will kill me.

A splinter had gone beneath one of her nails. She had been scratching at the floorboards. The wood was like a pencil box in grooves. They tied your hands and drove splinters up with hammers. He had held her head under his arm. They had walked round the kitchen in a sort of dance, her hands behind her.

The lower part of the key filled the keyhole. She took the hairgrip and held the two ends in her fingers. She steadied the newspaper with her other hand and pushed it further under the door; she lay and put her face flat and felt the wind and the newspaper moving. She put the blunt end of the hairgrip through the keyhole and pushed. She made a crying noise and rested her head against the door. There was silence. The rats and insects came out of their holes. She knelt up and looked through the keyhole and aimed at the key again and put the hairgrip against it and held her breath. It was like stabbing. She pushed and the key fell out on to the floor at the far side. Her heart jumped. She pulled the paper and it came back through the door and the key was on the paper, like a dog's mess. She didn't want to touch it. She would go to her bed and lie there. Would curl up into a ball. She would pull the blanket up and pretend to be asleep.

There was a sound of metal on stone, a scrape and clinking, coming from beyond the window.

The key was thin with two notches. Her knees were hurting. She picked the key up. She stood and went to the window.

There was the noise of a pick outside; someone digging. Digging her grave.

She went and sat on the bed.

She was waiting for herself to do something. They were watching her from behind the walls, the ceiling. She was open to an audience. She had to make herself believe they were not there. She walked across to the door. Her feet were one in front of the other as on a tightrope. Her heart was so violent it was in the air outside like a bell. She thought – A noise can kill you. She put the key in the lock and turned it. It made a bird-noise. She held her hand flat against a panel of the door as if someone from outside might rush in. She moved quietly backwards and forward as if on a swing. She opened the door. On the landing there were the banisters and the edge of the stairs. She would go along like the lady with the candle. She made faces as the boards creaked. She started going down the stairs with a hand on the banisters to the passage to the front door. She stopped halfway. The boy called Peter was out in the garden at the back, digging. The bottom of the front door had brown felt underneath it. There was a wall with a grey crack in the plaster. The bottom of the landing made an angle with the wall at the centre of her head. The landing came up and went over her: she was in the passage by the front door. Her arms were out on either side of her as if she had fallen. There was the wire cage of a letter-box; a Yale lock and a round knob. Beyond, the white light of the sun.

Outside was the path going up through weeds to the hedge and the gatepost. She had shut the front door behind her and had begun to walk up the path. The door had not shut. She wanted to go back and shut it. There was a car coming up the lane. She was going back to hide from the car. She wanted the car to come along so that it could rescue her.

She went up the path towards the car.

She was standing on the edge of the gravel and cinders.

The car had stopped in the lane by the cottage.

She was holding on to the gate which was falling off its post.

In the car was a man with a mackintosh and hat. He was looking at her. People always looked at her. They saw right through. They knew what she was thinking. The car was a black saloon. The man sat there. Mary heard herself saying – 'Can you help me?'

The man seemed to be trying to hide his face. He was starting up the car. He held his head sideways with his hat screening it.

She ran to the front of the car and put a hand on the bonnet. 'Please!'

She wanted to get away.

The man looked behind him. He had one hand on the steering wheel as if he were about to reverse.

Mary said 'I'm being kept here!'

The man turned the engine off. Her voice had shouted. His face was cut by the pillar of the windscreen. He said 'What's your name?' He had a foreign accent.

Mary stepped back from the bonnet of the car.

He was opening the door and putting his feet out. He had polished brown shoes beneath the car door. She was walking away along the lane between the thick hedgerows. The road crumbled away towards a ditch. She held her arms by her sides. She had done this before. The man was coming after her. She heard the slam of the car door. Her heart raced and her body seemed to stay where it was. The man took her by the elbow.

He said 'You're alone?'

She shut her eyes. She was on a wheel, with the old torture being repeated.

He said 'Where are the others?'

He had turned her round. They were facing the gate and the cottage. She took hold of his fingers and tried to pluck at them.

He said 'You're not hurt?'

He had a round face with small pale eyes. He was taking her back through the gate to the front door.

He said 'I knew you were here.'

She said 'Oh I see. Good.'

Coldness fled out into the air. She leaned slightly on his arm.

They walked round the side of the house to the back on the cinders. The path went down towards the willows.

Mary said 'He's gone.'

'Who?'

The man held her close.

Mary said 'He's digging.'

Her heart jumped. She couldn't remember what she had thought. The man had a foreign accent. She hung from his hand, going down on one knee.

She said 'He's got a gun.'

'He kept you here?'

The boy, Peter, was coming up the long grass from the willows. He wore a white shirt and dark trousers. Mary said 'Let me go.' She and the man were by the back door arm in arm. He had blunt fingers and a ring. She pulled away from him; pushed her hair back. Peter had stopped among the nettles. He bent and laid something on the ground. The man spoke in a foreign language. Peter looked quietly at him.

There was the leaning wooden hut in the garden. The ground was broken as if the hut had once fallen and spread rubble. There were blue flowers with thick smooth stems. If she had hidden when the car arrived she could have walked up the lane towards a village. She could have gone round the side of the house and waited. Peter and the man were talking with voices that were at the backs of their throats. Beyond the land there was a haystack; she could have lain with her legs curled up: could have gone along the road and found a telephone. The man in the car would have come after her and she would have hidden at the bottom of the telephone box: broken putty would have been at the edges of the cracked windows. She was standing in the garden with the man holding on to her. He wore a long grey mackintosh.

Peter came up the path and went past them into the cottage. He did not look at her. They followed. Peter went upstairs. The man took her into the kitchen and they sat at the table. He let go of her arm. She sat opposite him. She thought – If I get out of this I will promise anything; I will do anything; I will keep it. Peter came downstairs and he and the man went on talking in the foreign language. They were having an argument. Peter was red in the face. The table had grooves in it like a railway station. She had thought this before. She could have hidden under the stairs in a wedge-shaped cupboard with brushes. Peter and the man were arguing about her as if she wasn't there. They were pretending not to notice she wasn't there. She could have gone on from the telephone box and would have come to a village. There would have been a store with a short fat man behind a counter. She would have said – Please help me. He would have gone into a back room to telephone. She would have known too late he was one of them; he was telephoning to the man in the grey mackintosh. They were everywhere: they were taking over. She was clawing at the window trying to get out. There were the piles of tins and groceries. The windows were all thick glass with splinters. They ran up under her nails.

She was in the cottage with the two men making arrangements. Peter had been digging. He had lain the spade upon the ground. His sleeves were rolled up. The sides of the grave were slippery with water.

There was something changing inside her head. She pressed with the tips of her fingers. She thought – I am disappearing. There was a phrase running through her head – Goodbye Piccadilly. She was being carried along on a cart. Peter was looking at her as if he had not seen her before. When people looked at her she had no protection. She put her hands in front of her face. He said in English 'You are Mary?' His eyes and mouth pushed at her. She would put her head under the blanket. She was being driven home up the front drive past the rhododendrons. There was a man on duty by the stables. Connie would open the door and would kneel with her arms out. She would rush into her, crying. Peter held out a hand; she backed away. Connie would take her along the long corridors and closed doors to her father's room. She had said 'You must ask your father.' The tall doors were lined with velvet: there was the dark chair with its tray and glasses of water. Her father came out of the conference room stooped and smiling. He had his back to her. He said – 'They didn't keep you?' She fell down on the ground. He would kneel over her dying body.

Peter said in English to the man. 'She didn't tell me.'

Her father looked at her over the tops of his spectacles. When her mother had died she had run and hidden her face in his lap. She could not remember her mother. A woman with a long skirt and pearls. His hand had stroked down her head and back. He had touched her.

She said 'I must go out now.'

They were still looking at her.

She said 'Please.'

She was walking to the back door. The man in the mackintosh stretched across the table. She went out into garden with the cinder path and nettles. There was the branch to the left towards the leaning wooden hut. Peter had come to the back door and was watching her. She was going through the nettles with her arms raised. She came to the door of the hut which leaned at an angle. Her insides curled up. There were flies and the thick darkness; the edge of the door in cursed splinters. Holding her breath, and keeping her eyes away as if it were a slaughter-house, she went in and felt she was going to faint and bolted the door behind her. She was safe where she most hated. She leaned with her back against the side wall and it rocked; she flung out an arm against the wood. The bolt on the door was new and shiny with the shaft through an old rusted staple. She let her breath out and turned to a crack at the door for air. The nettles had come alive and were blowing poison through the walls as if they were of a gas chamber. At school she had been like this and they had come outside the door and laughed. They had seen through the walls; but with the bolt she was safe from them. There had been a noise like water to drown her; her towel like a bandage; things hard and crusted like wood. Your hands were on the white stuff; the thin blood. If you held your breath long enough you would die.

Opening her eyes she saw the upright wooden hut about three foot square at the bottom, the roof sloping overhead, the door with the bolt which she had locked. She wanted to sit. She slid her back down the side wall till she squatted keeping herself above the ground. At the back was the seat with a lid off. The wood had cracked. There was a dark flood on the floor. She had stood in the bath with a towel in front of her. Her father had said – Don't be ashamed. She had said – I'm not ashamed! There had been the white stuff, soft and crusted. She had been naked.

In the hut there was a wire with bits of newspaper hanging. On one of the bits was a man grinning with lines going out from his head like sunshine. The wire was a hook that had caught him through his mouth. The hut was burying her. Peter had dug her grave. They put you in and you were safe then you were struggling to get your knees and arms up. You were in the coffin alive. She wrapped her arms round her knees and hugged them. They would have to pry her apart. There were people talking quietly outside her door. She lifted her head to the smell, airlessness: Peter and the man in the grey mackintosh. Her father would come along in the car with the big windows like a hearse. She was sitting on the ground in mud and ashes with her head against her knees. She had wished she were dead, so then they would know whose fault it was. Her father would stand over her with his tired eyes; would read from a prayer book. Once at home she had run away and had locked herself in a cupboard. You pretended to lock yourself in a cupboard so that they would come after you and think you were dead. Peter was knocking on the door and asking if she was all right. She had only been in ten minutes. People were always knocking and asking if she was all right. There was the blood and the white stuff and elastic. Now no one would find her. She had the pain again and dug her fingers

97

into her knee. She imagined herself shouting – Just a minute! She began to pull at herself like unsaddling a horse. When she stood her head was as high as the roof; she was scraping and backing into a manger. She closed her eyes. Veins on her neck stood out. Specks floated in front of her like water. There was a noise like a crack and bits of dust floated down. The earth at the bottom of the hut was moving. She shouted – Wait! She was being dragged into the daylight. Peter was pushing at the walls of the hut; he was going to push her whole world over. Her back legs were apart like those of a horse. There was daylight appearing at the bottom of one of the walls. She could hear him struggling. Her inside was falling out. She could feel the whole hut coming off her. She folded her hands over her head to protect herself; felt naked from the waist down; the hut was being peeled off like a sheath. He would take her at the back of the neck and hit her. Mud would fly up in front of her eyes. Light rushed in over her neck and ears. She was squatting on all fours. The air was blinding. The whole hut had crashed over, just missing her head. She was on a small square of brown earth amongst broken cinders. The hut had disintegrated sideways into a pile of rubble. Peter was standing over her holding his wrist. He and she were on their own. His hair was over the collar of his white shirt. He wore black trousers. His shoes were pointed, with soft wrinkles. He was twisting his arm as if it hurt. He said 'I was frightened.'

23

Colonel Wedderburn stood on the front seat of a Land Rover holding a small megaphone. In front of him in an open ride in the woods were men in army uniform and a few civilians with big sticks. An officer stood with his hands behind his back. Colonel Wedderburn blew through his megaphone and made a noise like a hunting horn. The trees were like bright green weeds. The officer lifted a stick and shouted 'Hold it!' Colonel Wedderburn bent over the windscreen; raised the megaphone and shouted 'Can you hear me?' The soldiers stood at ease in a long line; behind them were men with walkie-talkie radios. Colonel Wedderburn said 'We are looking for a girl, fourteen, fair hair, medium build, about five foot seven; last seen entering the wood on horseback at a point just left of where the ride meets the road on your right – ' he pointed: the men looked away from the trees, the bright green sea ' – at about ten-fifteen yesterday morning. She went towards the top of the hill – ' he pointed in front; they moved from leg to leg, raised hands discreetly and coughed ' – where there are signs that she tethered her horse: from there, we've not much trace. The horse came back on its own.' His voice travelled into the distance; faded; the megaphone waved. 'What I want from you is a thorough search of the woods and scrubland – ' sweeping an arm round 'leaving no bush, no square inch, where she might have fallen. She might be hurt. There might be other signs of – ' the megaphone breathed ' – her whereabouts. Your officers will have emphasised to you that there is strict security. You will talk about this to no one: you will answer no questions about what you are doing, who you are looking for. But I am able to tell you that there may be some signs, conceivably, of a struggle. You are to look for anything in the undergrowth; of tracks being made. You are to talk of this to no one.'

He put the megaphone down. The voice disappeared in the wind.

The officer put a finger into his ear.

Colonel Wedderburn said 'You've got it on the map.'

The officer said 'To the road Wancote, Hassington village.'

'Then turn. Boundary 017 – '

A sergeant major came up and stamped. He shouted 'Sir!' The officer waved. The sergeant major spun and stood to attention and leaned above some bracken. The line of soldiers moved off into the woods.

The officer said 'Here beginneth the shooting season.'

Colonel Wedderburn raised the microphone and shouted 'Keep your distance!'

The officer said 'Hen bird only.'

The sergeant major span round and stood to attention and shouted 'Sir!'

The officer said 'What?'

'Can the men smoke?'

The men had disappeared into the woods. Behind them men with radio sets sailed along with waving aerials.

Connie came walking up the ride from the road. She saw Colonel Wedderburn standing on the seat of the Land Rover with his megaphone. She thought – He acts like Nelson.

The sergeant major stamped and disappeared into the wood.

Connie came up panting with her hand on her heart. She leaned against the Land Rover. The megaphone had a leather ring which fitted over Colonel Wedderburn's mouth.

Connie said 'Charles – '

The metal of the Land Rover burned like a gun barrel.

She cried 'Charles, this was supposed to be secret!'

He shouted 'See they cover the ground there!'

Connie said 'I've run all the way. You know he didn't want – ' Connie bent over her heart.

Colonel Wedderburn lowered the megaphone and said 'I know what he wanted.' He sat in the front of the Land-Rover. He wore a brown duffle coat. The driver, in uniform, sat with his hands on the wheel.

Connie said 'Charles, I heard you halfway to the village!'

'Can you find a track on the right driver?'

Connie stretched out a hand; said 'Charles, I'm sorry.'

Colonel Wedderburn stared through the windscreen. He said 'I was given orders last night.'

Connie said 'I know what orders last night – '

Colonel Wedderburn said 'I know you do.'

He raised his chin slightly. He held his stick upright between his knees.

Connie said 'Charles can I talk to you?' She began climbing into the back seat.

'You can go along by the fence, driver.'

The Land Rover started. Connie held on with two hands. She bounced on the metal. She said 'She's been traced to the roadside anyway.'

Colonel Wedderburn's neck bulged over the back of his duffle coat. He held on to a pillar of the windscreen. They were going down a track through overhanging branches. The branches whipped at them.

Connie said 'Please!'

They ducked beneath a rush of leaves like swords.

The Land Rover came to another wide green ride parallel to the first. Colonel Wedderburn held a hand out and the Land Rover stopped. He stood up; gazed back over Connie's head with his megaphone.

Connie said 'Charles I've said I'm sorry! You've broken my wrist!'

Colonel Wedderburn said 'I've got fifty men waiting at the village, Connie. We're taking the woods on from there. I'm covering a lot of ground.' He raised the megaphone, shouted 'Keep in line there! Hold it!'

The soldiers had reappeared from the woods. They stood on the edge of the ride looking back at the green and grey light. A few pheasants flew up with a whirr and clucking. The officer appeared and raised his stick and said 'Bang!'

Connie said 'I'm only trying to help you Charles.'

Colonel Wedderburn said 'You help me then Connie.'

The sergeant major was standing to attention, leaning slightly forwards, in a ditch.

Colonel Wedderburn said 'We're going to take the whole county to Fordingbright. I've got two counties working. I've just come from a briefing. They're going through empty buildings. I'm going to find this girl even if you can't.'

Connie said 'But we know she isn't here.'

Colonel Wedderburn shouted 'Move on there!'

The officer wandered up to the Land Rover.

Connie said 'I'll try to fix it with Simon then.'

Colonel Wedderburn said 'You do that, Connie.'

The officer put his stick against his hat, facing Connie. He said 'The iron station wagon!'

The men were disappearing again into the woods.

Connie said 'You know what he'll say. He'll be furious.'

Colonel Wedderburn said 'They're so frightened of the press you'd think they were a load of rabbits!' He said to the driver 'On up the track then.'

Connie said 'Let me out!' She put one leg over the metal of the Land Rover; hopped with the other leg trailing like a hurdler. The Land Rover set off bumping over the rough ground. Connie put her hand on her heart; bent over as if she were wounded.

24

There was a movement on the terrace in front of the french windows of the country house the glass opening and the group visible beyond, the round faces and some with their backs to the outside and in the middle the two figures one tall with grey hair and the other a short white blur. They came into the sun. Across the valley were the line of dark and pale green trees and the puffs of clouds. Sir Simon held out an arm and guided Korin along the terrace past the grey stone walls and creepers; men on either side, behind, looking from side to side, for something to do. They came to the end of the terrace by the tennis court and moved on towards outhouses, a conservatory, a long low building like a cowshed. In the distance was a line of soldiers with white belts and gaiters standing at ease. Sir Simon came to a door in the wall of the long low building and swept his arm round and Korin went in first. Inside were two long wooden runways of a bowling alley. At the far end were old wooden skittles. Some soldiers stood at ease behind the skittles. In the space at the front were wooden pegs to hang coats on and bare brick walls and a blackboard and chalk. At the far side from the door, in an alcove, were a crowd of men holding cameras. They raised their arms and flashed.

Sir Simon said 'The only one in the south of England.'

The man in the striped suit came up and spoke in the foreign language in Korin's ear.

One of the reporters said 'Sir, can you tell us what the forces in the woods – '

Andrew Seymour stepped quickly forwards and held a hand up; said 'No questions!'

Korin spoke quietly to the man in the striped suit, who turned to Sir Simon and said 'In my country we have this game with automatic equipment. After each – ' he waved his hands.

'Strike' Sir Simon said.

Andrew Seymour said 'Frame.'

The man in the striped suit said ' – the skittles are picked up – ' he moved his hands in the shape of a bottle.

Sir Simon said 'This is an eighteenth century bowling alley!'

One of the reporters said – 'What are they looking for sir?'

Sir Simon picked up a ball and handed it to Korin. He said 'You have the first.' Korin turned the ball round and round. He spoke to the interpreter.

The interpreter said 'There are no holes.'

Sir Simon took the ball back: he said 'No holes.'

Flashlights went off from the alcove.

The interpreter said 'There ought to be three.' He jabbed his fingers and thumb against the wood.

Sir Simon said 'One more than usual, what?'

One of the reporters said 'Sir Francis Drake!'

Sir Simon stepped, crouched, swung his arms, ran forwards, sent the ball rolling down the alley. It veered off into the side groove and went past the skittles banging from side to side. Sir Simon stood with his thumbs in his waistcoat pockets.

Korin was examining a row of balls at the side of the platform. Flashlights went off. He took a ball, bowled, and knocked over the two end skittles on the left. He remained crouching, an arm on his knee.

The interpreter said 'It is not possible this way to get bias'. He moved his fingers in a curve.

Sir Simon said 'Do we need that?' He made his face with his jaw drooped and his eyebrows raised. Some of the people behind him laughed.

Sir Simon said 'In the eighteenth century the game was imported from Holland. It originated I think in Egypt. Walpole played here. Also Madame de Staël.'

A reporter said 'What are the differences between this and the modern game?'

Korin had taken another ball: it knocked down a pile of skittles leaving only two upright. The soldiers at the far end set up the skittles. Korin clapped and waved.

A reporter called 'Can we have a picture of Miss Mary sir?'

Sir Simon put a hand in his waistcoat; took out a watch.

Korin was holding a ball out; took Sir Simon by the arm; pressed the ball on him.

Sir Simon said 'Lunch time.'

Korin led him by the arm to the end of the right-hand alley. Sir Simon dropped his top lip; peered over his shoulder. Korin pointed at the skittles.

Sir Simon took off his jacket, undid a cuff-link, rolled up one sleeve, laid his jacket down. Flashlights went off. He stepped, swung: the ball went quietly to one side of the leading skittle and knocked them all down.

The reporters cheered. A soldier began picking up the skittles.

At the other alley, on the left, Korin picked up a ball and bowled it fast. It veered to the right, bounced, shot over the dividing line, caught the right-hand skittles which the soldier was setting up, scattered them, and one jumped up and hit the soldier in the face.

The soldier sat down with a hand over his eye.

The reporters leaped on the right-hand alley, pressed past two men in uniform, trod over the ramp, the gutter, their cameras like guns. Flashbulbs went off. They crouched on the wood, clicked; arrived at the far end around the soldier and aimed. Soldiers began pulling at them from the back. There was the screech of rubber shoes on floorboards. Korin picked up Sir Simon's jacket; dusted it. Sir Simon said 'Strike!' and drooped his jaw. Korin took hold of his wrist and began talking earnestly. Sir Simon leaned towards the interpreter. The interpreter said 'Please let me know the name of the injured man.' Sir Simon said 'Certainly.' The reporters were being forced back from the far end. They suddenly broke for the door where they had been let in; tripped; banged against a wooden railing. Sir Simon flung out an arm and shouted 'Get those men out of here!'

25

Andrew Seymour was walking at the back of the house past the rhodedendrons and a line of parked cars when a man called to him making him turn; a fat man with a round face, squeezing between two cars, wearing a tweed coat in the hot weather. He said 'Mr. Seymour sir – ' Andrew Seymour waited. The man came up with his hands out; gazed anxiously at Andrew Seymour. He said 'What are you looking for'

Andrew Seymour said 'The john.'

The man looked at the sun. He had a small flat nose. He said 'What's the fuss?'

Andrews Seymour said 'Always a fuss.'

The man said 'The word went out.' He bounced his hands in his pockets. He spoke slowly, separating the words: 'You'd – lost – a' then rushed the words together as if tickling a child 'very-important-piece-of-merchandise.'

Andrew Seymour beamed through his spectacles.

The man said 'And not to say anything about it. Why?'

Andrew Seymour bent a little: put his head to one side. 'Not to say?'

The man flung his arms out. 'Not that we would!' His coat opened as if he were showing the lining like a conjuror. 'We're reasonable. But we've known it since last night.'

Andrew Seymour said 'Of course.'

The man looked behind him; said quietly 'We got a photograph.' Then hunched his shoulders and put on a false voice: 'You like a nice photo?'

Andrew Seymour said 'You know me.' Smiled.

The man looked over his shoulder. He said 'Now. What can we be looking for? With half the bloody army!'

Andrew Seymour said 'What photograph?'

The man came closer: said 'Now. We don't want to do anything we shouldn't. We're on your side Mr. Seymour.'

Andrew Seymour said 'You're the guardians of the public conscience.'

The man stepped back.

Andrew Seymour said 'We're just the machine. You shove it into the in-tray and we shove it into the out. It's you who're the myth-makers.'

The man's eyes went dreamy, as if he had been hurt.

Andrew Seymour said 'We've had quite a busy morning. The Yemen, a hundred or two Europeans about to be murdered in Masonville, the first signs for twenty years of a break in Eastern Europe.' He smiled. 'What photograph?'

The man said 'You don't like us do you Mr. Seymour?'

Andrew Seymour said 'On the contrary, I think you're absolutely necessary like bile in the guts. One of the mysteries of life – very important.'

'I was trying to help you Mr. Seymour.'

'I mean it. What photograph?'

'I can't help you then Mr. Seymour.'

'I didn't think you could.'

106

'What about Miss Connie Johnson then Mr. Seymour?'

Andrew Seymour stopped: turned with his head down.

The man said 'Very busy nowadays? Can't look after her job?' He held his hands out. 'Mr. Seymour sir!'

Andrew Seymour said 'Good morning.'

'Good morning.' The man stood like someone preaching.

Andrew Seymour walked on. He thought – I shouldn't have lost my temper. Then – But I meant what I said.

Connie walked along the corridor past the statuettes and bowls of roses. She said to herself – Simon, I'm thinking of the girl. You can't just leave it like this. Charles Wedderburn's got to get some men going properly through those woods. She may be lying there. Or if she isn't she might be – anything – lost her memory. Simon, you've got to let it be public. If she's somewhere, people must know who she is. Someone must have seen her. You ought to let it out on the news. I'm thinking of the girl, Simon.

She knocked at the door. There was no answer: she went into the room with the leather chair and the table with a tray of whisky and water. He would say – Are you going to ruin a whole line of foreign policy –

Connie put a hand to her head.

There was a noise in the passage and he was coming in. He shut out the group that was with him. When he came into a room it still seemed to fill with a faint rush; an aura of people watching him. He went to the table with the bottles of whisky and pills. He looked exhausted. The flesh under his eyes was like leeches.

Connie said 'Simon, you've got to do something. For your own peace of mind.'

He was drinking water as if very thirsty. His skin seemed transparent. She thought – He is a victim.

Connie said 'I've been thinking, Simon, wouldn't it do something for the talks if you made it public? You know how unpopular the whole thing is – all the criticism you get – and you want a bit of sympathy. You know how unpopular Korin is. Wouldn't it be good if you got people's attention off this and on to something else? You know what a bad press you've been getting. This is the silly season, they've got to write something. But you really do deserve something better.'

Sir Simon took his glass to the window and hung his head. He seemed to have grown smaller.

Connie said 'This isn't the point of course. But you would get sympathy. They'd think it was the demonstrators. Or just that she was hurt. You'd get the public. And would be doing the best for Mary.'

She watched him. He seemed slightly luminous; his soft hands and skin.

Connie said 'Someone must have seen her. They must know where she is. But they won't know who. She's probably even waiting for this sort of thing, to come home. You know what children are. It's a way of getting attention.'

She thought – He suffers.

She said 'I only mention this because I thought it would help. I know you're carrying a tremendous burden Simon. And it's only really fair on Charles Wedderburn. The press are bound to get it sooner or later anyway.'

Sir Simon said 'I've thought of that.'

He came away from the window and banged his glass down on the tray. He said 'It's difficult for children who have to put up with their parent's public work. Inevitably they suffer. I must spend more time with her.'

Connie put her hand on her heart and raised her eyebrows.

He said 'All right. Tell Wedderburn. And Andrew can get out a statement. Let me see it.'

She said. 'Simon I'm sure you're right.'

He said 'There's so little time. The areas in which we can influence things are so small. It's a question of priorities.'

Connie stood with her legs apart, her skirt hitched slightly at the back.

Sir Simon said 'It's one of the fantasies of our time, this feeling of control. I don't think the old people had it. Tolstoy was right, you can't beat the Gods. It's the small things – the warf and woof – that make up the pattern. And how much influence do we have over the small? Now that's a theme for a modern writer. The influence of the minuscule over the macrocosm. Not in the ridiculous way, of course, of the muck heap. But in fact what does happen? Not the way people think it happens.'

Connie thought – He must have a rest.

Sir Simon said 'We should pay more attention to the Gods. They don't care what a man does, they care what he is. But out of the chaos comes a line. Directly from this. Yes go and tell Andrew and Wedderburn. We must learn.'

Connie went to the door. Outside she leaned against a wall and theatrically wiped a hand just in front of her forehead. She looked along the corridor, as if someone might have seen her.

Andrew Seymour saw Connie in the corridor and said 'Connie I must talk to you.' Connie said 'I must to you too.' Andrew Seymour said 'The press know, we've got to get out some statement.' Connie said 'Yes I've just been told to tell you to do that.' Andrew Seymour said 'How did they know? How many men has Wedderburn got in those woods?' Connie said 'I had a tremendous time persuading him, you know, he's been against it all along.' Andrew Seymour said 'What did he say?' Connie said 'I don't think we can possibly blame Charles Wedderburn.' Andrew Seymour said 'I'm not interested in blame.'

They went into the room where there was the harmonium and the picture of a dog with a dead bird in its mouth; a coffee urn and a row of mugs.

Andrew Seymour said 'There was a general in the Spanish Civil War whose son was captured by the enemy and they threatened him with death and they blackmailed the General, and the General just said – "Carry on".' Connie said. 'Andrew that's a terrible thing to say.'

Andrew Seymour said 'Well I don't know, Connie, this is politics, and someone always gets hurt.' Connie said 'I don't think that's true.'

Andrew Seymour said 'All this talk about truth, Connie. Do you know at the moment we're giving an undertaking to all our allies that we've not entered into any discussion about eastern frontiers and we're doing just that, and they don't even think we're not. If we didn't or they didn't, the thing would collapse. Do you expect Simon to show what he feels?'

Connie said. 'As a matter of fact Simon feels very deeply.'

Andrew Seymour said 'It's absolutely essential that one keeps up formal pretences Connie. What does it matter if Simon pinched her bottom?'

Connie said. 'What on earth are you talking about Andrew?'

Andrew Seymour said 'Of course she may have been taken by some absurd students. I'm not saying that. But it's the attitude, Connie. You're saying it's wrong she was allowed to go out riding. But I think it's absolutely essential for children to get out at an early age. They're competent enough heaven knows. I was in America last year where they are supposed to be so precious, and they were very repressed and fat.'

Connie said. 'I said nothing about her not going out riding!'

Andrew Seymour said 'And there's another thing I ought to tell you Connie. People have got hold about you and Simon. This doesn't matter: the press can't use it anyway. But if you do hear anything just shut up like a clam. They've got nothing to go on. Or have they? There isn't a photograph is there?'

Connie said 'Andrew I shall hit you.'

Andrew Seymour said 'No I think that's of Mary. They say they've got some photograph, do you know anything about it?'

Connie said 'What photograph?'

Andrew Seymour said 'Now there's another thing, Connie – ' he broke off. 'Does he really want a statement?'

Connie said 'Yes.'

'All right – now when they do find Mary, Connie, this

might be one of the biggest things for months. There are bound to be wild rumours. And if we don't get at the truth, we'll have to construct it. We'll have to make the story before we begin. Everyone nowadays thinks you've just got to tell something and out comes truth. Well it doesn't.'

Connie said. 'What are you trying to tell me?'

Andrew Seymour said 'I know you Connie. And I'm devoted to Charles Wedderburn. But I wish there was just a little more common sense in all this. We've got to make up our minds. Then carry it through. This is what everyone knows at the centre. And you are at the centre, Connie. It's all much too important for people's feelings and opinions. Simon knows this. He's a great man Connie. I want you to be careful. I just don't want him hurt.'

Connie had gone red in the face. She was smoothing her hands down her thighs.

Andrew Seymour said 'Do you know what I mean?'

Connie turned her back and walked away along the corridor.

26

In the afternoon the sky went dark with rain. Mary lay in the upstairs room with her head underneath the rug. She had fallen from her horse and was crawling through gorse bushes. There were tunnels with black branches on either side. Under the earth were caves with stalactites. She was on a ledge above a precipice. The precipice was of cardboard.

From outside, beyond the willows and the green slope of the field, came the noise of motorcycles. They were going up and down over hills, never getting any closer or further away. Sometimes the noise was like a mechanical saw cutting through wood and the flesh of her head.

He had taken her by the arm and led her up to the room again. That was hours ago. He had found the key in the pocket of her riding-breeches. She had felt his hand against her groin.

Later, she had heard them talking.

There were people at the centre of the world like this in groups, in underground cellars. Lines went out from them tunnelling like moles.

He had locked her in the room again. He had told her to wait. She had lain on the bed and dozed and woken.

The sound of motorbikes was going over and under the hills. When fear came it was like cold starting from her stomach and flowing each way to her head and feet. When it reached her head it circled and exploded like a rocket. Stars fell in burning ice. She was under the rug, her knees drawn up, her hands stiff on either side.

They were going to kill her. There were people like herself all over the world in prisons, on boards, waiting for footsteps in the passage. The sounds of hands at the lock and the moment before they got the key in.

Last summer she had started building her house in the tree; coming across it with the planks, the nails, already there; carrying the wooden boxes and the biscuit-tins; a taste of old rope, damp; going on a long sea voyage with the tide and a square sail; one oar against which she steered. She was going to a country with flowered restaurants and a band with rattles. A hurricane beat down the palm trees. The sea was rough and the fish rose from a deep blue. A whale darted like clouds beneath green and silver. There was a cone going into the centre of the earth, the hollow of a whirlpool.

They would come into the room and stand by the bed around her. The cold went into her heart, her centre. When they put their hands on her she would shoot out rigid and they would pull her by the arms and legs: trembling like a spider.

She thought – I want to die then.

She heard footsteps going away on the path outside. From the door, from the downstairs passage. The noise of motorcycles came and went over the hill. A car started. An enormous voice floated on the wind.

Footsteps had moved before in the passage, the kitchen. Voices and the scraping of iron. They had been pulling the grate out: lifting the flagstones. The thump of hair; of skulls.

Footsteps were coming up the stairs now.

Pressing her head down by her knees she did not think she could bear it. Fear was in a white light of magnesium. It had burned her eyes and mind out. The hands were at the door. The eternity before they put the key in.

Her knees were pressed into her face so that she thought she might have melted.

He was standing over her. She burned and froze. She had held her breath so long it was as if she were being strangled.

His voice said 'Can't stay in bed all day!'

Something flat seemed to hit her just below the heart, bruising it.

He said 'Waiting for servants to bring it to you are you?'

There was a piece of rug in front of her eyes like a forest. Light trailed down in creepers.

He said 'Living off the fat of the land!' He put on a high-pitched voice: 'Tea and crumpets!'

He was trying to pull down the rug like a scab coming off. There was the grey wall with whitewash.

He said in a rough voice. 'Come on get up!'

She leaned on one elbow; opened her mouth and breathed again.

He said 'Aristocrat!' He bent down and pulled. He was smiling.

She shouted. 'What's the matter?'

He was carrying a plate with food on it. His white shirt was open to the waist.

Mary moved her jaw; stretched her neck about.

He gave her a push below her shoulder.

She shouted 'Let go!'

He raised an arm. She bowed her head down on the

mattress. He said in a cooing voice. 'I'm not goin' to hurt 'oo!'

She turned on her back with her arms folded. She said 'I'm not an aristocrat!'

The boy blew his lips out and made a bubbling noise.

She said 'My grandfather was a clerk in a shipping firm as a matter of fact.'

He had put the plate on a chair by the side of the bed. He walked round the room. She watched him: she had forgotten what he looked like.

He said. 'You've got to get back.'

She said 'Yes.'

He said 'We've been hanging about all day. What have we been doing?' He turned and stared.

She said 'What?'

He smiled lopsidedly. He said 'Come on.'

They were playing games again.

Mary said 'Nothing.'

He said 'How did we get here?' He came to her bed, put the plate of food on the floor, sat on the chair.

Mary said 'On a motor bike.'

'Yes.'

He had dark gentle eyes. Thick lashes at the bottom going different ways.

Mary said 'Oh I see!'

'Come on then.'

She said 'I came here on a motor bike. I didn't see what happened.'

'What happened?'

'Nothing.'

He said 'Something must have: otherwise how did you get here!' His eyes were hurting.

Mary said 'I mean nothing about you. The gun.'

He said 'What gun?'

'You were shooting rabbits.'

There was a softness moving behind his eyes; things trying to speak, frightened.

Mary said 'Oh you weren't there at all! I came with someone quite different!'

'Who?'

'I don't know.'

He went to the window. There was the noise of motor bikes like the buzzing of insects.

He said 'I came down for the cycle racing. D'you hear it?'

'Yes.'

'It's on Saturday afternoon.' He walked back to the bed. He said 'I found you here.'

She stared. He was trying to say something different.

He said. 'You'd been taken here.'

'Who by?'

'I don't know. Do you?'

Mary said 'No.'

He said – 'I can't trust you!'

Mary sat up and shouted 'I told you you could!'

He walked away.

Mary stretched her hands out of the mattress beyond her drawn-up feet. She cried 'I do mean it!'

He suddenly put his clenched hands against his head. He said 'There's no trust.' He banged his head gently. The room seemed to be floating. 'There are such terrible things!'

She said 'Tell me.'

He said 'I had a friend.'

He was standing facing a wall, his clothes hanging loose like those of the dead. There was a black line around him.

He said 'This friend was taken and shot. But before they shot – '

As he spoke he seemed to be fighting to keep upright against the wall.

' – They put her upside down in a coffin.'

Mary found that she was stretching her eyes and opening her mouth as if horrified.

He squatted down on his haunches by the wall. His white shirt was pulled tight at the back. In the room there was pressure like sickness.

He said 'They kept her like this for a long time. The head – ' He made an enormous circular gesture with his hands.

Mary brushed her hair back. She watched herself doing this, repeatedly.

He said 'If you don't fight you die. There's such cowardice.' He spread his hands out. 'They sell one another. No truth.' He was whispering.

Mary said 'Oh I know!'

He shouted 'What do you know?'

Mary found herself crying; the tears down her cheeks and salt in her open mouth.

He said 'Nothing!'

Mary said 'I do! What d'you think I've felt – '

He whispered 'I need – ' put a hand on the wall as if to stop himself overbalancing.

She found herself holding her breath again. A tight band round her throat, her heart. The sensation of being able to swim.

She said 'Don't you believe you can trust me?'

He went on to his knees: he hung there with his head between his arms.

He said 'I could have rescued you.'

She said 'What?'

'When I came here. I found you.'

'Oh yes.'

She couldn't see his face. The top of his head, his hair, was a black hole.

He said 'Is that all right? You can tell them. Then I can be sure you won't betray me.'

Mary lay back. The cold had come in again. She thought – I thought it was different.

He lifted his face. He said 'It's true in a way. That man might have – '

'Yes.'

' – killed you.'

The room settled down again. She stretched her arm down the mattress, to something that had disappeared.

He said 'Why don't you say something?'

'What?'

'I have to make sure.'

She shouted 'All right!' She put her hands over her face.

He said 'I wanted to tell you something about my country. What it's like.' His head swayed like a dog. 'There is nothing there. You have to fight.' He seemed to sneeze.

Mary said 'But not kill.'

He shook his head as if getting rid of water.

Mary said 'Or you're the same.'

She watched him.

He said 'All right.'

She said 'You promise?'

After a time he said 'Yes.'

Mary said 'Then I promise.'

She saw her fingers on the mattress pointing like gun barrels.

He said 'I'll take you back and you can say I rescued you. You were taken here by people. Crazy people.' He went on shaking. 'No killing.'

He looked up. His gentle eyes were still trying to tell her the things that were different.

She said 'What's wrong?'

'He said 'I don't know.'

She said 'When are we going then?'

'Not till after dark.'

'Why?'

'It's not safe.'

He looked round. There was his mouth and the flat profile with the line around it like a medal.

She said 'It was nothing to do with my father then?'

He said 'No.'

She said 'I thought you would have just trusted me.'

27

Sir Simon sat in the small room with the tray of water and decanter of whisky. The reading board was in front of him. He read –

Three groups, or categories, are for separate reasons interested in the removal of Korin: first the old Soviet-trained wing of the party still working for subservience to the USSR and who see the recent rapproachement with the West not only as a betrayal of communist policy but as a serious threat to themselves: second, those non-communists remaining from the purges of the 50s obviously few in number and not in important positions but said to be feeling confident enough now to re-emerge with their own contacts: and third, the various youth organisations that have been allowed to reform after the Students' Rebellion which undoubtedly still feel the scars of this but which share in the renewed sense of freedom throughout this part of the communist world. How strong, or effective, are any of these groups singly or in contact with each other is not known. In the present situation the old alignments are breaking up: Korin, in this particular gamble, has alienated extremists on both sides and relies on the solid and nationalist central front – which has never probably been as hostile to the West as they have had to make out for the last twenty years. However there is little organised resistance for this same reason; from the centre, Korin can ensure that his enemies disagree. There have been reports of growing political organisation however amongst the young: also, a growing ODS leniency towards them. A debate took place at Lov university at the time of the Chi Min crisis which was remarkable for the way in which the participants seemed to split equally between those who were critical of Korin for his rapproachement with what they held to be the decadent West, and those who were critical of him for his continued intransigence at home. In the peculiar state of change it seems possible that there might even be a tie-up between the students and their old enemy the secret police: in which case it will not be the first time that there has been a cynical exploitation of the young by the old –

Sir Simon dropped the paper on the floor. He rang a bell.

When Andrew Seymour came in he said 'Why they can't get a bloody man to write English.'

Andrew Seymour picked up the papers.

Sir Simon said 'Have you got those telegrams?'

'Yes.'

'And the statement's gone out?'

'Yes.'

'They'll be all round the bloody house soon.'

Sir Simon ran down a page of paper with a pencil. He said 'In my time the standard has gone down appallingly. One used to get papers from people like Bridges that were little masterpieces.'

Andrew Seymour said 'Despatches from Defoe.'

Sir Simon said 'It would be worth someone's while collecting them and finding a publisher.'

Andrew Seymour shuffled the papers and sorted them into a box. He said 'Do you want to see Wedderburn?'

Sir Simon went on reading.

Andrew Seymour said 'Which way'll Korin totter?'

Sir Simon said 'How long'll he last, that's the question.' He pushed at the reading board: stretched his legs; said 'Here we are with the Teds against us one side and the Bluebell Boys on the other, but at least they won't shoot us.'

Andrew Seymour said 'He's a wicked communist plus a fascist beast.'

Sir Simon said 'I wish we could put him over. If we manage, the Americans might lump it.'

Andrew Seymour said 'Isn't there anyone better?'

'Not on the horizon.'

Andrew Seymour poured out whisky; brought two glasses.

Sir Simon said 'The day after tomorrow they could come with television. He'd be good at that.'

Andrew Seymour said 'Here?'

Sir Simon said 'A performing monkey. To charm the Romans as we make peace with the barbarians. Suggest that. On Monday morning.'

Andrew Seymour took out a notebook and wrote.

Sir Simon said 'It's a load of bloody nonsense! That's what runs the world now. We dress up like clowns.' He added – 'But I wouldn't have it different.'

Andrew Seymour said 'Who do you think might get rid of him?'

Sir Simon said 'Of his own people?' He looked vague.

Andrew Seymour went on writing. He said 'Wedderburn's waiting somewhere.'

Sir Simon sighed 'All right.' Then – 'There's so little time.'

Andrew Seymour went out. Sir Simon picked up the bell-push by his chair and rang it. The button came off stuck to his thumb. It had a small wire underneath like a hair-spring. He stared at it.

Colonel Wedderburn came in.

Sir Simon said 'What the bloody hell's this?'

Colonel Wedderburn looked round. He said 'Precautions sir. It'll be on the news. Then they'll be down here en masse. I've got men – '

Sir Simon shouted 'Are you more concerned with finding my daughter or protecting yourself from the press?'

Colonel Wedderburn stood to attention.

Sir Simon said 'They'll find out soon enough. Don't think they won't. Do you feel happy about bringing us all into ridicule?'

Colonel Wedderburn said 'It wasn't my idea sir.'

Sir Simon said 'You insisted in bringing in the press.'

Colonel Wedderburn said 'No sir.'

Sir Simon said 'Will you send someone to get this bloody bell mended?'

Colonel Wedderburn said 'Is that all?'

Sir Simon said 'As usual it will be left to the politicians to sort out the balls-up made by the army and the police. But don't think we're going to underplay this Wedderburn! We're going to have the full enquiry. If anything's happened to the girl it will come out.'

Colonel Wedderburn said 'I've followed my instructions sir.'

Sir Simon shouted 'Are you a pen-pusher or a soldier?'

Colonel Wedderburn said 'After this is over, sir, I shall ask to resign.'

Sir Simon jumped up and walked about the room. He said 'I'm an old soldier Wedderburn. This girl's my daughter.'

Colonel Wedderburn straightened his shoulders.

Sir Simon said 'It's not going to be a joke, Wedderburn. Not just a student's prank. Now tell me – ' he put a hand on his arm ' – what are your ideas?'

Colonel Wedderburn said 'Well they've been round the house two days, sir. The students.'

'What'd they do?'

'Just keep her sir'

'What else?'

'Could be more serious sir.'

'Are you checking the loonies?'

'Yes sir.'

'Both ends?'

'Yes.' Colonel Wedderburn put a hand to his mouth and coughed. 'Of course she could have just fallen.'

'I'm fed up Wedderburn with hearing she could just have fallen.'

'Yes sir.'

'Or that she's run away from home at the moment when I'm working for a united Europe.'

'Yes sir.'

'This is going to be serious whether anyone likes it or not.'

He paced up and down. Colonel Wedderburn watched; after a time said 'Police are carrying out searches in every unused building in the district sir. The news is being put out in terms of anyone who has seen anything suspicious, an exact description – '

Sir Simon said 'There'll be a lot of uproar. Politicians can stand anything except ridicule.'

Colonel Wedderburn said 'Yes sir'.

'You go along then.'

Colonel Wedderburn turned in a military manner and went out.

Sir Simon looked at the end of his thumb. He picked up the bell-push and jabbed at the hole with it.

Andrew Seymour came in.

Sir Simon said 'Keeping old jackboots on the hop!'

Andrew Seymour said 'Has that awful thing broken?'

Sir Simon sat down. He drummed on the arms of his chair. He said 'We've got to play this right. It is possible.' Then – 'Mustn't be beastly to Wedderburn! Shall I have him back for a drink?'

Andrew Seymour said 'Oh I shouldn't worry about Charles!'

Sir Simon said 'He says it wasn't his idea to bring in the press. Whose was it then?'

Andrew Seymour said 'I think Connie's.'

'But she must have talked to him.'

Andrew Seymour said 'Oh I'm sure she talked to him!'

He brought over a glass of whisky.

Sir Simon said 'What do you mean by that?'

Andrew Seymour tidied papers, put them on the table, went to the window and straightened the curtains.

Sir Simon said 'What grounds have you for saying that?'

Andrew Seymour ran his hands up and down the edges of the curtains, like a woman.

Sir Simon leaned with his head on the back of the chair. He said 'The child's been gone thirty-six hours now, Andrew. I was very close to her. People didn't see that, but I was. I didn't give her much time. But she was very close to me after her mother died.'

Andrew Seymour straightened cushions of a seat by the fireplace. His hands shook slightly.

Sir Simon struck out his lower jaw. He said 'I lost one person close to me. I don't want to lose another one, Andrew.'

Andrew Seymour said 'Are you tired sir?'

Sir Simon said 'No.' The loops of flesh under his eyes were like wounds.

28

At night there was a movement along the road running through beech trees; cars with their headlights rushing up over the earth like meteorites. After they had gone they were small and unremarkable, square backs fading into the darkness.

As they approached the lodge gates there was a looming as if an accident; other cars backed off the road top heavy in the soft earth and their lights swinging like girders. Cars stopped and men climbed out and walked forwards kicking against gravel; greeting each other and rubbing their hands as at some war. The trees moved slightly like the sound of shells disappearing in whispers. Beyond the cars were the lodge gates and a line of police. The police had their hands behind their backs and were smiling. The men from the cars moved from foot to foot as if for warmth.

Opposite the gates, at the beginning of the farm track that went up the hill, was the group of three young men and a girl carrying their banner. Two of the boys had long hair over their shoulders; the third a crew-cut. The girl had long black hair and dark jeans. They were like medieval singers. The headlights of a car turned on the girl and she shone like water. Above them the dead banner sagged; a hammock in which no one was sleeping.

From the side, along the road through the beech woods, came a large green van with gold lettering and steps up the back to the roof. The lights of cigarettes wandered at the sides of the road like fireflies. The van pushed its way past and came to a group in the middle of the road who turned their backs on it and huddled. The van flashed its headlights. One of the men put his hand to his heart and made a noise like a gun going off; tripped and staggered into his companions.

Some men moved into the darkness at the side of the road and there was an order from the police and suddenly the barking of dogs. Through the trees a figure ran bent; crashed with twigs and feet, a brown hat as if between antlers. A man emerged on the road and glanced behind him quickly. He brushed at his legs as if they had been through wire.

The van with the ladder to its roof had backed into a gap beneath the trees and the back door opened and a television camera was carried out. A man climbed to the roof with the camera over his shoulder like a rocket; crouched below overhanging branches and called to men below; lights went on and lit him. There was black cable being taken out of the back and a man with a spade and a saw like a bow and arrow. The headlights of the car went off. The cable slid on the ground in a black snake.

The three boys and the girl with the banner suddenly found it caught by the wind. The groups of men ducked slightly. One felt underneath his chin; another did a small dance with his hands in his pockets.

From above the van with the camera on it there was the sound of wood being sawed. A branch cracked; a huge shape came down like a pouncing animal. Men put their hands up: the branch fell across the roof of the van and hands pulled it with twigs and leaves pattering.

Another van was coming up the narrow road between the wires and parked cars; of a different colour and with different lettering but a similar ladder at the back to the roof. It stopped where the men were handling the branch across the road; its headlights lighting them as in some frieze of men struggling with chariots. The first van turned its lights on and there was a square of criss-crossed shafts like a pit in which men were digging. The men carrying the branch got it clear and they came and stood in the square of light and faced the van which had just arrived. From the back of the van came more men who walked to the front. The two groups were made thin by the light as if seen from the top of a watchtower.

The line of police had broken up and were mingling with the groups; were silhouetted against the flares and tree trunks. Someone had lit a small stove and was brewing-up. People gathered round the flame with their hands out and face glowing. Above them was a bright star like Christmas.

More cars were coming through the beech woods. The second van backed up the track towards the hill; its lights swept the three boys and the girl who backed into the ditch as if in front of flame-throwers.

The long line of cars stretched through the night; more and more doors slammed and there was the noise of feet on gravel: tramping down the long road they were like refugees, with their carts and horses; and above them the wind like machine-guns.

Some time later in the night it began to rain. The men went back into their cars, put tarpaulins over the wires and cameras; sat hunched eating out of packages and smoking. The police went into the lodge by the gates and reappeared with capes like bats. Gradually the lights of the cars went out and the black shapes seemed to lean against one another as if ruined. Sometimes the fireflies of cigarettes would glow through glass: the only survivors of a battlefield in which everything else was destruction.

29

Colonel Wedderburn moved a finger down the spine of Connie's back feeling the ridges of a mountain, the long cold air in between. Connie lay on her front with one side slightly raised as if by some earthquake; showing a hipbone and the side of a breast against the sheet. Her skin was gold till it reached her neck where it became redder; like a mask or a mask having been taken off, leaving ground unused to air. Down where the top sheet was pulled off were two soft bruises like pears. Colonel Wedderburn said 'Was that the Land Rover?'

He moved his hand down. Connie watched where it brushed like clouds across a landscape.

He said 'You like that?'

Connie lay flatter: the mountains became expanses of soft plain.

His hand moved like a bulldozer.

He said 'You're not on duty tonight? When is it, every other?'

Connie put a hand sideways and clawed at his thigh. She had short nails painted silver.

He said 'What do you do with him then?'

Connie rolled over on her back. She put a hand to her face as if light was hurting her; then stretched her eyes and stared at him. She had grey-green eyes heavily painted above the lids with blue. Her eyelashes were like spikes. He put out a hand and pressed his palm over her eyes.

He said 'You're sure he's sleeping?'

Connie's room with the brown polished furniture and flowered curtains smelled slightly of dust, of sour wood.

He said 'He took his pills then?'

Connie turned her head away. In profile there was her strong chin and the full flesh underneath. She was like a bird with a full crop. She held her arms out with her hands flat on their backs; the flesh between armpit and breast bunched as if with a taste of bitterness.

Colonel Wedderburn pressed her waist with his thumbs and fingers. There was a faint pale line between his lips. Her body did not move. She swallowed: stretching like a fish against a hook.

He said 'What is it?'

She turned and faced him again, her hair spread out,

staring with the grey green eyes moving from side to side to each of his own repeatedly. He thought – Her hair is like snakes.

He said 'Come on.' He pressed her.

Connie held herself still: looked down at his hand touching her.

He said 'It isn't him then?'

She said 'No!' The skin round her mouth trembled.

He said 'What is it?'

She turned on one side; said 'Can't you think of Mary?'

He took her two wrists and pulled them under her back; held them both with one hand while he pulled the lower part of her body up on his forearm and pushed her legs so that they were round her head. From between her knees grey-green eyes stared at him.

He said 'I'll give you a lesson.'

Connie felt herself compressed and exposed all at once; her face went whiter.

Colonel Wedderburn's voice, slightly muffled, said 'Small arms manual.'

Connie got her hands free and wrapped her forearms around the backs of her knees. A hand dragged at a calf muscle as if she had cramp.

Colonel Wedderburn said 'What does he do? The old goat!'

Connie began to vibrate as if something was passing in a tunnel far beneath her. It moved to and fro beneath the surface seeking for a way to get out. A shaft would be sunk down to a trapped miner waiting for air. The point would burst into the hidden cave but might destroy what it was rescuing. The trapped man would have a stake driven through his heart: a witch had a stake through her heart at a lonely crossroads.

Colonel Wedderburn said 'I could tell you a thing or two!'

Connie said 'Stop!'

She took a breath; then the pressure came in again. The drill, when it landed, would expose a vision of herself.

127

Connie thought – I want to be destroyed. But I am destroying him.

Colonel Wedderburn said 'Don't like me talking? People do.'

Connie waited. Where he pressed against her there was a spit, an iron bar, upon which she began to turn. As in a gyroscope there was a force from this point to the centre of the earth; this held everything together; herself and the point upon which she turned. She rolled slowly with the earth rolling inside her; went sideways, the hard end slipping on the pain.

Colonel Wedderburn said 'Does it hurt?'

There were shadows passing on the inside of Connie's face. White spots on the blue of her eyelids.

Colonel Wedderburn said 'I could you know.'

The iron passed between Connie's legs, the small of her back, the centre of the earth, cut into her, stretched and tightened with the pain. She clung upside down like a sloth. Otherwise she would lose it and go tumbling for ever through the darkness. Rolling her head and looking for earth, for safety, she began to feel herself alive, ascendant, rising from flames.

The telephone rang beside her bed.

Falling, she clung as if to life: the ringing was at the centre of her, at her point of balance.

She put her arms around him and held him; suddenly found how beautiful he was; skin, ribs, body, man. He was groaning. She opened her eyes and stared at him, as if terrified. His head went down past her line of vision, soft hair like a line of fir trees being crashed into by a plane. As the crash came there was the hard earth of his back and legs: he was burying himself in her snow. She put out an arm and pushed the telephone to the ground.

The ringing stopped.

He made a noise like someone dying.

She seemed to wake up on her back beneath fir trees and the sky of his weight on top of her; she could not move.

128

The sun and the ploughed-up snow and something that had been crying. There was so much beauty.

She ran her hand down his back. The ridges of bright mountains, the cold air in between.

He said 'I suppose you better answer it.'

She reached out an arm, but the telephone had gone. She struggled.

He pushed. 'Wait then.'

She leaned over the side of the bed and found the telephone.

She said 'Hullo?' Then – 'No of course he's not.' She put a hand over the mouthpiece; pointed with the other hand to the door.

Colonel Wedderburn said 'Simon?'

Connie said into the telephone 'Andrew I told you – '

Colonel Wedderburn lifted himself on his hands and smiled.

Connie said 'Oh I see!'

Colonel Wedderburn whispered 'It's for Simon then?'

Connie began pulling the top sheet over her. Colonel Wedderburn held it down. Connie was on her side; her skin from her knee to shoulder.

Connie put her hand over the mouthpiece and said 'They've found Mary.'

Colonel Wedderburn climbed off Connie and began feeling for his clothes.

Connie said into the telephone 'Yes I'll find him. He'll ring you back in two minutes.'

She began moving off the bed.

She said 'Where did you say – the police station?'

She was beginning to dress while holding the telephone between her ear and her shoulder.

She said 'She's all right?'

Colonel Wedderburn had put some clothes on and was going towards the door and waiting there.

Connie said 'How very good.' She put the receiver down.

'She said 'She's been brought into Cowdsdon police station.'

Colonel Wedderburn said 'Who by?'

'I don't know.'

'I'll fetch her.' He waited. 'Will you come?'

Connie said 'Yes.'

Colonel Wedderburn said 'How did he know I was here?'

Connie said, dressing 'He knows about us.'

'Connie – '

'Shouldn't we go then?'

Colonel Wedderburn waited by the door.

Connie looked into a mirror and saw her face streaked as if with tears.

Colonel Wedderburn said 'She's all right?'

Connie said 'Yes.' Then – 'What do you call all right?'

She opened her bag, looked, put her hand in, felt around, shut it; went to the door.

Colonel Wedderburn said 'Dearest Connie.'

He put a hand to her cheek and stroked it. She had grey green eyes. She went out of the door in front of him, her back striding along the corridor like a boxer.

30

Sir Simon appeared at the bottom of the stairs in dressing-gown and slippers; an old man not quite sure of his movements, his neck coming out of its shell and hardly connected with it; holding on to a banister and one foot groping as a blind man might. A woman in a black coat and skirt came past with a tray of tea in mugs. A man in a boiler suit stood in the background with a spanner. Sir Simon took a mug and blew on it and tears came into his eyes. There was the ringing of a bell; a corridor with men in uniform and old prints of battleships.

Connie came down the stairs and put a hand on Sir Simon's arm; she leaned on him for a moment, her coat wrapped around her as if she were cold. Colonel Wedderburn walked quickly along the passage with his stick under his arm; spoke to a man in uniform who stood to attention. Colonel Wedderburn came on to the bottom of the stairs and stood in front of Sir Simon and Connie. They all held mugs of streaming tea which they stirred with sugar-crusted spoons.

There was a chandelier that lit the hall around the staircase with its banisters and bowls of roses and bronze statuettes. It seemed to keep the objects out of sight so that the people underneath were in another role, another dimension. Connie looked up at Sir Simon as if in some goodbye; waiting for a train to go, the faces of officials along the carpet of a station platform. Colonel Wedderburn was checking his watch as if against the movements of the earth and stars. Sir Simon, as all great leaders, tottered slightly; seemed held from the roof by invisible wires.

There was the sound of cars on the gravel outside. Colonel Wedderburn held out a hand to Connie. Squeezing Sir Simon's arm, she smiled bravely. Stepping down the last stair and moving round to the archway to the back door she knew she should not look back with everyone's eyes upon her. Colonel Wedderburn spun half to attention; feathers nodding on horseback and a still plain. The woman in the black suit collected the mugs of tea: the man in the boiler suit clutched his spanner. Sir Simon was left on the last step of the stair; in the ruined house, too old to fight, while all the young went off to glory.

Outside it was a bright night with stars. There were two black cars drawn up on the gravel. Colonel Wedderburn put his head through the front window of the first and said to the driver 'Go out of the gate turn right go slowly round the wall. Right again to Hassington. Some way along there'll be a block. We go through. Then on to Cowdsdon. You know it?' The driver said 'Yes sir.' Colonel Wedderburn walked to the car behind: there were two men in front and two at the back. He said 'Right?' One of the men said 'Right.' Colonel Wedderburn went to the first car and held the back door open for Connie. Connie stepped in holding her overcoat wrapped round her; a glimpse of white ankles and head disappearing as if it might carry a tiara.

They sat on the back seat with a space between; royalty; the car going over the grassland towards the lodge gate where there were the mass of lights as if at an accident. The gates were closed and beyond it police and the crowd pressing. The car slowed. The driver flashed its lights and the gates were being opened; the police with hands joined, and faced and bodies bending over their arms. Colonel Wedderburn said 'One of these days!' As the car reached the gates and went through Connie put a hand up to the side of her head and flashlights went off and shadows seemed to move inside her face as if it were hurting. A blaze like a searchlight suddenly shone from the top of a van and a man swivelled a camera like a machine-gun. Colonel Wedderburn gripped his seat as if he were in a motorboat; his face flat and luminous with spray. He said to the driver 'Go on!' There were men raising cameras and stepping in front of the car; Connie said 'You'll run over them!' The car turned right. They went past the black shapes and men ran at the side of the car, their bodies bouncing in the rectangles of windows and their hands out to steady themselves close to Connie's and Colonel Wedderburn's heads. The car went faster and the men dropped behind, pushing at the car; then there was darkness and the arches of beech trees. Colonel Wedderburn leaned forwards and took a microphone from a rack at the back of the front seat and said 'Can you hear me?' There was a crackling noise and a voice said 'Yes.' Connie looked out of the back window where the second police car followed and beyond it the headlights of other cars starting up, the beams swinging along the beech trees like a scythe. Connie said 'They're following.' Colonel Wedderburn looked through the back window and said 'We'll rub their noses.' The road was going along the side of the park wall. In front of them was a barrier, a red light in the middle and torches coming forwards on either side. The car slowed. Colonel Wedderburn wound down a window and put his head out and a man with a torch shone it into his face and Colonel Wedderburn shouted 'Wait till we're through!' The barrier was a red-and-white striped pole on trestles; policemen lifted it and it swivelled; the man with the torch stood back and swung his arm and Colonel Wedderburn said 'Now fast!' They went past the barrier and Connie looked out of the back window and saw the men running to close it again in the headlights of the following car; the car stopping and policemen getting out and turning and facing the way they had come. In the further jungle of headlights hacking like matchet blades there were the other cars piling up; the whole scene lit as if by lightning, the cars in tiers, the night sky pulsing as in an air-battle miles away.

Connie leaned in her corner. Shivered.

Colonel Wedderburn said 'Have you brought her any clothes?'

Connie said 'Yes. Do we know what happened?'

Colonel Wedderburn said 'A boy found her.'

Connie looked out of the window. They were going fast through the wood; the road was a tunnel with the car on rails. Then the road opened out to a switchback over downs: a white line and cat's eyes which the car went over and killed. Connie thought – I must do better. They were travelling through the night, the dead time, over the world between one event and another. She opened her mouth to speak. Mary in a ditch; being put on a gate with ribs broken; lifted under the shoulders with the sharp weight cutting her. Connie thought – I am still in my room at home; we know nothing, do not want to. She said 'Is there anything else I should know?'

Colonel Wedderburn shook his head and pointed at the driver.

The car was going through a village of thatched houses like toys: a church with a stone wall and the noise of tires. Connie thought – We are ourselves only when we travel: at either end we are taken over by surroundings. The car slowed at a crossroads: Colonel Wedderburn looked out at a signpost: a gibbet, a grave. Connie had the image of the witch with a stake driven through her heart. The car went on. She thought – I must love Mary. She had been on a spit with the iron running through her. Charles Wedderburn's face in profile was an axe. Connie thought – It takes only an effort to love.

They were coming to a town. There was a steep hill with raised pavements and railings. The car slowed. A motorcyclist waited by a lamp post. A clock tower said five past one. The motorcyclist started up and went past with a roar like a bombardment. Connie thought – We are arriving.

Colonel Wedderburn put a hand on her knee and said 'Get her straight into the car. Don't ask her anything. Put her to bed. I'll follow later.' He had thick hands with a ring; rather yellow.

The driver was looking for a turning. On a corner was a group of men standing. As the car turned the group broke up; men were running on either side of the car again, their bodies bouncing in the rectangles of windows and putting out hands close to Connie's and Colonel Wedderburn's heads; seeming to push at the car like a chariot. Colonel Wedderburn said 'Sweet God!' Connie put a hand up; shadows moved inside her face like pain. She said 'I thought they didn't know!' Colonel Wedderburn said 'They didn't!' Men were prancing backwards at the front with cameras raised; spiders about to be squashed. Colonel Wedderburn said 'I'll get someone for this!' He shouted to the driver 'Go on!' Policemen were trying to clear a way; flashlights went off into the car like grenades. Colonel Wedderburn was shouting 'On!' He pressed against his seat as if it were a horse. The car reached the steps of a police station with a blue light above; the crowd was being held back by police and was leaning over their arms like nettles. Colonel Wedderburn climbed out of the car and straightened himself; voices called 'Colonel! Mr. Wedderburn sir!' He looked carefully round, his hands on the buttons of his coat, manipulating and stroking with fingers and thumb. There was a man on a van with a ladder at the back; he spoke silently into a microphone. Voices called 'Is it correct – ' Colonel Wedderburn put out his hands like a prow against the surf; said 'Thank you gentlemen thank you!' The headlights lit him as he pushed forward, affable, a head on medallion, smiling; the crowds with their arms raised like laurel leaves. He went up the steps of the police station. Connie followed out of the car and she had one hand up to her face and the other lifting her skirt as if she were a queen, above a puddle and under the blaze of arclights. She said 'Thank you, thank you!' She went up the steps with railings on either side and claws sticking through; a catwalk.

Inside the police station was a passage with yellow walls and notices in black letters and a poster of a policewoman. There was a room with a yellow wooden counter and yellow lights. Colonel Wedderburn shouted 'How the hell did this lot know?' There were men standing about in suits and uniforms; a frieze of water-pipes, a switchboard, a concrete floor, papers in baskets. Colonel Wedderburn shouted 'I took all precautions, they didn't follow us, don't think they did!' There was a woman in a hat with a tray of mugs of tea.

In a corner there was a boy sitting with dark hair in a fringe and the sides coming down over his ears like feathers. Connie looked round; said 'Where's Mary?' There were people standing round Colonel Wedderburn; he hit his stick against his leg, the narrow sheath of his trousers. Connie went up to the woman in a flowered hat and said 'Where's Mary?' Someone said 'The frogs came over in a helicopter.' Connie looked at the boy: she thought – He is like a medieval singer.

The woman had taken her by the arm and was leading her through to a doorway at the back. There was a passage with a grey floor and a wall bright green halfway up: on the other side a row of doors to cells. The doors were open like empty looseboxes. Connie thought – Something has gone wrong. The woman put a finger to her lips; a hand flat on a door of iron and woodwork. Connie went in. Mary was lying on a wooden bed with blankets underneath her

and one on top. She had her back to the door. She was
wearing riding-breeches. Connie thought – People are like
this all over the world, in cells, in hospitals. She trod over
the floor quietly. She said – 'Mary?' The fair hair was out
on a pillow, a blanket pulled up just below her eyes, her
mouth hidden. Connie knew she was not asleep. Connie
sat down carefully. She thought – Waiting for footsteps.
She put her hand on Mary's shoulder and said 'Mary my
darling!' She pulled at the blanket gently. Mary held it.
Connie took her hands away and held them theatrically in
front of her eyes for a moment, the palms turned in as if
she were praying. Then she leaned over Mary and tried to
take her in her arms. Mary's shoulder, neck, were rigid.
Connie thought – That is what love is like. She put her
cheek down on Mary's, the airplane coming down in the
snow, the soft rush of fir trees. She stared at the grains of
a blanket like a battlefield. She said 'It's all over now my
love!' Mary suddenly swung round and buried her head on
Connie's shoulder; struggled with an arm to get it up round
Connie's neck to hold her. Connie got a forearm propped
beneath her back. Connie thought – She is too big a girl
for this: then – Dear God, I must love her. Mary was
rocking backwards and forwards with some violence in her
like a fish that has been caught on a line. Connie said 'Come
along then I'll take you home.' She put out a hand to stop
herself falling; past the line of Mary's hair saw the floor as
if far below and the wooden supports of the bed like a
bridge. She said 'We're going back my baby.' She pulled
her bosom up; tried to clutch Mary's head underneath.
With tears, while the traffic shook, you hung on to the
bridge and miles below was the foaming sea and small ships
and the wind and rocks. Connie saw that Mary had stopped
shaking; was looking past her shoulder quietly with open
eyes. Connie pulled her head back to see Mary's strong
rather masculine schoolgirl's face. Connie said 'Tell me.'
Mary dropped her head; a curved soft mouth like a singer.
Connie said 'No, tell me later.' She began pulling herself
away, wrapping a blanket round Mary, holding her,

keeping her warm. She said 'Can you walk darling?' She thought – Of course she can walk. There was a patch of wet on Connie's coat where Mary's mouth had pressed against it: soreness between her legs, her hips. Mary's jersey had come out of the top of her jodhpurs where there was a circle of white flesh with a hair and mole. Connie thought – She might have been raped. Connie in the room with her legs raised. Connie theatrically passed a hand in front of her eyes. Mary was moving as if sleepwalking towards the door; Connie's arm round her. There was a distant crash of glass; shouting outside. Mary looked up. Connie thought – The first time she has noticed anything. They clung to each other. Connie said – 'Don't be frightened!' They went into the passage, the bricks like green seaweed. In the front room men stood round the boy with hair like feathers. Colonel Wedderburn held his stick horizontally at his back. The boy had large dark eyes. Colonel Wedderburn said 'Got the name and address?' A man wrote in a notebook. Colonel Wedderburn said 'Came down on your bike did you?' Connie and Mary stood in the doorway: two women with a blanket like long skirts and a bonnet. Colonel Wedderburn said 'Hullo hullo Mary, none the worse?' Mary was not looking at Colonel Wedderburn or at the boy. She listened. Outside at the front there was more shouting and a flashlight went off. Colonel Wedderburn said 'Mary have you any idea how the press got to know?' Connie pulled the blanket over Mary's shoulders; settled her on a bench. Colonel Wedderburn said 'All right, in the morning.' He turned back to the boy. He said 'And when did you arrive?' The boy spoke with a slight foreign accent. Mary straightened herself; said 'I don't want –!' Connie said 'What?' Mary said 'To see them!' Connie said 'No you won't.' Mary went limp, hung her arms between her knees: a refugee, being offered tea and crusted sugar.

A man came from the passage and said 'I'll get the car to the back.' Colonel Wedderburn said 'Is there a back?' The man said 'Can't you send the boy out first, that'll draw them.' Colonel Wedderburn stood in front of the boy and said 'We'll send you home in a car, but I don't want you to say anything, absolutely nothing, is that understood?' The boy looked at him brightly. Connie thought – A prisoner, knowing he is winning. Colonel Wedderburn said 'Then we'll see you in the morning, we can't do anything here.' The boy had not looked at Mary. Connie said to Mary 'Where did he find you?' They were like two people caught in an elopement at Gretna Green. The boy had stood up and was going to the door with Colonel Wedderburn. He suddenly turned and looked at Mary. Others stood back and watched; some parting scene, as at barrack gates or a railway station. Mary did not look up. He went out of the door. Directly he had gone Mary looked up and pushed her hair back and blinked violently as if to focus. Connie said 'Who were you with, have you told them?' Mary said 'Yes.' Connie said 'Tell me darling can't you?' Colonel Wedderburn came back and stood in front of Connie and said 'Now don't let anyone see her and don't let her talk.' Connie said 'Right.' He hit with his stick against his leg. A man ran in from outside and said 'He's talking to them!' Colonel Wedderburn said 'Sweet God!' He went along the passage to the front door. The boy was on the steps holding on to the railings. The crowd beyond were on a lower level, a posse facing the sheriff and the man in handcuffs. They were saying 'Is it true – ' 'You found her?' The boy was saying 'Yes.' His head moved from side to side quietly. Colonel Wedderburn put on his smile and straightened his overcoat; stood in the light with his hand on the boy's shoulder. A voice called – 'And you are going to see Miss Mary again?' The boy said 'Yes.' Colonel Wedderburn put a hand out as if he were stopping traffic; tried to move the boy down the steps towards the car. Lines of police opened a way through. The boy had his hand on the railings. A voice called – 'Was there a struggle?' The boy smiled. Colonel Wedderburn said 'Come along now.' He thought – They always want this: the crowd, the glory. He was ahead of him down the steps, the boy standing in the spotlight pale and rather beautiful. A voice called – 'Are you going to see Sir Simon?' The boy said 'I hope so.' He was peering into the dark, the flashlights going off in his face. A voice – 'When?' The boy said 'Mary – ' Colonel Wedderburn pulled at him. Voices said 'Mary?' Colonel Wedderburn said 'I insist'. He took him by both arms and dragged him; the boy's hand white on the railings. Looking into his face, his large eyes, Colonel Wedderburn thought – He is afraid. Holding him in an embrace, slightly underneath him, almost lifting, Colonel Wedderburn said gently 'Don't be afraid.' A voice called – 'Sir Simon's going to thank you? Personally? Mary said so?' The boy looked around; shouted 'Yes!' Colonel Wedderburn had him by both arms; the thin cloth dry as paper. There was a smell of sour dust about him like war. Colonel Wedderburn thought – Dugouts. They were down on the pavement by the car. The door was opened and Colonel Wedderburn pushed him in. With his hand on his back he was like a woman, stroking him. He waved the car forward. He said 'Gentlemen! Gentlemen!' He stood in the arclights fingering the buttons of his overcoat.

In the police station Mary sat with the blanket round her neck and her white rather dreaming face like a boxer's. A man at the switchboard spoke into a mouthpiece and said 'Ferec. Yes. Peter Ferec. F.e.r.e.c.' Colonel Wedderburn came back into the room and said 'Where's the car?' Mary stared at the ceiling; blinked as if trying to focus. Through the glass of a skylight, in the high roof, was the face of a young man with fair hair in a fringe; sad, rather close-set eyes. Connie took hold of Mary's shoulders. The young man seemed to be aiming through the skylight something silver like a cannon. Mary ducked. Connie was dragged forwards and said angrily 'Come along now!' There was a flash and the room lit as if a small bomb had gone off. Colonel Wedderburn put an arm above his head. The room went darker, and settled. A man came running from outside and said 'They're on the roof!' Colonel Wedderburn looked at the skylight. He shouted 'Get her out of here!' He ran to the door and switched the lights off. A voice called – 'Put her in the car with a rug over!' Connie and Mary moved in the dark. There were lights outside at the front like a fire, and a crash of glass. A voice shouted 'They're after them!' Connie and Mary went into the passage that led to the back; a hand took them and said 'This way Miss.' They moved out into the air, the quiet night with stars; iron steps with dustbins; a car. Round a corner into the yard came people running, feet on wood, the hooves of cavalry: in the other direction laughter sudden turned to a jeer. Connie said 'Lie on the floor Mary.' Mary went into the back of the car on her hands and knees and lay there and Connie put a rug over her and there were bits of lights trailing down in creepers. There was a carpet underneath with wool that stuck up like fir trees. Mary pulled at the wool and it came out in her fingers. The car started and she could hear it going through the crowd. Connie's hand was on her back. Mary smiled at some memory.

In the police station the lights were on again and people were standing looking up at the skylight. A blue trouser leg had come through and broken glass was on the floor. Other figures stretched above the skylight. More glass tinkled and the bottom half of a man appeared through in dark blue trousers, a leather jacket, a white shirt like skin between the trousers and the jacket. His thin legs hung like stamens of a flower. He seemed to be dangling from his neck on the broken glass; arteries on the jagged edges. Colonel Wedderburn called – 'Drop him!' The circle underneath stepped back; a face appeared at the edges of the glass and scraped past; a long boy's face with fair hair cut in fringes like feathers. Then he fell. The glass had torn the skin of the leather of his jacket. He landed on the concrete floor, crooked, with one leg underneath the other. There was a crack. Squatting, as if doing exercises, he rolled sideways with his breath going out like a balloon. He lay on one elbow, a dying swan, his fingers on the concrete fluttering. A policeman stepped forward. Colonel Wedderburn said 'Leave him.' They were standing round watching in the yellow light. The noises on the roof ceased; faces loomed above the skylight and disappeared. Someone said 'Bust his leg.' The young man's head sank to the floor, one hand above the knee and the other pulling at the leg that stretched the wrong way impossibly. He whispered in French. The policeman said 'A frog.' Colonel Wedderburn said 'Lift him.' The policeman said 'Get a stretcher.' Colonel Wedderburn said 'No.' He bent down and took the man beneath the armpits: said 'Give me a hand.' He began pulling. The man opened his mouth and made a sound like rattles. Policemen bent down and put their arms around his hips; struggled as if with the enormous weight of a piano. Colonel Wedderburn said 'Sit him on the bench.' They carried him and put him with his back to the wall. His white face went from side to side, his eyes white like a blindfold. Colonel Wedderburn said 'They're used to this sort of thing.' The policeman stood as if to attention: Colonel Wedderburn held the young man upright with a hand in his hair. He said 'Now, where are we?' The young man on the bench was trying to raise himself with fingers pulling at his trouser leg like spiders scratching against the wall of a bath. Colonel Wedderburn rumpled his hair and said 'Ca va?' Outside was a noise of cars being started and lights swinging past the windows. Colonel Wedderburn said 'Get through to Hassington and tell them the car's coming back.' The man's face on the bench, fingers slipping on a rockface, seemed to be going to sleep. Colonel Wedderburn said 'You don't like it?' Then – 'I could really hurt you!' He pushed at the man's head and the man swivelled off the bench again and screamed and Colonel Wedderburn said 'All right fix him.' A policeman came and touched him tenderly. Colonel Wedderburn went into the passage to the front door and looked into the night, the stars, the sounds of battle far away. He pulled from his pocket a pair of gloves and put them on, pressing down each finger and thumb as if the glove were skin. There was one parked car left in the street and beside it two men in dark trousers and leather coats waiting. Colonel Wedder-

burn stood with his legs apart on the steps: a statue of a
statesmen.

31

Sir Simon came on to the terrace in the early morning light
and saw the landscape dark and pale green; the long sweep
of grassland to the boathouse and lake and on the far side
the line of oak trees. Each angle of light and shade stood
out from its background in pillars and icicles and crystals.
He walked on the gravel in his dressing-gown; came to a
bench by a stone urn and sat on it and took from under
his arm a bunch of newspapers. A cold wind blew through
his dressing-gown and tingled in his skin, chest, spine. The
blue sky pressed against the trees and they opened like
anemones. There were distant bells. It was Sunday.

He unfolded one of the newspapers and saw a huge
picture of a girl in a riding-cap, blurred. There was a
headline WHERE – then Mary with her horse, holding its
head in front of railings. Her face under the riding-cap was
curiously white and concave. He read MYSTERY OF THE
NIGHT IN—: turned to the back page, where there were
cricket scores. He pressed a hand against his side where a
pain pressed him. On the front page the story began 'It
was announced last night from Hassington Grove that Mary
Mann, the daughter of the Foreign Secretary Sir Simon
Mann, has been missing from home since Friday morning.
She went out riding at 9.30 a.m. Her horse returned alone
a few hours later.' Sir Simon looked to where there were
willows over the lake in the valley; reflections of clouds,
pigeons making tired and lonely hooting. England was like
poetry; bugles and cattle in a churchyard. Further down
the page he read 'The mystery deepened on Friday night
when it was reported that Mary had been seen sleeping out
by searchers in the woods. This was later denied by an
official spokesman. Several units of army and police were

active throughout Friday night and yesterday morning. The official statement asking for the public's help was issued at 7.15 p.m. but before this an anonymous telephone call had been received in this office . . .' Sir Simon put the paper down; the pain, cold, blew through him. On the left of the valley there was an electricity pylon like a ruined steeple; the while smoke of an airplane fading. He read '. . . gave the news of Mary's disappearance. The call was traced to a call box in the Kensington area. No details were given. But it seems at least that Mary is safe and well. After exhaustive two-day searches, the theory that she might have fallen off her horse and been injured has been largely discounted.'

'The public are asked – ' Sir Simon picked up another paper. Mary's face was heavy, powerful; she photographed badly. She had big breasts like a much older woman. The headline said THE CALL GOES OUT. FIND – ' Lower down there was a picture of himself and Korin in the bowling alley: a caption – 'Sir Francis Drake.' He was holding a ball like an anarchist bomb: Korin had a hand on his arm, as if pleading. He read 'Meanwhile there is no rest for the anxious father. The deadlock reached in the current talks – '. In the next column – 'Text of the Official Announcement.' Beyond this – 'Mary is an only child. She goes to school at Harpenden, Herts: fees £450 a year.' He thought – That's not correct. Above him was a slight rustle down the side of the house; dust drifting through creepers. He looked up and saw the silhouette of a man on the battlements; his head curiously flat like a penny. The head disappeared. Sir Simon put the papers under his arm. He stood up and walked on along the terrace till he came to the conservatory; went in, smelled heat and airlessness and greenness growing. Camellias flowered round a small fountain. He sat on the edge of the fountain and put his nose against a flower; he was in the east, a back street, anonymous. He trailed his hand in the cool water and touched a lily. There were camellias and palms pressing

143

towards the roof; pushing the glass and flattening and the glass going green, a heart with blood trying to get out.

He opened another paper and read 'Police at the moment hold no theories. The presence of demonstrators near the lodge gates and the general circumstances of protest with which Dr. Korin's visit has been surrounded . . . still say there is no reason to think . . .' he skipped, his eyes freewheeling down the page '. . . a close friend of the family . . . Mary has always been an impulsive girl. I do not expect it is anything more than . . .' Turned a page. There was a picture of a woman in a bathing dress, her breasts hanging out. Could get your fist between them. In the fountain were goldfish swimming with small jerks of their tails. On the centre page was a cartoon of Korin dressed in an Eton jacket holding his bottom; a tall man behind him with a cane. Sir Simon put the paper down. He took a deep breath and held his stomach and felt his ribs, his heart. Pressing through the bones there was something soft like a cuttlefish. A door opened at the back of the conservatory; a man whistled: a gardener: footsteps moved beyond greenery. Sir Simon stood up quietly; crouched, and began hiding behind the camellias. There were other noises in the distance; dogs barking, a horn, fingers trying to get through. Putty had fallen from glass and lay in triangles. The whistling ceased; a door clicked. Sir Simon sat on a white metal chair under a palm tree and opened another paper. He turned to a centre page and read 'The peoples of Eastern Europe this week for the first time since the war have some hope of nationalist aspirations being backed by more than sweet words and good intentions. At Hassington Grove Sir Simon Mann and Dr. Korin have succeeded where so many others have failed – in establishing working proposals for a detente in Central Europe without threats of reprisal. That such a possibility should even be contemplated is due to the untiring efforts of Sir Simon Mann . . .' He turned the sides of the paper back, folded, patted; himself upright on the hard metal chair with the bones sticking through. Bruised like old leather. He made a square of the paper: a warmth of blood in his heart, lungs. There were flags and the crowds going down like corn before the cutter.

Connie appeared on the gravel outside. Sir Simon sat quietly under his palm tree. Through glass, Connie came along looking carefully from side to side; wearing a bright summer dress, her hands back, fingers behind her like feathers. She was moving past the conservatory silently, the morning making the glass clear, beyond it the droppings of sun and lime trees. Sir Simon put the paper carefully behind his back. Connie turned and looked at him. He did not know if she could see: light was reflected from bright surfaces. Connie bent as if looking under a horse. Sir Simon opened his paper and appeared to go on reading. He studied a list of engagements, of church services, of movements of royalty. Connie had moved to the door and was coming in. There was a clink on stonework: the smell of goldfish, flowers, the skirts of leaves.

Connie said 'Good morning.'

Sir Simon made two lines with his fingers down the centre of his forehead: 'Good morning.'

Connie looked at the papers; said 'Thank heavens it's Sunday!'

Sir Simon pulled the skirt of his dressing-gown over his knees; said 'Why?'

Connie picked up a paper; said 'There's nothing yet.'

Sir Simon turned a page to a headline – MIDNIGHT DRAMA. The picture was of a girl looking naked, like Eve, in front of tree trunks.

Sir Simon said 'Isn't there?'

Connie looked over his shoulder and the air became misty.

Sir Simon said 'That's not Mary?'

Connie took the paper; said – 'No.'

Sir Simon took the paper back. Hands at her breast, groin: a smell of heat and sandalwood.

Connie said 'Have they told you?'

Sir Simon rustled the paper. The conservatory was like

a railway station, lines appearing and disappearing through glass and arches that looked down on nothingness.

Connie said 'They were there last night when we fetched her. All over the place.'

Sir Simon said 'Who were?'

Connie said 'We don't know how they heard. They'd had an anonymous telephone call.'

She sat down on the bench. Sir Simon moved to one side; pulled at his dressing-gown; put a hand to his hair and pushed the skin underneath it.

Connie said 'The boy had been down to the motorcycle racing for the day. He found Mary in this cottage. They told you?'

'Yes.'

'He's some sort of Central European. We told him not to talk.'

Sir Simon said 'What do you mean some sort of Central European?'

He rearranged his legs. His calves were white. The sun came over the roof of the house and caught the top panes of glass like fireworks. They sat side by side: outside was the man on the roof, the gardener, the distant line of oak trees.

Connie said 'He had to force his way in.'

Sir Simon said 'I know. What are we going to do now: in the present.'

Connie's dress was of black and white flowers; dark patches with solid holes through.

Sir Simon said 'Dear God. I'll have to ring up Malcolm. I'll have to see Bradbury. I'll see him personally. He can do the press.'

Connie said 'She was taken by some people to this cottage, after she'd left her horse. She didn't see who they were. They treated her quite well. They gave her a bed, fed her.'

Sir Simon said 'I imagine that.'

Connie looked at him: the red and white veins under his eyes like make-up.

Sir Simon said 'Have you got the memorandum for Paris?'

Connie put a hand up to her forehead like a humming-bird in front of a flower.

Sir Simon said 'It's perfectly obvious that there's more in this than meets the eye. I don't particularly want to hear it.'

'Mary won't say.'

'I don't suppose she will.'

Connie said 'Oh Simon, what is it?'

He took a paper and banged the edges back and tried to fold the centre forward. It collapsed in the middle like soft cloth.

Connie said 'Let me.'

He took the top of the paper in his mouth.

Connie said 'She must have seen them. They drove her in a car. They didn't talk. They just said they wouldn't hurt her.'

Sir Simon said 'Come on you better tell me.'

Connie said 'I'm telling you everything!'

'Was she in with them?'

'I don't know.'

'What a time! They choose it well don't they?'

'Oh Simon I don't think so!'

He said 'What are they going to get out of it? Publicity? Money?' He appeared to be reading.

Connie said 'As a matter of fact this boy did say something to them after we had told him not to. On the steps. Charles – ' She looked at him sideways.

Sir Simon, in profile, was pulling at his top lip. His eyes were moving backwards and forwards quickly. He said 'Wedderburn seems to have made a series of mistakes, doesn't he?'

Connie folded her hands between her knees; blinked at the glare. She said 'Mary's quite safe. That's the main thing.'

Sir Simon turned pages and smoothed them.

Connie said 'There seems something odd between Mary and the boy.'

Sir Simon said 'Naturally.' Then – 'Wedderburn's through.'

Connie said 'I'm trying to talk seriously. Are you going to talk to Mary?'

'What for?'

'She is your daughter.'

Sir Simon said 'I pay you to look after her.'

Connie stood up. She brushed at her skirt. She bent down for a moment to pick at cotton. She stood among the flowers with the thick green smell; the water with the impression of iron and excrement.

She said 'Am I through too?'

Sir Simon was reading a page of the newspaper about jobs in universities in Australia.

Connie said 'I'm sorry. I came out specially to find you. I'm very tired. Please don't take it out on Mary. I don't want it to hurt your work.'

Sir Simon said 'You don't care about my work.'

Connie said 'I do.'

Sir Simon said 'No one's thought much about me.' He stood up and smiled; put a hand quickly to the back of the bench.

Connie said 'What is it?'

He said 'Are you sure she's all right? No after effects? Tell me quick; in a few words.' He pressed his side.

Connie said 'Where?'

He said 'Will you?' He smiled brightly.

Connie put a hand to her head. Said 'Oh. She was taken to this cottage. Haven't I said all this? She's described the people. Three. But she won't really. She might have gone with them voluntarily. Yes. I don't think so. They kept her in one room. They never told her what they wanted. Then this boy came along. The others panicked. They ran.'

'Is there anything else?'

'Oh yes. What time did he come along. Apparently – '

Sir Simon said brightly 'Does it matter what time he came along?'

'Yes I think so. They waited two or three hours.'

Sir Simon said 'Are we going to give him a medal or something?'

Connie stared at him. She said 'She did say you'd thank him as a matter of fact.'

Sir Simon said 'Of course. I haven't got much else to do.'

Connie said 'Simon, has Andrew been making trouble?'

Sir Simon said 'Andrew's a loyal servant.'

Connie said 'You know he's half in love with you.'

Sir Simon said 'Oh is everyone homosexual nowadays? I thought that went out of date. With Proust. I thought it had been discovered that one or two people were not.'

Connie said 'I just don't want you to believe everything.'

Sir Simon said 'I believe the evidence. People come to me with their evidence, their factual evidence, and I have to judge.'

Connie said 'This was supposed to be our nice holiday.'

Sir Simon said 'I don't have a holiday. Will you tidy up here please and bring the newspapers to my room. I now have to ring up Malcolm. Then I'll have to get in touch with Bradbury. Will you see about the car at about twelve. Check in my diary. Is that understood? Right.'

Connie said 'Are you going to see Mary?'

Sir Simon said 'When I have time. There is always the matter of time.' He moved towards the door, his head down, scraping his slippers. Connie picked up the papers and saw the picture of Mary under the riding-cap pale and military. Sir Simon was going off along the gravel like a captured general. Connie thought – They are alike, father and daughter. She put the papers under her arm and at a distance followed him. There was a man on the battlements moving in and out of the embrasures like a target at a shooting range. A sprinkle of dust fell through creepers. The gardener appeared with a watering can. Sir Simon went past with the skirt of his dressing-gown flapping. Connie thought – Like a butcher.

32

Amongst a row of parked cars along a street in West London, in one, a dark blue Vauxhall, a man in a brown suit and brown felt hat sat reading. He turned the page of a newspaper every few minutes and looked at advertisements for jobs in universities in Australia and vacancies for engineers. At the bottom of the newspaper was an open notebook with writing in English. Out of one of the doors with grey pillars came a young woman pushing a pram. The man in the car looked at a watch; wrote in his notebook. The woman lowered the pram down the steps pulling it back like a horse. Dark hair, dark complexion, about twenty-five. He turned a page of the newspaper: there was a photograph of racehorses with the jockeys wearing goggles like headlamps. The woman wore a dark green jacket.

The houses were tall with slight variations in doors and windows. A boy with a ladder came bicycling up the street. The race had been won by Pearl Fire, with second Drake's Green and third Ornithologist. A red Mini had stopped opposite the house with grey pillars; a man in a grey mackintosh got out. He locked the car and went up the steps quickly. The time 11.22. He turned at the top of the steps and looked across the street. The man in the Vauxhall had pulled out a cigarette lighter: was looking through the viewfinder of a camera. He bent and felt in his pockets for cigarettes. In the viewfinder was the pillar of the windscreen and the reflections of trees. He wound down the window. He was lighting a cigarette with his hands cupped. The man at the top of the step was peering at a row of bells. His figure, crouched, came into the viewfinder. The man in the Vauxhall flicked the camera and the flame almost took his eyebrows off.

The man on the steps had gone into the house. Smoking, the man in the Vauxhall wrote down the number of the red Mini. Thickset, middle-aged, wearing a grey mackintosh. He wound on the film in his lighter. The street was quiet. Raising his eyebrows, and patting his pockets as if for matches, he suddenly got out of the car. He wandered up the street towards the Mini picking the tobacco off his teeth, a man looking perhaps for a house for sale. In the back of the Mini was a paper bag with blue and white stripes, a street map, gloves. Turning to the door between grey pillars he had noticed a house that he liked; or belonged to an old friend; or something had reminded him of something. Putting his cigarette out casually under his foot he went up the steps, saw the row of black bells, appeared delighted. There were cards in the slots. A door scraped open in the basement: he turned, whistling. There was an old lady with a basket. He ran lightly down the steps and across to the house opposite. He had got the wrong number. There was a removals van: he was waiting for it on the doorstep. The old lady was closing a gate in the area railings. Peter Ferec suddenly appeared at the grey door between the pillars, wearing black trousers, white shirt, a brown leather jacket. He ran down the steps and up the street with the door not closing behind him. The man in the doorway opposite walked quickly after him. He had left his notebook in the car. That was an error. Peter Ferec was disappearing round a corner into a wider street with shops. HADDON ROAD. On Sunday the stalls on the pavement would be empty. You could always tell a Sunday. Reaching the corner, he saw Peter Ferec had stopped by a milk machine and a notice-board of advertisements. The man put his hands in his pocket, sauntered to the notice-board. There were models who gave Swedish lessons: no callers after 7 p.m. Peter Ferec had turned and was coming straight past him. A young boy with a white intent face. For a moment looked at him. He walked to the milk machine. There was the shop next door; EDWARDS; piles of groceries with pictures of alligators on tins. Peter Ferec had run across the road to the brick wall marked GENTS. The time, 11.27. The man began sauntering slowly back down the road. A quiet Sunday: people ought to be all in church. He would go to the lavatory; would be taken with a pain in his inside. Before crossing he looked up and down the road – a good citizen. Suddenly he had stiff legs, his face grimaced, he heaved at his clothes as he went down the short flight of steps. In concrete were a row of miniature looseboxes. His mackintosh had buttons going one way down the front and a small one the other way at the bottom. There was brass and grey stonework and a central pillar. No sign of Peter Ferec. He went in, bolted a door and began reading the walls from habit. *Would anyone like. . . . I have a sister . . .* He felt in his pockets: patted: his eyes got accustomed to the dark. Bending down, he tried to see under the bottom of a dividing wall. There was a pair of black shoes such as Peter Ferec might have been wearing. Straightening himself, he saw in front of him the drawing of a woman. In the correct place, like a gun, was the peephole to the next compartment. He jerked away, pressing his back against the wall and raising his hands slightly.

33

Mary was underneath the bedclothes where she could stretch on her stomach with her hands gripping the edge of the mattress and one knee raised in the position of a dancer; her stomach against the cold white sheet and her body still dirty from the old rug and striped mattress. Last night, when she had come in, they had not made her have a bath. She had pretended to be asleep. You let your head droop, your mouth open, stumbled on the staircase. She had stretched out in the clean bed and held the edges of the mattress. She had pulled the top sheet over her head. Then you were safe, with no one watching you.

Already that morning they had come in to look at her.

Connie had stood and had said quietly – 'Mary?' You breathed with your mouth open and a slight flutter beyond your lips. Connie had gone away; her quiet hands on the door like an executioner.

Mary felt her body hot where his hands at the neck and wrists had pulled at it. There was a bruise on her thigh from the motor-scooter: a lump on the side of her head where he had hit her. Her body was an ache against the cold sheet and her teeth pressed against her bottom lip. She was back in the room with the rug and striped mattress and the taste of damp dust and mud. Her hands were held by her sides in the darkness.

He had said – There are forces working through you.

In front of her mouth, where she breathed, was the white fabric of sheet like a bandage. He would be in London; in a back street with chimneys. There were tunnels connecting them through the earth; an army of unseen helpers. No one knew; people moved on the surface, laughing and chattering. She pretended to be asleep. Underneath they worked ceaselessly.

He had said – You can't escape it.

Someone was coming along the passage again. Connie would come in; might pull the sheet down from her eyes. She would flutter her eyelids; hold her mouth open like a film-star. The footsteps stopped; the door opened quietly.

A man's voice – 'Mary?'

She went hot and cold. The executioner.

A hand was pulling down the sheet. She pretended to be terrified.

There was a grey face with spectacles.

She jumped up. She said 'You frightened me!'

Andrew Seymour said 'Calmers! Go to sleep for another minute!' He walked round the room.

She turned her head and began pushing her hair back.

He said 'Better?'

She was wearing pink woolly pyjamas with white frills. She said 'What time is it?' She wobbled her head: an eccentric.

He said 'Well how are you? Tell me all!' He picked up objects on her dressing-table.

She said 'Oh I'm so sleepy!'

He said 'They're round the house like the siege of Paris. You've become a legend in your lifetime!'

Mary waited: then did a high-pitched giggle.

He said 'The biggest story since – ' He looked at her out of the tops of his eyes. 'Not for your ears!'

Mary shouted 'Oh I know!'

He said 'Well, what was it?'

'What was what?'

'What *really* happened.' He went round the room in profile; drawled and nodded.

'I've told.'

'Like Joan of Arc.'

'No.'

'Well that was lucky.' He smiled. 'Your father had to go to London early. But the police'll come. Can I help you?'

Mary lay back and swallowed.

He said 'They've got to find out. You know. Your father's very hard worked.'

Mary said 'Hard luck.'

'What?'

'Nothing.'

'I thought you said "hard luck".'

Mary licked her lips.

Andrew said 'Yes. It is. Oh dear. What'll we do now?'

Mary said 'Will you torture me?'

Andrew Seymour had stopped at the door of her cupboard. He pulled at it and gramophone records fell out.

Mary shouted 'Can't you look!' She jumped out of bed and knelt by the records at his feet.

He said 'Did they talk about torturing you?'

'Who?'

'What did they talk about then?'

Mary got the records into a pile; held them to her front and went to the bed. There were several with covers of a shiny boy with long hair.

She said 'We talked about religion.'

Andrew Seymour smiled. He watched her as she sat crosslegged. He said 'You know there've been these very careful precautions. A great deal depends on them. Certain people object to Dr. Korin's visit, and we've got to know who they are for safety.'

Mary said 'Don't you know then?'

'We know some. We want yours.'

Mary arranged the records with their edges aligned.

He said 'Will you answer questions yes or no?'

'Perhaps.'

'You went away of your own free will, didn't you?'

She put the records nearly by her bed.

He said 'It wasn't serious?'

Mary said 'If I answer one question then you'll know when I don't answer another, won't you.'

Andrew said 'Then I do know.'

'You are clever.'

'And you're loyal.'

She said 'Don't you like that?'

He said 'I like playing these games.'

He smoothed his hair at the sides. He was wearing a black suit with a gardenia in the buttonhole.

Mary said 'Oh politicians!'

Andrew Seymour had a pale speckled skin. His eyes behind his spectacles seemed to be watering.

He said 'What did he do to you?'

'Who? What are you talking about?'

He said 'I read your diary.'

Mary put her hands to her temples. Gasped.

He said 'I had to. You might have been kidnapped. Dead. We do care about you, you see.'

Mary bounced back on her elbows on the bed. She said 'Read my diary!'

Andrew said 'Where did you go then? This boy – '

He had his hands in his pockets. His hips looked wide like a woman's.

He said 'You're a big girl now. You promised not to tell?'

'Yes.'

'Who?'

Mary said 'I thought you said I was loyal.'

Andrew said 'Someone's going to find out, you know. This thing's serious.'

He trod round the room cautiously; a step like a giraffe.

Mary said 'Why don't you find out then?'

He said 'Tempers!'

'Who's tempers?'

Andrew said 'A promise isn't a promise if it's made the wrong way. Under threats or misunderstanding.'

'It wasn't.'

'It was a promise then?'

'I've told you. But I might be lying, mightn't I?'

Andrew Seymour smiled. He said 'What's all this about politicians?'

She said 'Oh they're so boring. Blah blah blah. They never say what they mean.'

Andrew Seymour said 'Who does?'

'Some people do.'

'Oh I see.' Then – 'You better talk to your father.'

Mary said 'I don't want to talk to my father.'

'Why not?'

'He never talks to me.'

He stopped by her dressing-table: peered in the glass. He said 'You don't feel appreciated. But you've found someone at last?' He put a finger up and smoothed the side of his mouth. 'You're keen on him?'

Mary shouted 'Oh you would think of that!'

Andrew Seymour stood at the foot of the bed. His spectacles had rings in them like catharine wheels. He said 'Ultimately, your father's work matters and you don't. That's the point.'

Mary lay back and put her hands above her face at arms' length and moved the fingers as if she were making shadows on the ceiling.

Andrew said 'I'll send you up breakfast.'

Mary said 'I don't want any breakfast.'

'I'll send it up anyway.'

'I'll throw it out of the window.'

Andrew Seymour laughed. His front teeth overlapped like a rabbit's. He said 'Then we'll smack you.'

Mary said 'You and who else?'

Andrew put a hand down and touched the shape of her foot under the blanket. It shot away like a fish. Mary sat up and clasped her knees. Andrew said 'Well you seem inviolate!'

Mary pushed her hair back; her mouth opened on small white teeth.

Andrew said 'Nothing much can have happened then.'

34

Sir Simon and Colonel Wedderburn sat in the back seat of a car driving up a dual carriageway on the other side of which were three rows of cars in a traffic jam, the occupants like cardboard cut-outs. Sir Simon's car went slowly past wire netting and advertisements with pictures of tigers. Colonel Wedderburn said –

'The story is this, the boy rode down from London leaving ten-thirty arriving at Woolcombe soon after twelve, spent the afternoon watching the motorcycle scramble, he has this motor-scooter himself; then went off on a ride cross country and came out at this cottage which he says he wanted to explore. There he found Mary, the others either had left or were scared off when he arrived on his bike. This was the evening. She told him what had happened and they decided to wait till after dark. Then he rode her to the police.'

Sir Simon said 'Why wait till after dark?'

Colonel Wedderburn said 'They say they were frightened. That part of it's fairly clear.'

He and Sir Simon sat in opposite corners of a car with a partition that separated them from the driver; enclosed like fish in glass.

Colonel Wedderburn said 'But the rest of it I've got mainly through our own sources. My problem is, sir, I don't know how much is better not to be known.'

Sir Simon said 'For me? I can forget it.'

Colonel Wedderburn looked out of the window.

Sir Simon said 'I suppose it's something disreputable.'

Colonel Wedderburn said 'This boy Ferec is in contact with Grigoriev.'

Sir Simon said 'Who's Grigoriev?' Then – 'Oh yes.'

Colonel Wedderburn said 'Grigoriev must have known where she was.'

Sir Simon said 'Dear God.'

Colonel Wedderburn said 'He must have realised that whatever happened, it was a mistake. Not in his interests.'

Sir Simon said 'You mean he knew the people who had her?'

'I think so. It's a bit conjectural.'

'What are your sources?'

'We've been having these embassy men watched. Also something when I saw Grigoriev.'

Sir Simon looked out of the window. They were passing a skating rink with huge pictures of wrestlers. He said 'None of this does us any good.'

Colonel Wedderburn said 'I don't see it like that sir. She was rescued as it were by one of their own people. That's the story.'

'Go on.'

'Look at it like this. One, there's Mary's story. She was taken by people she can't identify and was at this cottage till this boy rescued her. Why should she tell a lie?'

Sir Simon said 'Do you mean why should she tell a lie for her own advantage or why might people think she is telling a lie?'

Colonel Wedderburn said 'Sorry?'

'Go on.'

'That is what people think, sir. Perhaps she did make up a bit of a story. But still.'

Sir Simon said 'Then how would Grigoriev have known?'

'I admit that. But she still might be in sympathy with these people. And Grigoriev might have known them.'

'Students?'

Colonel Wedderburn said 'They're good at keeping an eye. You know – thieves and policemen. They're in touch with a good few people against them. The nuts.'

Sir Simon said 'Aren't you covering up a bit for our own mistakes?'

Colonel Wedderburn said 'I'm trying to see it sir. If Mary and the boy corroborate, no one else can say any different.'

Sir Simon said 'Correct.'

'Now as I understand it this suits your book. One, you don't want this to be a prank which the papers will ridicule. Two, you don't want it connected badly with Korin. In fact, the opposite. You want Korin to gain public sympathy.'

Sir Simon said 'Certainly.'

'Well, you've got it.'

The car was stationary in a queue in front of which, like a dragon, a machine was pouring hot tar on to the road.

Sir Simon said 'What exactly do the press know?'

'Just the story.'

'What are the chances of their getting any other?'

'Practically none sir.'

'Then what you mean is, that I should thank this boy, as he says I will, thus gaining good publicity, and I know nothing more about it.'

Colonel Wedderburn said 'Yes sir.'

'Tomorrow.'

'Yes sir.'

Sir Simon said 'Isn't anyone, even the idiots, going to notice the coincidence of where this boy comes from?'

Colonel Wedderburn said 'I don't think so. Coincidences

are common. Nowadays no one asks why. They don't want to.'

Sir Simon said 'Mary wasn't in any danger was she?'

'I don't think so.'

'Then why did she say I'd thank him?'

'I suppose she thought you would sir.'

'This is a bit complex. You'll come out looking a bit of a fool, Wedderburn.'

Colonel Wedderburn said 'Not the first time sir!' He smiled.

The car was moving into a wide street with railway bridges. On the other side the rows of cars were wedged like bricks. The air around them shook with smell. Above, on a railway bridge, a passenger train had stopped and faces looked down through glass.

Sir Simon said 'I must say I think you've handled this extraordinarily well Wedderburn. I'm afraid my family – ' he heaved forwards and back as if embarrassed ' – are an extraordinary assignment. I'd just like to thank you – ' he pressed at the sides of his hair ' – for your loyalty.'

Colonel Wedderburn said 'Oh it's nothing sir!'

Sir Simon said 'I depend very much on the loyalty of the people who work with me. I know of no other way in which great events, and those working for them, can be guarded.'

Colonel Wedderburn moved backwards and forwards; pressed a hand to the side of his hair.

Sir Simon was looking out of the window. He could see his own face in the glass. On one side was his cynical expression when he drooped his jaw; on the other his teeth seemed to be clenched, his head raised as if in a high wind.

35

In a church with a high baroque roof and angels with seashells men in dark suits and uniforms sat on each side of the aisle as at a wartime wedding. They faced into the distance stiffly where banners hung in a dead wind; three trumpeters appeared in an organ loft and raised their trumpets and blew; the congregation rose soft and still in the air like paper. At the top of the aisle Sir Simon emerged in morning dress with a white carnation; generals in uniform were on either side of him as if on leashes. The gallery was hushed with a quiet coughing; footsteps stamped outside and there came through the high doors at the back, the congregation too disciplined to turn, a posse of men with a new banner, the shaft held erect from the waist, strutting up the aisle with quick boots as if to a commemoration or execution. The men reached the top of the aisle and halted; beyond, through an iron screen by the back choir-stalls, priests like white sea-birds flitted in a cold mist. From the pews opposite Sir Simon a group in brown suits stepped out; among them Korin. One began to speak in a foreign language. The priests came down through the iron grille sweeping as if on broomsticks; lined up beyond the banner clasping their hands against the cold. When the voice stopped the trumpeters blasted again and the man holding the banner, in a dark uniform, turned and stamped towards Korin. Korin reached out. The banner was detached from a ring and Korin took it. He moved slightly forwards as if on a tightrope with the weight. One of the men in brown uniforms had an arm to steady him; they were round him like gangsters guarding a boxer. Korin moved towards Sir Simon with the banner dipping in the dark and cobweb air, Sir Simon ducking slightly from the dust, the shaft of the banner swinging vertical and the rectangle of grey and gold sagging. Sir Simon clasped the shaft above Korin's hands and for a moment they seemed to be climbing it, like powder-monkeys. When Korin let go Sir Simon swayed and one of the generals came forward to support him. The general took the banner, Sir Simon stretched his fingers down the sides of his coat, Sir Simon and Korin bowed, an organ played suddenly splashing music as if in a waterfall. The general moved with the banner up the steps towards the iron screen; two priests came down to take it into the darkness. Sir Simon had turned and was facing the distant altar; Korin, a few paces away, had still one arm out as if grasping after something fallen into the sea. The men in brown suits, around him, were carefully to attention. Korin touched Sir Simon on the arm. One of the men in a brown suit stood close to Korin. Sir Simon put his head down: Korin spoke. The organ was thin and reedy and dry as a smell; at the bottom a deep and almost soundless series of explosions. Sir Simon looked round, half of his grey face quizzical, made a move to the pew behind. The man in the brown suit had a hand on Korin's arm: Korin moved his shoulders. A man came from the pews and stood by Sir Simon and Korin; Sir Simon gazed over the two of them to the gold mouldings at the tops of columns like candlesticks. The organ suddenly stopped: in the quietness by the dark altar a priest was intoning. The man from the pews spoke to Sir Simon. Sir Simon looked pale and amused; a medieval saint with his insides screwed out. The priest's voice stopped. People began to look round for their hats. Sir Simon said to one of the generals, his eyebrows raised like skiing sticks, 'I think I'm asked into the vestry.'

Korin came forwards again and was almost pulling Sir Simon by the sleeve along the top of the pews and into the shadows of pillars; it was as if he had some urgent message. Men in brown suits quickly followed. One of the generals said 'A shotgun wedding.' The other said 'Repent at leisure.' When Korin and Sir Simon passed a side door of the church there was a confused noise from outside of a crowd, cars hooting, a revolution round some corner. A priest came out of the shadows: Sir Simon said 'I wonder if we could use your vestry.' A man in a blue suit came up and said 'They can't get the cars through; there's a crowd of several hundred.' The priest said 'This way'. They went through a side door into a room with wooden benches and cupboards and a wash-basin. Sir Simon flipped his tails back and sat on a bench. Korin stood in front of him. Their heads were almost at the same height. Korin said, in English, 'I wish to say, I accept, in principle, the provisos of the general schedule apart from – ' he frowned, waving a hand behind him. The men in the brown suits had come up: one of them spoke in the foreign language. Korin was looking beyond for someone who had not yet come in. Korin turned back to Sir Simon and repeated in English 'I wish to say I accept.' He held his hand out. Sir Simon took it; stood up; put his other hand to the side of his hair. Korin turned with Sir Simon towards the door and posed as if there were photographers. There were the men in brown and blue suits and behind them a few men in uniform. Someone said 'Do you want the snappers?' Sir Simon said 'Good God no!' He turned to Korin and said 'Could we please discuss this, I'm very pleased, very gratified – ' Korin had taken him by the lapel and seemed to be lifting himself up on him. Korin said 'No time.' Sir Simon said 'I didn't know you spoke such good English.' Korin said 'I have made it clear?' He spoke some words in the foreign language. Sir Simon said 'Yes.' Korin was looking towards the door again. Sir Simon said 'I'll try to find him for you.' He waved over the heads of the men in brown and blue suits. A man came in carrying a suitcase. People made way and he set the suitcase down on the bench and opened it and took out a bottle. The bottle had gold paper and wire over the top and a picture of a castle. Sir Simon said 'I wanted the interpreter!' In the case also were six silver glasses like large thimbles. The man began screwing the wire off the top of the bottle. Korin pulled at Sir Simon's sleeve and stood facing him with his back to a cupboard of vestments. Sir Simon said 'Tomorrow we'll make a public statement.' He looked round with his smile gone black at the edges like a mask. Korin had taken one of the silver glasses and filled it and he handed it to Sir Simon. Then he stood back and clapped. Some men in brown suits leaned together whispering. One of the generals had come in and stood at the side of Sir Simon: he said 'Unholy matrimony.' He put a hand up to his moustache. Sir Simon raised his glass: his coat rose at the back like a pendulum. Korin had taken a glass; raised it: said 'Historic moment.' Sir Simon said 'Historic moment.' Some of the men standing round were given glasses. From outside there was the bell of a fire engine or an ambulance. Korin drank, tossing his head back. Sir Simon copied him. With his eyebrows pressed upwards and together like sand castles he began to say 'I should like formally to thank on behalf of the British people the gift of St Georgi's standard from the people of the People's Democratic Republic – ' Korin had turned to Sir Simon and had taken him by the elbows. Sir Simon looked round for somewhere to put his glass. Korin suddenly stretched up and kissed Sir Simon behind the ear. When he smiled he had tiny teeth like seashells. Sir Simon put up a hand to his moustache. Korin moved to the other side of his face; seemed to murmur into his ear. Outside there was a shout from the crowd. Behind Korin, in the line of Sir Simon's vision, were the men in brown suits watching. Sir Simon thought – Like the three murderers in the cathedral.

36

Colonel Wedderburn was shown into the room with yellow walls and bowls of red flowers and the large brown desk: behind it was the man with close-cropped hair wearing a white shirt and white tie. He said 'Colonel!' Colonel Wedderburn said 'Sorry to come on a Sunday!' They shook hands. Colonel Wedderburn sat at the side of the desk and took out his gunmetal cigarette case and tapped and leaned forwards to get it back in his hip pocket. The man behind the desk said 'Coffee?' and Colonel Wedderburn said 'No thank you.' He looked at the end of his cigarette and moved his tongue and picked a bit of tobacco off it. He said 'You've done us a good turn Grigoriev.'

Grigoriev was looking down at his seat and adjusting it like a pianist.

Colonel Wedderburn said 'The girl was well. Then there was this boy.'

Grigoriev straightened an inkstand; the telephone.

Colonel Wedderburn said 'He found her about nine p.m. He didn't bring her in till after eleven. In the meantime someone had rung up the press. We don't know who did this.' He still picked at his tongue.

Grigoriev waited; the look of a prisoner used to verdicts.

Colonel Wedderburn said 'Have you heard the news today?'

Grigoriev said 'On the radio?' He pressed a bell.

While they waited Colonel Wedderburn said 'You know the boy?'

Grigoriev said 'Do you not want publicity?'

When a secretary came in he spoke in the foreign language. The secretary went out.

Grigoriev said 'It is necessary.'

Colonel Wedderburn said 'One of your people went round to him at ten today.'

The secretary returned with typed sheets of paper. Grigoriev took them. He held a sheet and read aloud '. . . a cottage, where she had been taken by still unidentified – ' He looked up. 'You have not identified?'

'No.'

Grigoriev read '. . . probably students hostile to the visit . . . this disrespect for law and human decency . . .' He put the paper down: said 'This is not serious.'

Colonel Wedderburn said 'You knew?'

Grigoriev looked away. 'It is the boy who is important.'

'Did you know the students?'

'No.'

'Was it students?'

Grigoriev picked the papers up again. He said 'I see that he says Sir Simon will see him.'

'That's not in the news.'

'No.'

Colonel Wedderburn said 'Oh well, he said that for publicity I suppose.'

'He will earn money?' Grigoriev smiled.

Colonel Wedderburn said 'I hadn't thought of that.' He rocked forwards trying to catch Grigoriev's eye so that he could smile at him.

Grigoriev said 'Probably the girl told him.'

'She did.'

Grigoriev had turned away; it was as if there were some fear around him.

Colonel Wedderburn said 'Who did ring up the press?'

Grigoriev waited; then stood up and said 'This girl being taken by students could have upset the whole purpose of the visit. She was allowed to go out riding when it was known there were hostile elements at the gates. These people are allowed to wait in the countryside for an opportunity – ' He spoke quietly.

Colonel Wedderburn said 'From your country, who, over here, would be hostile?'

'What are your theories?'

Colonel Wedderburn smiled. He said 'You'll vouch for the boy?' Then – 'You must have planned this. You didn't mind us knowing at ten o'clock.'

Grigoriev said 'The boy is a matter for security.'

Colonel Wedderburn said 'Yes. Tomorrow at eleven o'clock they're having the television and press down. They were having this anyway. To celebrate the cementing of friendship between our two peoples.' He bent his head; determined to make Grigoriev look at him.

Grigoriev said 'Did you not get someone who they say broke his leg while falling through a skylight?'

'He did break his leg while falling through a skylight.'

Grigoriev said 'That sometimes happens.'

Colonel Wedderburn said 'Then the boy can be there, tomorrow, all right?'

'He will meet them both?'

'Naturally.'

Grigoriev walked up and down behind the desk.

Colonel Wedderburn said 'We're agreed? You do not know the boy – '

Grigoriev took a handkerchief out of his pocket and coughed. He said 'It is her story that she was taken by students?'

'Yes.'

'Naturally a father will want to thank – ' He broke off. 'It will suit our two countries. To celebrate.'

'Exactly.'

'But we have to take precautions. You understand.'

Colonel Wedderburn said 'I hope you don't think I don't realise this.' He stood up.

Grigoriev said 'I take it then that this is between ourselves?' He looked at him suddenly with eyes that had no depth nor meaning.

Colonel Wedderburn said 'We're in no position to act otherwise are we?'

Grigoriev smiled. His face wrinkled like a rubber mask being pulled off. His mouth opened. Colonel Wedderburn found himself backing away suddenly and holding his breath.

37

Mary walked past a cedar tree towards the conservatory where her father sometimes sat with his cloth cap and cape and a reading rest in front of him. Through the glass there were pelargoniums and fuchsias and blue daisies. Behind, and stopping when she stopped, was a large man in a blue suit with a round shiny face. Mary looked across the park towards the line of pale and dark oak trees. The man looked at right angles to the tennis court. Mary wore a skirt and white socks to the knee and a dark blue boy's shirt. The skirt was of pale cotton and ended above the knee. When she walked it was like a bell and her legs the stamens of a flower.

Past rhododendrons was a swing from an elm tree and a see-saw with one end rotting. When she walked the man followed her and pretended not to watch. She was on a stage; an audience of trees. One day long ago she had come here with her parents and her father had pushed her on the swing and she had gone so high she had called to him to stop. He had gone on pushing and her mother had called and he had laughed in that way as if spray had got mixed with his moustache. She had flown off the swing trying to put a foot down and had landed in the sandpit with one wrist underneath her. She had rolled over as if it were broken. Her mother had kneeled and had looked at her father above: they had quarrelled. Mary had known how to hurt them like this; writhing, her eyes carefully watching the grains of sand that were like mountains.

The sandpit had almost disappeared. There were marks in the long grass like earthworks; the hump of a grave.

The man in the blue suit had stopped just behind her. He said 'A swing and a see-saw!'

Mary held one of the ropes. She lifted her feet and dragged them above the ground. The heat of the rope cut into her.

He said 'Shall I swing you?'

She lowered her feet and pushed her hair back: moved on again with each hip drooping as she walked.

He said 'A bit old for that I expect!'

She moved through rhododendrons and fallen branches, bark hollow with fungus and deadly nightshade. The path led down to the valley where there was a railing and beyond it a green field. She trod through nettles with her socks and bare knees; leaned with both arms on the railings and looked past the curve of wood and meadow to the lake. In the grass were patches of thistle and grey dust. The white pony was at the far side; it trotted in a diagonal with its mane and tail flowing. Mary shaded her eyes and called in a voice like a bird 'Coom alon oop Silver my beaut Silver!' The man in the blue suit leaned beside her. The pony went in a semicircle with its hooves and head tossing. Mary held out her hand. The horse came up and blew, its soft eyes distrustful. It pressed its mouth against Mary's hand and showed yellow teeth, hairy lips moving like part of an engine.

Mary said 'Can I ride?'

'I'm afraid not Miss.'

'Oh why?'

'Well I haven't got a horse have I?'

Mary climbed on to the bottom rung of the railings and leaned over and put her arms round the horse's neck. Her skirt was pulled up at the back.

She said 'Coom a kiss what did they do my beaut, Silver!'

The man smiled; held on to the top of the railings.

Mary said loudly 'Have you been with Dr. Korin?'

The man said 'Oh I have a bit!'

'What's he like? I mean what sort of person?'

'Well it's difficult to say exactly.'

'I mean what are these stories about him? Is he cruel?'

'I don't think that's the way to look at it, Miss.' The man's face had gone dark, as if he were hiding.

'Does he murder people?'

'Is that what they told you?'

Mary pressed her mouth against the horse's neck; said 'Coom alon did I leave you then, oh I do love you!'

The man said 'What did they say to you then?'

'Who?'

'The people you were with.'

Mary pressed herself up with her hands on the top rail, her arms straight, her feet clear at the back, her body arched as if on a parallel bar.

She said 'Oh lots of things!'

'What?'

Mary said in a sing-song voice – 'Back in, shoulders square, come along Mary – ' She pushed herself off, landed on the ground, stood to attention.

The man said 'Did you try to get away?'

'Of course.'

'What happened?'

'I hid under the stairs.'

She stood with her feet apart, hands on her hips, legs

straight, chest out. Then plunged the top part of her body down with her fists on the grass in front, between her legs, in front, alternately; whispering 'one, two, three . . .' appearing to gaze up at the man, who was behind her, through her legs.

When she stood upright again she said 'I got the key out by pushing a newspaper underneath the door.'

He said 'And then what?'

'They found me.'

'How many of them were there?'

She rolled her shoulders about, hands on hips, her face pale and cut off by her hair.

She said 'What I don't understand is what we're doing with Korin, we were against him once weren't we?'

'That's nothing to do with me Miss.'

'That's the trouble, it's nothing to do with anyone.'

She turned, clicked her heels, and stood facing the railings again. Pulled down an imaginary jersey at her back. Went up on her toes; lowered herself on her haunches.

He said 'Can you give me a description?'

She said 'Dark hair, rather good-looking, long hair at the sides and back.'

'What age?'

She said 'Oh why can't you leave him alone? He's not done anything!'

He said 'This is a special person then?'

Mary, standing straight, did a jump for the top rail of the railings; caught it and hit her thighs hard, slowly sliding down and screwing her face up.

The man said 'Hurt?'

She crouched with her stomach, arms, down by her knees. The pony suddenly swirled and cantered away.

The man took her by the shoulders. She was looking carefully at bits of earth round her fingers. She said 'Agony!'

The man let her go.

She got to her feet and limped a few steps. She said 'Anyway who's side are we on? I thought it was him who killed all those students. Nobody keeps to anything. They're crazy.'

The man smiled like a bruised apple.

Mary said 'We all tell lies. Of course I'm against violence!' She clutched her skirt between her legs and hopped.

The man said 'Did you go into the woods with them?'

Mary put her fists to either side of her head; pulled her eyes into slits; shouted 'What?' Then – 'No one makes sense!' She began striding up the path through nettles and bracken.

The man called after her 'You talk to your father!'

Mary shouted 'I don't want to talk to my father!' She held her hands stiffly by her sides as if there was a crowd watching her.

38

Sir Simon came into the conservatory with the pelargoniums and fuchsias and limped to the wicker armchair with the reading rest. He wore the trousers of his morning suit but over his shirt an old cardigan. He leaned back and closed his eyes at the sun which came through glass and with blind hands took off his tie and collar. He seemed to sleep, his hands trailing down his shirt like someone shot. A maid came in carrying a tray of coffee and biscuits. She moved quietly, put the tray on the ground, arranged a table, picked the tray up. Through closed eyes Sir Simon said 'Put that thing down and get out.'

Later, Andrew Seymour came in carrying papers. He moved slowly, lifted the tray, put the papers down, rattled. Sir Simon said 'Put it down and leave me.'

Alone, he pulled the reading rest close and took the sheaf of papers in one hand and the coffee cup in the other; brought them together spilling a drop of coffee on to his cardigan; watched it with his moustache drawn up from his large yellow teeth; drank, holding the saucer, gripping the cup with his long upper lip.

He read –

The ground upon which the uneasy pyramid of power rests in the People's Democratic Republic has recently been shaken. If Dr. Korin wishes to see something of the writing on the wall he only has to reflect on the extraordinary phenomenon that took place in Gheorghi Square last Tuesday on the anniversary of the students' revolt. A crowd estimated at twenty thousand stood bare headed for two minutes while the police were powerless to disperse them. It is one of the ironies of the present situation that whereas in the past Dr. Korin has exerted a malign and even savage influence upon the policies of Eastern Europe it is now, when he seems to have seen the light, that his position is for the first time in danger. The relaxation of terror has meant that forces hostile to him have been able to emerge – not only who still see him as the architect of repression but also those who see betrayal in his present liberal policies. There are no signs, even, of those two strange bedfellows – the old nationalists and what might be called new liberals – coming together in an effort to depose him.

There is no prospect that any change of government at the present time would be helpful to the West. For obvious reasons a government by 'liberals' is not possible: any change would be a reversion to the old Left-Wing and they, undoubtedly, would kill all hope of the present *détente*. For all his actions in the past and his reputation as a reactionary it is clear that Dr. Korin now is aiming genuinely at the establishment of a neutralist federation in Eastern Europe: that he alone of post-war satellite leaders has the ability to do this in spite of the violent opposition of Peking and the faint-hearted objections of Moscow: and that now is the time to achieve this, when the Moscow-Peking conflict has reached a crisis in which a re-alignment in Europe is not only possible but advantageous. There is no doubt that Dr.

Korin sees in this policy a chance of his place in history as the architect of a new world power-block. To this end he has an ambition the characteristics of which are modern, but the roots of which go far back in history.

What opposition there is to Korin from the Left is of course undercover. Efforts to oust him would come probably from the secret police and the army, and the details of such efforts would be lost in the murk of communist politics. There are many facets of the story that we cannot know and never will. But what is significant at the present time is the extent of the unrest against him that is evident – and this from the very people who might be thought to welcome a neutralist *détente*. These are the young still imbued with resentment engendered by the Students' Revolt; those who ape Western manners and Western culture and whose hostility to the regime is one of boredom and revulsion. These people are a-political: they do not see the present situation in terms of power which might be to their advantage: their characteristic is a revolt against power itself – after twenty years indoctrination they are sickened. In this atmosphere certain groups have taken on an almost religious and mystical aura – for the first time the young are in revolt not against failures of materialism but against materialism as such. There are certain brotherhoods, for instance, dedicated to standing out against cynicism and corruption in government rather in the manner of extremist sects in the eighteenth century – or during the decline of the Roman Empire. This is a phenomenon at the moment unique but perhaps increasingly to be expected in a world which has cut off its religious instinct but not buried it. Korin of course has little to fear from such groups on their own: the machinery of oppression is still overwhelming. But the danger to him may come if ever the Left-Wing elements decide to use these groups of the so-called "Right"; and this again is a situation not unknown in history.'

Sir Simon placed the piece of paper carefully to one side;

lay back frowning. He picked up the paper again, took out of a pocket a red pencil, drew a line down the margin of the last paragraph.

He picked up another paper and read –

There is no denying that at this moment of summer when usually all is quiet on the international front the struggle between the great power-blocks has come to an unexpected but decisive crisis. With the Prime Minister away and not yet fully recovered from his illness and with most of the world's diplomats either on holiday or only just returning to their desks it has been left to Sir Simon Mann to bear the burden of what must surely in the future be seen by historians as one of the decisive meetings in post-war diplomacy. It is true that the present talks were occasioned ostensibly by the crisis in the Middle East and the dissension between Moscow and Peking. But the context is much wider, and it is to the lasting credit of the two principals that they have seized the opportunity thus presented.

No praise can be too high for Sir Simon Mann. As Foreign Secretary he has in the past come in for a good deal of criticism: it has been said that his methods are too sedate, too conventional, for the speed of the modern world. It looks now as if such prognostication could not have been proved more wrong. During the past weeks Sir Simon has shown us the value of patient effort, dogged determinism, and a brilliant aptitude for spotting the crucial occasion. His qualities are the traditional ones now so often despised – an unshakeable reason, an optimism, and an ability to work hard for the best while not being scared by the prospect of the worst. There is no other politician in the West better equipped with these qualities, nor is there a task at the moment which more calls for them.

At the same time credit must be given to Dr. Korin who also and with much more reason let it be said has come in for hard knocks from his critics. But now is not the moment either to go into the past nor find excuses for it. What is of importance in the present is the lessening of tension and the withdrawal of troops in Central Europe. Without the change in Dr. Korin's attitude over the last two years perhaps the people of this country would not take kindly to the present proposals: but let it now be said clearly that Dr. Korin is as vital to these negotiations as they are to the peace of the world. It would be helpful if those individuals and organisations who profess to care about peace would think carefully on this, and would then perhaps extend to Dr. Korin that respect or even welcome which is traditionally given to those willing to risk their own political future for the sake of a wider issue. What is required amongst young people of today is more of an attention to practical issues and less of a romantic attachment to the past.

Sir Simon laid the paper to one side. He hovered over it a moment with his red pencil then replaced it in his pocket. Then he took up another piece of paper and read –

It was a fine summer morning when tall, fair-haired Mary Mann decided to go on the ride that made news round the world and might affect history. Mary went out against the express orders of her father and of security chief Wedderburn: but Mary is a schoolgirl (Harpenden, Herts, £520 a year) well used to disobeying the letter of the law. At Harpenden today Vice-Principal Miss Helen Boddy said 'Mary is a spirited girl. I wouldn't say she looks . . .

Sir Simon began to skip

. . . left the house at 9 a.m. . . . no one . . . at Wool-combe corner . . . by mid-afternoon . . . identity . . . was taken to Oak Tree Cottage which stands in rough ground away from the road on the Aldington estate. In a bare room with old iron bedstead . . . roof . . . in the kitchen . . . being taken with the utmost seriousness by the authorities. Suggestions that it is part of just another student's demonstration have been largely discounted. Mary says she was kidnapped and kidnapped she . . . One of the peculiar features . . . by people who took

175

good care she should get no . . . It is still not certain
how . . . horse . . . fed through the . . . woke . . .

Sir Simon screwed the piece of paper up and hurled it
into the daisies. He took a sip of coffee. Picked another
piece of paper and read –

Oak Tree Cottage is the scene of intense activity.
Police are keeping away onlookers who have arrived in
large numbers. Likewise Hassington Grove has the
appearance of being in a state of siege. Sir Simon Mann
goes to London today for the presentation of St. Georgi's
flag to the people of London, but behind the high wall
which surrounds the Hassington estate Sir Simon's staff
and his family are saying nothing.

. . . the purpose of the abduction can only be . . .

. . . on identity of the culprits which . . .

. . . it is probable that the true story will never be . . .

. . . Peter Ferec, 25-year-old student, was in Bagley
Wood on Saturday afternoon. Why? Peter Ferec, son of
a Central European father and Irish mother, was born
in Gradov in 1941. Both parents disappeared in 1949 –
in what circumstances is not known, as with so much of
this story. Peter Ferec was taken to a state orphanage in
Gradov. In 1955 contact was made through the International Refugee Organisation with Ferec's grandmother, who had been making enquiries for him and
who lived in this country. He was allowed to leave the
country of his birth during this period of general East-
West thaw. He came to live with his grandmother at
Baldon, Norfolk, and finished his schooling there. Later
he was apprenticed to the engineering firm of Loveboy.
His grandmother died in 1960. Since then he has
revisited the country of his birth at least once – in 1961
when he attended a rally of the League of Youth in Lov.

The question remains why was Ferec in Bagley Wood
at the time . . . his Saturday afternoon outing to . . . he
says, the motor-cycle scramble at . . . From there he
rode across country to the station at Aldington. It was
on his way there that . . . but Ferec, like the other prin-

cipals in this story, is not available for questioning. He was driven last night to a secret address by police and neither last night nor this morning . . . except for his one brief appearance at Cowdsdon police station. In fact it is the secrecy around this case that gives rise to . . . Why it could not be divulged for instance . . . surely a case for complete . . . tomorrow . . . is it not coincidence . . .

Sir Simon screwed the paper up and hurled it into the daisies.

Gazing through the conservatory windows, towards the dark valley and the distant line of oak trees, he saw on the near horizon of green Mary in her blue shirt walking and behind her the man in the blue suit. Carefully, in order not to attract attention, Sir Simon picked up pieces of paper and shielded his face as if he were reading. He put his hand horizontally in front of his eyes to make a roof from his face to the paper: through a narrow slit like a defence-work he saw Mary's long legs in the white socks and the pale skirt go round a corner; the man in the blue suit following her.

He sipped some cold coffee with a hand held underneath the cup like a tray.

He read –

Memorandum of disposition of military forces and installation in WPP on 30 June 1965 . . .

When he looked up again he saw hopping on the path in front of the conservatory a rabbit, its head down by its paws, its face red and swollen with disease. It pulled itself along on its front legs while its back legs quivered slowly after them. Sir Simon gripped the sides of his chair and raised himself and began moving quietly along behind pelargoniums. There was a large parasol propped by the door into the garden. Sir Simon took it; went out. Outside the evening sun was in his eyes; the rabbit had hopped to the edge of the lawn and was nibbling grass. Sir Simon went up to it, held the parasol round the ends of the prongs, put the spike against the back of the rabbit's neck, raised

177

the parasol and brought it down hard. The rabbit quivered. A man had come along the path and was standing just beyond the rabbit, watching. Sir Simon turned the parasol round and gripped it by the spike; the prongs lethargically opened. The rabbit stretched its legs out. Sir Simon swung another blow with the handle and caught the rabbit on its back and it rolled over. He beat it on the head. The prongs flicked up the gravel.

The man on the path said 'That took a lot of doing!'

Sir Simon rested with his hands on the spike; drew his moustache back from his teeth and said 'Who the hell are you?'

The man said 'Carstairs B.T.V.'

Sir Simon said 'Talk Queen's English can't you?'

The man had a small spectacled face above a huge body. He seemed to have found chewing-gum in his mouth; groped with his tongue.

Sir Simon shouted 'Who gave you permission to come into my house like some bloody peeping tom to take I suppose a picture of my daughter in her bath?'

The man put a finger into his mouth; sucked it.

Sir Simon raised both arms and shouted 'Out!' The prongs of the parasol flapped open.

The man turned sideways and gazed across the valley. Sir Simon picked up the rabbit and held it by the back legs. He advanced on the man with the rabbit held in front of him. The man walked away. Sir Simon threw the rabbit and it hit the man at the back of the knees. The man stopped and looked at the rabbit on the gravel. It still kicked. Sir Simon, smiled, as if he had run someone out in a game of cricket.

39

Peter Ferec lay on an iron bedstead in a room with white-painted wooden furniture and brown-stained boards with a rug. The window looked out on the crumbling wall of a basement area; a yellow space above which footsteps walked like shadows. He lay with his hands underneath his head and his feet crossed. From time to time he arched his body so that his back rose a few inches from the bed. He took deep breaths; becoming slower until it seemed he might be dying.

Wiping stillness over the surface of his mind like mud he began to imagine scenes from his childhood. The windows of the orphanage, yellow with painted brick, had looked out over a railway yard across the wastes of which women had moved hunting for coal. Men stood on the low platforms with wicker baskets containing chickens. Trucks came past with their bumpers clanking, the cold air burned, smoke rose from wooden faces. In the orphanage there had been a laboratory with a case containing ants and their eggs; he had watched them struggling with the soft white things at the smell of chemicals and honey. On the platforms the men had small steel spectacles and hair growing in tufts. In his home there had been the smell of paper and thin clothes: paper all over the floor where the drawers had been turned out. His mother's and his father's desk; his mother's clothes. When they had been taken away he had wanted not to cry, but to kill someone.

His father had had red hair on each side of his head like a clown. He had sat at the head of the table eating stew from a bowl with his sleeves rolled up; had made a sucking noise, his eyes like fish behind his steel spectacles. They had lived in a big block of flats in the only part of the town that had been rebuilt since the war. At the back was a space of rubble with iron railings like those of cattle pens. He crossed it when he went to school carrying food in a satchel with his schoolbooks. He sat with his knees hunched to keep the food secret: bread fell down and birds waited to peck it. There were bodies sometimes at night that lay in the street; vans with low engines that took the bodies away in the mornings.

Once he had stood with his father on a platform and

cheering crowds had raised their faces and the wind came through their brains like cornfields. On the platform they had lifted their fists; short thin men in crumpled suits. When they kissed, their spectacles became flattened against their eyes like snails. Behind the block of flats there was a roundabout worked by an old man turning a windlass. The horses had wild cruel heads with black eyelashes. The wind came through your clothes and burned you like paper. The boys wore peaked caps and long jackets with their arms held close; stood around and watched him eating.

Dark ash came down in the white sky and settled on the snow like fingers. In the block of flats there was heating from a boiler; stone stairs guarded by an iron gate. The wood for the boiler came from rubble; you were not allowed to take wood from the rubble, carrying it under your coat meant death. The wood was hard against the skin; scratched and would not heal there.

His mother cooked in a white bowl with a ladle, her big red arms with the sleeves rolled up. He had said – There are people starving. There were voices in the sitting room; his father's jacket hanging dead on the back of a chair. His father had come through the room without seeing him, followed by the men in brown suits. All his mother's and father's clothes had been left behind in the sitting room and bedroom; the washing-up in the basin.

The orphanage was through a countryside of huge fields and dusty roads like cattle trails. A woman in a grey overcoat had taken him. The fields were cut in wide strips with the women bending over with black handkerchiefs round their heads. In the village people sat outside their houses by puddles like ice. He had asked – Nothing. There were no young people in the village. The vans came with their low engines and collected vegetables.

The windows of the orphanage looked out over the railway yard where the women moved looking for coal. Men had questioned him and had run their fingers through his hair. They had said – Is this your mother's or your father's writing? His mother's backwards-sloping writing in which she did the accounts. They said – Tell us, not your mother's but your father's writing. His father with his squashed steel spectacles when he leaned and shouted at his mother. They had said – It will be better for your mother. A man had taken him into the bathroom; had said – Give me your belt.

In the big block of flats the clothes and the papers had been tidied and the washing-up had gone from the basin. He had stood with his head down and his hands curled at his sides. One of the men had the belt with the soft leather buckle. They had gone to the place where the papers were hidden beneath the floorboards. They had not looked at him. They had run their fingers through his hair. One of them had taken him into the bathroom.

From the orphanage he had seen the railway yard where chemicals and fertilisers were transported. There were the huge plains and the ash falling down like butterflies. Men in grey coats moved across the lines to the trucks where white powder fell out of the cracks in doors. He was a small boy in grey shorts with a belt and grey stockings. His mother used to scrub him in the bath with her strong red arms. He had heard her voice in the sitting room. She had not had time to say goodbye. They had killed his father and his mother.

He was lying in the room in London with the squares of windows floating against the basement wall. There had been the butt of the gun against his shoulder and the front of the large country house and the sights moving up and down across the blue sky and the grassland. He had held his breath: the iron of the rifle against his mouth, his tongue.

At the orphanage they had played a game which was underground in cellars at night with the boiler wrapped up like a mummy. He was shown into the room and the boys were sitting round like candlesticks. He had knelt in the dust with his hands raised and they had held a sword in front of him and he had said – I swear. The sword had writing on it which said – freedom, love, truth. They had given him blood to drink. He had held the cup in his hands and had breathed and it had gone dark and his inside was coming out in fire, a red stream. The liquid in the cup seemed solid; a grey island that was said to be from graves.

He had won a prize at school; stepped on the platform with the faces of the crowd cheering. Later a man had come to talk and he had said – Yes. They had taken him to the station where the silver lines ran into the wheatfields. The man had said – You understand? You will help us? There had been a woman in a grey coat with a white-and-red band on her arm. In England there was the quiet world with borders round it; the villages neat and green and the spires over them like watchtowers.

He had gone back once to the town where he had lived in the big block of flats, and the town was built up again now with cafés full and men leaning over tables and pushing words down each others' throats like hooks. The streets were full of young: fathers and mothers and their families. He had been carrying letters; handing them to a man in shirt-sleeves up the stone well of a staircase; his grey hair growing from his head in tufts. He had said – What more can I do?

At school in England they had laughed at him: said – Go back to where you belong.

In London he had gone to the part where there was a man in a grey mackintosh and children had played on a pond with boats. The man had said – He had been supposed to forget what the man had said. There was the taste of blood and his mother's red arms where she had washed him and where the skin had come off. His father's spectacles were squashed into his eyes and his own heel was upon the glass. The man in the mackintosh had said – We want you to kill. The man had been standing at the corner of the cottage with the girl hanging on to him like a child. The man had said – You have the rifle?

He was lying in a basement in London with the light going darker and the movement like moles above the grating. There was the taste in his mouth as if the skin was coming off and his father's eye which he had his tongue around and the bits of glass cutting him. He could not close his mouth and his palate swelled. It choked him at the back of his throat and he could not breathe, could not live, he would put an end to it. Once he had seen a pig killed; it was held by the neck and tail, under the tail pink flesh like a sea-shell; it had been himself kneeling. He had been in the bathroom and their faces had come down at the back of him like birds. He sat up on the bed and threw himself sideways with his head against the wall; his hands with its nails drawing up his thighs in scratches. He was digging with his fingers at the stony earth for the rifle he had buried; to put the end in his mouth and burst it where his tongue was swollen. He had held his breath so long that he thought he at last would die; then the blood and the grey flesh would be rid of him. He leaned over the side of the bed with his head down and his mouth wide but nothing came out, there was a scuffle on the floor like rats, the pink sea-shell of the pig again and only a slight smell and pressure. He thought – These memories, life, are unendurable; in my head is a darkness like the sun.

40

Colonel Wedderburn and Andrew Seymour and Connie sat in the small room with a tea urn around which there were white mugs and a jug of milk and sugar. Andrew Seymour took from his pocket a flask of whisky and offered it and when the others refused poured some into his tea. Colonel Wedderburn said 'There is no problem, nothing more to be said, it's arranged and just a matter for security.'

Connie said 'Tomorrow?'

Colonel Wedderburn said 'He's got to come, they expect him. I thought the plan was that this use should be made – '

Connie said 'But it's absurd!'

Andrew Seymour said 'What isn't?'

Colonel Wedderburn said 'Can I finish?'

'Certainly.'

'As far as I'm concerned, there's no objection.'

Connie said 'Is that all?'

'Yes.'

Connie said 'But we haven't found out anything. We don't know what happened, who took her, how the boy knew, why they waited, who told the press, who is this boy – '

Colonel Wedderburn said 'I do have information about that which unfortunately I can't divulge.'

'For goodness sake!'

Colonel Wedderburn said 'I've discussed it with Simon, and that's good enough for me.'

Connie said 'What have they found in the cottage?'

'I'll be getting a report tomorrow.'

'I suppose today's Sunday.'

'Yes today is Sunday.'

Andrew Seymour said 'Now let's hold our horses. Connie – ' He smiled.

Connie said 'I'm just trying to ask something basic which I know is unpopular. The question – why. The truth.'

Andrew Seymour said 'People can have odd reasons. Don't we know in our odd life!'

'Why did they just let her go?'

'Why indeed when they could have kept her?'

Connie stared at the ceiling; pressed her lips out.

Colonel Wedderburn said 'But haven't we agreed she's covering up? She probably went quite willingly – '

Andrew Seymour said 'And we've got our own sources of information Connie.'

Connie said 'There's nothing in her diary!'

Andrew Seymour drooped his smile and his lower jaw like Sir Simon did. He said 'Well I've got to get on. Did I tell you Korin's agreed to the basic proposals?'

Connie said 'Do you want me to worry nothing more about her then?'

Colonel Wedderburn said 'Oh I forgot, sorry, Harris,

who was with her this afternoon, got her chatting and says he definitely had the impression she'd been with someone she wanted to protect and was doing this quite willingly.'

'Who then?'

Andrew Seymour said 'Isn't one much the same as another?'

Connie slowly looked from the ceiling towards two corners of the room, down at the table, drank some tea.

She said 'Isn't anyone going to wonder about this boy?'

Andrew Seymour said 'This is politics. Indeed, why are we thanking him? Why has Simon got to dress up like an old queen with make-up to go in front of the telly and tell them a lot of soap? Because they like it. And they'll believe it. They'll believe anything. It doesn't matter how unlikely it is, if it's put on right.'

Connie blew on her tea. She said 'The point is, none of you really want to know what happened to Mary.'

Colonel Wedderburn said 'We spend so much time talking about children. I think it must be put across they aren't of such importance. They can sulk, run away, but ultimately it doesn't matter.'

Connie said 'There's something between Mary and this boy. I saw it in the police station.'

Andrew Seymour said 'I suppose she's a virgin?'

Colonel Wedderburn said 'So much of what goes on in adolescent brains is fiction rather than fact. Freud has taught us that.'

Andrew Seymour said 'You've got too lively an imagination Connie!'

Connie said 'Better than none.'

Colonel Wedderburn shouted 'Touché!' He waved his cup.

Connie, with tears in her eyes, said 'But we're not even trying!'

Andrew Seymour said 'Anyway the purpose of this exercise has always been quite plain. Simon's worried about the hostility in the country, he wants to discredit it and gain sympathy for himself and Korin and this is the chance to make out Korin's opponents the bullies, the wicked kidnappers, and us for once the innocent protectors of the young. And Korin too, That's all.'

Connie said 'By using his daughter?'

Colonel Wedderburn said 'Why in God's name shouldn't he use his daughter?'

Andrew Seymour said 'She uses us. Sitting here like three old witches!'

Connie said 'You're so obsessed with your own schemes – '

Colonel Wedderburn said 'And to cap it Simon's now got to go and spend hours talking to her when he's very tired and has better things to do, because no one else can get anything out of her.'

Andrew Seymour said 'Well said!'

Connie said 'The extraordinary thing is, when you two get together, you each begin to talk like the other.'

Andrew Seymour said to Colonel Wedderburn 'You'll brief them in the morning then?'

Colonel Wedderburn said 'Yes. I'm getting an extra load of men.'

Andrew Seymour said 'Splendid.' He stood up.

Colonel Wedderburn said 'You'll do the mob?'

Andrew Seymour said 'The knobbly mob. The mobbly knob.'

Colonel Wedderburn said 'I'll say goodbye then. A domani!' He went to the door. He did not look at Connie.

Andrew Seymour said 'Attende!' He jumped up and followed. They went out like two schoolboys at the summons of a bell.

Connie was left at the table with her head on her hands; one wrist turned inwards like the neck of a swan.

41

Mary sat in front of a mirror in her bedroom brushing her hair and watching her head jerk from side to side; making faces at her face in the mirror as if it were in pain, having a dialogue with it, the triangular shape with the two lines of straight hair looking out as if from tent-flaps. She put the brush down and held on to the ends of the hair and pulled as if it were bell-ropes; pushed out her bottom lip and glowered. Behind the mirror were pale curtains with dark folds and ghosts. She wore her pink pyjamas with lace frills round her neck and wrists and ankles. By crossing her forearms in front of her throat she could make her head look as if it had been cut off and was on a cushion.

Appearing to hear some noise above and behind her and getting up from the stool and being drawn across the room as if to the edge of a stage she arrived at the door, acting surprise; put a finger in her mouth, bit it, crossed her legs and stood on the outside of her ankles. She opened the door and looked out on an empty passage. There was an unshaded bulb above a staircase. She put her hands behind her and pulled down her pyjama jacket. Closing the door, and going to the middle of the room, she did an arabesque; held on to the back foot and pulled it towards her neck; drew her breath in. Then she walked to the bed and picked up a telephone and dialled two numbers and said 'Connie?' Then – 'Oh nothing, do you know where she is?'

She had lifted one foot on to her lap and was looking at the sole; leaned down and bit a piece of skin off.

'No, I'm in bed. Going to sleep.' She spat through half closed lips. Shouted 'Good night!' Put the receiver down.

Sitting up on the bed cross-legged, her feet on her thighs, she listened, held her breath, closed her eyes, watched the insides where there was an area of grey and a white band and dim lights changing. Curves came down from the top corners and bulged. Behind were scraps of sentences that did not quite turn into words. A man's hand was over her mouth and she bit it. It tasted of bread. There was the man's arm from which she had hung. He had had short square fingers and a gold ring. On the cinder path through the nettles.

She let her breath out, pressed her hands to the sides of her head and said aloud – 'Help!'

She rocked herself forwards on her knees and with her head on the bed looked through her legs, her feet still on her thighs, a pressure in her throat as if she were being strangled. She was an arch with trains going over her. She put her arms behind her back and clasped them. She was a cellar under the stairs with feet stamping. Footsteps were coming along the passage. For a moment she got the sound confused with her imagination; she was stuck, could not move. She forced her hands away from her back and pushed, rolled on to her back, her feet still on her thighs. She dragged at them. There was someone at her door turning the handle. The top of her pyjamas had come out at the waist. She was sweating, her knees in the air.

The door opened and her father came in. He looked at the bed. He seemed bewildered.

Then he held his arms out dramatically.

She struggled off the bed: ran and buried her face against his waistcoat.

He stroked her back.

They began walking towards the bed, three-legged; taking care he should not step on her toes.

He said 'Helen of Troy! In the firing line. Won her medals early. What?' He laughed.

They sat on the bed, his arm around her, his face drawn back from her hair. He said 'All the king's horses and all the king's men. They didn't hurt you?'

She said 'No.'

'You're sure?' He felt her arms and sides.

'Yes.'

'They didn't do anything?' He cleared his throat.

There had been the scene when he had come in at the door. Mary had been on her back, sweating, her legs in the air.

He said, 'You must tell me. You know?'

She had her mouth against his watch-chain. She wanted to cry.

He said 'Who was it? Nelson the Neanderthal? Conrad and the Cavemen?'

Mary shouted 'Oh Dad!'

He said 'Not?' He laughed, making the sucking sound behind his moustache.

She was holding her breath again; beginning to tremble.

He said 'There. Home now. Safe and sound in piglet ground.' He squeezed her.

She watched his waistcoat where a bit of her spittle was falling, the gold chain like an umbilical cord against a black shroud. He patted her. She pushed herself away and sat up, stroked her hair down the side of her face into a pyramid.

He said 'Cover yourself up.'

She shouted 'All right.'

His face became hurt. He said 'This may be important.' She tucked her jacket into her trousers. He pursed his mouth. He said 'There are things going on, you know. Big things. All a great bore, a great nuisance. But you've got to tell me.'

She said 'What's a great nuisance?'

He said 'There are always some things in politics which are a great nuisance but unavoidable.' His hand still touched her leg. He said 'I understand you made a promise.'

After a time she said 'Yes.'

'I think it's been explained to you how we all sometimes have to say things we don't believe. There's nothing wrong in that. It just means you're not bound to them.'

'But I did believe!'

He said 'I think you've got to be guided in this by people of greater experience. There are so many other things involved. Affairs of immense complexity.'

She said 'Don't you believe in promises then?'

'This sort of problem crops up every day. We have to accommodate.'

She said 'Then what's the point?'

'If it does a great deal of damage – '

'But if it doesn't – '

He said 'Let me finish.'

'All right.'

His eyes drooped. 'If it does a great deal of damage, there's moral wrong in keeping a promise.'

'But if you know it won't.'

'You don't know it won't.'

She said 'I do.'

He moved from the bed and walked over to the chimney. He arranged one foot in front of the other. He took out his watch and laid it in his palm as if it were liquid. He lowered his head and gazed at her. She was hunched on the bed looking fat. There was a scene like this in a play: the strong father and the ill daughter on the sofa. He said 'You're going to tell me who you were with. Now.'

She said 'I don't know.'

'Quick.'

She said 'Students.'

'Who?'

'I don't know. I was going through the wood.'

'And they took you and you didn't see them.'

'Yes. One was short and dark and another was tall.'

'How many?'

'Two or three.'

'And they took you in a van?'

'Yes.'

'Then why are you keeping it quiet?'

She shielded her face by dropping her hair down.

He said 'Did you put up a fight or just give in?'

She lifted her head. 'Of course I put up a fight!'

'Have you got anything to show for it?'

'Yes.'

'What?'

'This.'

She pulled up a trouser leg. There were scratches, and a burn from the exhaust of the motor-scooter. It was red and blue round the edges. Her leg was white, with large pores. There was an impression of scentlessness. He said 'Have you had anything on that?'

'No.'

'Why not?'

'I didn't want to make a fuss.'

He said 'Did you see the number plate of the van?'

'BXC or something I think.'

'And they kept you in this cottage?'

'Yes.'

'Did you stay of your own free will or did they make you?'

She shouted 'Of course they made me!'

'Then why won't you help us?'

She rolled over on her stomach. He watched her. She said 'Oh all right they didn't!'

'Why do you say that?'

She said 'It makes no difference what I say!'

He said 'I'll tell you why it makes a difference. You've been a bloody little nuisance. You've had the entire police force after you for two days when they've got better things to do, much better things to do, and I'm not putting up with any tantrums from a schoolgirl now.'

She banged her head from side to side; showed her teeth.

He said 'What?'

She shouted 'They were going to kill me!'

There was a vein pulsing in his cheek like a tap dripping; moving through his head, his eyes, to where she lay on her stomach; into the dark, a waste pipe, with pale hairs around it.

He said 'Then what does this mean?'

She rolled on to her back: gasped 'Oh you're so stupid!'

He sat down and put a hand on her side. He said 'Come along. You're safe now. Absolutely.'

She shouted 'What would you care!'

He pulled at her.

She resisted with her arm in front of her eyes as if protecting herself from blows.

He tried to lift her head with a hand under her cheek, smiling.

She shouted 'All right I'm a bloody little nuisance!'

He pulled at her neck: tickled and said 'This little piglet went weenie weenie weenie . . .'

She screamed 'Sod off!'

He pulled his lips back from his teeth as if in a high wind; laughed quietly at the back of his throat; held her with one hand at the back of the neck and the other on her hip. His face crumpled as if he were weeping.

She waved her legs, twisting sideways and breaking away from his hands and rolling to the edge of the bed and standing and seeming to spin there like a firework. Then she swept all the objects on her bedside table to the floor. A china lamp fell and softly broke; the bulb flared, separated from the body and rolled. She moved to the dressing-table and hit with the flat of her hand against the mirror: some bottles and brushes slithered away like mice; the mirror teetered on the brink with flapping arms. She put her hands in her hair and pulled. Sir Simon came over and held her by the elbows. He seemed on tip-toe; perpetually hit in the face by spray.

She could hear a noise in his throat like a clink of metal.

He said quietly 'That's enough.' She hung from his arms; tried to knock her head back and kick his ankles.

He let go with one hand and swung a quick blow and caught her on the hip-bone. His wrist went numb.

She went down on to her knees and folded her hands at the back of her head.

Nursing his wrist, he put his foot against her bottom.

He sat down on the stool at the dressing-table. The dark curtains were behind him. The bed, with the counterpane off, looked like the scene of a murder. The wings of the mirror still swung so that lights flashed past. On a stage again, the woman at his feet, the dagger in his hand, the fallen curtains.

He said 'We do care about you. We care very much. I know it's not easy. You've got to grow up without a mother and this is very hard. When your mother was alive we were very close. I was able to leave a lot to your mother. She was a person of great sweetness and light. Since then, I'm afraid it hasn't been the same for you. We've all been a bit lonely. We all miss her very much.'

Mary had not moved. His hair was wild and his white shirt twisted at the neck.

He said 'Everyone in life takes these hard knocks. And now you've had to take another. I'm sorry. It's hard for the children of people in public life. I did my best to keep you out of it. I always wanted to keep your mother out too.'

Mary had taken her hands from the back of her neck and was rubbing her eyes.

He said 'I've always been so very grateful to have had a child.'

Mary said 'Oh Dad.'

She began clambering up. He took her by the shoulders; dragged her up his leg, his thigh, to where she hid her face; leaning back with an elbow on the dressing-table to keep his balance, looking down at her head between his knees, a smell of cheap scent and a memory of a mouth like a rubber band. He stiffened.

He said 'Old girl. You've had a rough time.'

He rumpled her hair; the skin of a dog.

She made a snorting sound.

He said 'All right we won't ask any questions. Not if you don't want. What would you like? A treat? A trip to London? Out on the tiles, Eh?'

She shook her head and pressed it tighter into his thigh.

He said 'What?' He was half on to his back like an oarsman caught in the stomach.

He said 'There's only this one more thing tomorrow. Then we might have a hol. We'll definitely have a hol.'

He heaved himself up and leaned over her. This was another scene, an old man and his daughter at the end of a long life, looking forward to the future, a feather to her lips, over her dead body and his mad eyes –

Mary said 'What's tomorrow?'

He said 'Well this boy's coming down.'

Mary said 'What boy?'

He looked at her head again. Her mouth had made the usual wet patch on his trousers.

He said 'The boy friend. The rescuer. The avenger.'

Mary said 'He's coming here?'

With her face startled as if she had been hit, he said, hurt again, for some reason he did not know, 'Isn't that what you want?'

She said 'Why?'

He said 'Well you said I was going to thank him.'

She said 'I said you were going to thank him?'

'Yes.'

'But I didn't!'

'Well someone did.'

She had pushed herself away. He closed his knees. He said 'Anyway, there it is.' He looked sad and old. 'All you've got to do is put in an appearance.'

He began fingering the bottles on her table. There was one called Dawn: a picture of a robin on a cherry.

She said 'I can't!'

'Why not?'

'Stop him!'

He said 'It's too late now. Why, what did he do?' His face pouted like a child.

She said 'He didn't really rescue me.'

He said 'Oh, what then. Or can I guess?'

She shouted 'Dad!'

He said 'Well sit up, can't you, and stop this hysteria. First it is and then it isn't. First he did and then he didn't. I'm accepting what you say. All of it. But I don't want any more now.'

She said 'But please – '

'What?'

'Nothing.'

He said 'Things are too important for this. We've made our plans and we're sticking to them. If you want to tell me, tell me. If you don't, don't. But tomorrow you'll just be there.'

She sat picking at the carpet. He pulled out his watch and it lay in the palm of his hand. This was the first scene again – A doctor in a frock coat and a prima donna dying of consumption.

She said 'Dad – '

'Yes?'

'I don't know what to do.'

He said 'About what?'

She was pulling a hole in the carpet. She said 'Why is everyone against Korin?'

He said 'Oh there are lots of reasons.'

'But I want to know. Does he torture people?'

He put his watch away. He said 'Torture is always terrible.'

She said 'Why are we making friends with him?'

'There's the history of a thousand years in that.'

'What will he do now?'

'Don't worry – '

She said 'But I want to!'

He said ' -about a naughty old man!' He suddenly lunged forwards and tickled her under the armpit.

She shouted 'Don't do that!'

He laughed, making his clinking sound.

She pressed her hands to the sides of her head. She rocked from side to side.

He said in a serious voice. 'There are many little things we have to do which we don't want.'

'Why?'

'For the sake of the greater.'

She said 'Then where's the truth?'

He said 'Into bed now. Quick. Pig in the poke.'

She shouted 'Don't treat me – '

He said 'I'm afraid in politics you don't have to like

people or trust them, you have to know what is in their interest and of what they are afraid.'

She shouted 'I don't believe that!'

He said 'Good.'

She said 'Something must be trustable!'

He had gone to the door and had his hand on the handle. He turned and saw her kneeling on the carpet as if she were praying.

He said 'You trust someone?'

She said 'Yes.'

He said 'Then that's worth something.'

'Is it?'

'Yes. Cling to it.'

She took a deep breath. She said 'All right.'

He said 'As long as you're responsible.'

He came back and took her by the shoulders, lifted her, and they went three-legged again to bed. He leaned over and tucked her up. She put her arms round his neck: he made a humming noise. He had a hand on her breast; her mouth was pressed against his cheek. The door had come slightly open and he could see behind him into the passage. Connie's room was at the other end; beyond the unshaded bulb on the landing.

42

Peter Ferec lay on the iron bedstead in the room with white-painted furniture and brown-stained boards with a rug. Outside the street lights lit the basement wall so that it gleamed like water. The front door banged; there were footsteps overhead on a landing, stairs. He folded his hands across his chest. Someone was outside his door and listening. There was the moment before the door opened: then someone came in and put on the light. He raised a hand as if about to be hit. A woman's voice said – 'Look at you!'

He turned his face to the wall and drew his knees up.

She said 'Lying there in the dark!'

He turned and let the light come in; saw by the window a girl with long black hair, black jersey, black stockings. She had her face to the window and was looking up towards the street, at the line of railings.

She said 'They're still there.'

He sat up in bed and moved his jaw; banged a fist against his head.

She said 'What will you do then?'

He bit a piece of skin from his finger; spat it between half closed lips.

She said 'Three men in a car.' She came over and sat on the edge of his bed. She said 'You haven't washed!'

He leaned down and pulled at his socks and yawned.

She said 'How are you going to go tomorrow?'

He said 'By car.'

'You in a car!'

'With an escort of cycles.' He smiled. The light was an unshaded bulb from the ceiling. There seemed to be a silver line round his dark head.

She said 'You don't know where you are do you!'

He pushed himself so that his back was against the wall; raised his bottom eyelids into slits and stuck his lower lip out.

She said 'You're like a girl!'

He put out a hand and she ducked off the bed. She laughed. She had a big mouth with big teeth; no make-up except dark circles around her eyes.

She went to the window and took hold of the ledge and kicked her leg back in an arabesque; went up on one toe, floated her arm back. Her skirt dragged at her knees. She dropped her leg, undid her skirt and let it fall to the floor. She wore black tights.

He said 'You'll see.'

'What'll I see?'

She went on doing ballet steps clumsily on the rug; her arms above her head in an oval.

He said 'I may be gone for some time.'

'D'you think they'll put out the red carpet for you? Ask you to stay or something?'

He said 'I got on all right.'

She said 'With a teen-age girl! Disgusting.'

He pulled his feet up on to his thighs and sat crosslegged; straightened his back and closed his eyes. He said 'They're all the same.'

'With you?'

'You'd be surprised.'

'I would.' She held the window ledge with one hand and swung her outer leg counting 'One, two, three . . .'

He suddenly said in a sing-song voice 'There I was carrying the flag up to the government building! Single-handed I took on two enemy tanks! Jumping on the bonnet I wrung the captain's neck!' He made a spitting noise; laughed.

She said 'Is that what you told her?'

'There were some reporters came over in a helicopter from France. They dropped by parachute.'

She said 'They don't drop by parachute.'

'They did.'

'Or why did they come by helicopter?'

He said 'Three in front, two behind, and two on the running board. Whee!' He made a noise like a siren and zoomed his hand to and fro.

She said 'You know, you're too daft!'

He said 'She had big breasts.' He smiled.

She said 'Oh come on, will you?'

He said in a sing-song voice 'He took her down to the dark dungeon and the door closed with a clang! Around the wall were the instruments of his dread profession!' He rolled on his back and kicked his legs in the air.

She said 'What have you been reading?'

He said 'Wham!'

'You're in a dream! Sit up. They've been watching you for days. They even follow me when I go out with the pram.'

He said 'I know.'

She said 'You need a mummy.' She leaned over him.

He said 'Oh, they look after you all right. I'd been in this cottage a day or so, but he came. He's clever!'

She said – 'Who?'

He said 'He had a plan. He was to ring up the papers. I was to keep her. Then I was to say – '

'What?'

'Yes sir, that's what she said to me! Yes sir, I hope I do see him!' He blew a noise through tight lips.

She said – 'When?'

'In I go. Walking on to the platform. They say – Thank you so much! All with their hats off!'

She said 'You're crazy!'

He said 'Come here.'

She said 'I want you to tell me. Seriously.'

He turned on to his side. He seemed to be listening for something. Then he said 'So that's it.'

'What?'

'Who's got hold of you?' He swung his feet off the bed. 'Have you told anyone then?'

She began picking her skirt up off the floor.

He said 'Leave that where it is.'

She said 'Stop it. Shall I get supper?'

She made a dash for the door. He caught her and got his arm round her neck. He said 'I'll kill you.'

She was pulling at his arm with her fingers.

He leaned against her: looked round at the yellow walls. He said 'Why not?' She was kicking at his ankles. Her hands went down and groped at his groin, violently. He fell to one side, dragging her.

She said 'Let go then!'

He lay on his back on the floor.

She got up and brushed herself. She said 'What's got into you?'

He rolled from side to side and chanted 'Oh I won the revolution single-handed!'

She said 'Go back to your girl friend.'

He said 'I will.'

She began combing her hair from side to side facing the

window pane. She put her head close to the glass and looked up into the street. The light came down and made her skin yellow. She had thick lips. He lay and pointed a finger at her and made a noise like a shot being fired. Footsteps went past overhead as if they were treading on gratings. He said 'You'll see tomorrow.'

43

Connie was in her bedroom in front of a typewriter. She typed with two fingers, fast, her eyes flicking between the paper and the keys. Sir Simon, in a dressing-gown, walked behind her. He said 'The more I think about it. You know. We were at the top of the aisle. He took me by the elbow. They wouldn't let him alone. He said he wanted to speak. We went to the vestry. He was trying to say something. He couldn't get hold of the interpreter. I was slow on that. They stopped him. And then what did he say? He said he accepted everything. He wanted me to know. To make it public; to have it recorded.'

Connie had stopped typing. She said 'What do you want me to put down?'

He said 'Nothing. If they did want to do him in they couldn't do better than here. The embassy people. He's popular at home. But here they can blame us even if he is at the embassy. Just one more night. And there's nothing we can do about it!' His eyes gleamed.

Connie said 'What could they do?'

'It's the reactionaries. How to stop the talks, get rid of Korin, and discredit us all in one. Quite an achievement. It's too simple!' He prowled up and down smiling.

Connie said 'Don't you think you see too much?'

'He wanted us to know it before too late. If he can hang on till tomorrow!'

'But they can do it whenever they like.'

'No, we've got to appear responsible. Then they're in

the clear. But if he makes a success of it tomorrow it'll be too late.'

Connie tried to stifle a yawn which made the muscles on her neck stand out and her head shudder. She said 'Have you seen Mary?'

'Yes.'

'How was she?'

'All right.'

'Do you want any more of this?' Connie lifted the paper from the typewriter.

He said 'When they shot Belek, in 1948, they framed it so it looked like western agents. It didn't matter what the assassin said, no one believed him. They didn't even think about belief. When you get to this level there isn't such a thing. You believe what you want.'

She said 'What can we do then?'

Sir Simon said 'If he's here tomorrow, I'm going to beat them at their own game.'

Connie looked at him. His face was transparent with exhaustion, like a thin boiler.

He said 'I can make a big show of friendship. A public circus. Then no one will believe it of us. We're too honourable.' He laughed. 'Then it doesn't matter what they do. They can or can't get rid of him. But everything depends on the show.'

Connie pulled the page out of the typewriter; read through what she had written.

He said 'What a business! Politics has become a commercial for deceit.'

Connie said 'Will this do?' She read 'I think it is fair to say that the ties of friendship that have been established – '

He interrupted 'They think we're no good at it! But we are. What matters is to win. And we're good at that. We've got something which they haven't – a tradition, style, which they despise. Truth. But they're naive. Ultimately, deception is naive.'

Connie put the bit of paper down. Her head swayed like a tree about to fall.

He said 'Oh well let's get back to the hard facts of life!' He took the sheets of paper.

She said 'You should go to bed.'

He said 'I don't sleep much.'

He sat on her bed, reading.

Connie said 'Well if you don't mind I must really.' She went into the bathroom.

He called out through the door. 'What's all this about you and Andrew?'

Connie came to the door of the bathroom and looked at him.

He said 'I mean, Charles Wedderburn?'

Connie walked to the middle of the room and closed her eyes.

He said, reading, 'I'm fond of you Connie. But as Caesar said – I am busy now, my child. Be good and patient.'

Connie went and lay on the bed beside him.

He said 'I've got my own alibi.' He chuckled.

Connie said 'What?'

He said in a drawling voice 'Dear Andrew.'

There were footsteps coming along the passage. Connie sat up. Sir Simon folded the papers and said 'This will do.' The footsteps stopped outside Connie's door: there was a knock.

Sir Simon shouted 'Come in!'

Andrew Seymour put his head round.

Sir Simon said 'Oh Andrew, we were just talking about you!'

Andrew Seymour said 'I wondered – '

Sir Simon said 'Are your ears burning?' He rolled his eyes.

Andrew Seymour said 'The speech – '

Sir Simon said 'All is ready. All is under control. Have you got any complaints Andrew?'

Andrew Seymour stared at him.

'Well we can't hang about, the housemaid might catch

us!' His eyes glittered. He handed the paper to Andrew Seymour.

Andrew Seymour said 'Sorry to barge in.'

Sir Simon said 'Anytime, you're welcome! Have you looked under Connie's bed?'

Andrew Seymour said 'Good night sir.'

Sir Simon said 'Good night, sleep tight!' in a sing-song voice.

After Andrew had gone Connie went to the dressing-table and put her head in her hands. She said 'You shouldn't have done that.'

'Why not? He's an old woman.'

Connie said 'He's loyal.'

He said 'When old Tab was Chancellor and his wife caught him in bed with his secretary, d'you know, he called it bolstering the economy.' He laughed.

Connie went to the door and locked it.

He said 'I was once trying to explain to old Tab how to make love to his wife. Those were in the early days, when he was a young chap, didn't know very much. I was drawing him an anatomical diagram on a piece of paper, when some secretaries came in. We were having a committee on armaments, on some naval gun, I think. And afterwards we found the piece of paper had been taken away with the other military material. Probably used to launch a rocket, what?'

Connie went into the bathroom and undressed. She lifted a leg on to the seat of the lavatory and manipulated between her legs.

He began 'When I was with Howard in the Middle East – '

Connie stopped listening. The hard thing, like cancer, was soft inside her. She came back into the room, turned on a light by the bed, turned off one on the dressing-table, set an alarm-clock, climbed into bed. His voice went on '. . . the unimportant things, how much we are dependent on the little things, at one of the meetings in Rome . . .' She closed her eyes. The bright light shone in her face, there was a tap dripping, they came to look at you every few minutes '. . . when negotiations were going on which would decide the future of Europe . . .' so you could not sleep, you broke down screaming '. . . and it depended on a vote, a single vote, Panelli didn't turn up because his mistress had torn up his trousers. We can work out a plan to its logical conclusion . . .' She felt sleep coming down like a blanket, a dentist's chair, a mask over her mouth like bread. '. . . but my point is, you can still play it by ear if you're attuned, and then it works for you.'

Connie was in a hospital and someone had died. The stretcher was being wheeled along on a trolley. The body had been cut off at the feet. Her legs were standing in water –

He had leaned over her ear and shouted 'Bo!'

She leaped up in the cell with her arms to her face to protect her from blows and the bright light.

He was making his clicking sound, laughing.

She thought – All this is a dream.

He began touching her. She rolled over on her stomach. When they did this to you you became limp. If you became soft enough, you could pretend. Then it might happen. It was only by forgetting that it happened. You remembered it and it went. She was in the cell with eyes through a peep-hole. He was good with his hands, lifting her with one underneath and the other on top of her. She was like a bun, being baked in an oven. She turned her head and looked at him. His face was curiously young; reflecting fire from her back, from a dark furnace.

44

In the lane at the gate through which the cinder path went down to the cottage was a man with hands cupped round a cigarette. A car came up the lane, voices laughed, lights swung through hedges like a scythe. The man flicked the top of his cigarette off and it glowed in the damp grass; he put the cigarette in his pocket. The car stopped; someone made a noise like an owl hooting. The moon rushed from behind clouds overhead and was like a surfboard on dark waves.

People climbed out of the car. There were whispers and choked giggles. A voice – 'Is this it?'

The man by the gate leaned over it. He wore a mackintosh and a brown felt hat.

From the car a tall young man came up through the dark and said 'Oh good evening!' There were girls behind him crouched in the headlights; their arms wrapped like mummies.

The young man said 'Cigarette?' He offered one to the man at the gate who did not move.

The young man said 'Are you police?'

One of the girls by the car called 'Come back do!' She came through the headlights with her hands in front of her like a sleepwalker.

The man by the gate said 'Move along.' The lights made the girl's legs thin as a bird's.

The young man said 'Is this the famous place? Can we look round? What's the story?'

The girl had come up. She said in a screaming voice 'Oh the spooks!'

The young man said 'Can you give us the low-down officer?'

The girl shrieked 'You poor man!'

The man at the gate said 'What are you doing here?'

At the back of the cottage from the dark trees that dropped like breakers there was a faint chink of metal on stone: a cough. The man by the gate turned to listen.

A voice from the car said 'What's up?'

The young man said 'They won't let us in. Isn't it pathetic?'

the girl shrieked 'It's the house of Usher!'

The man at the gate said 'Get that car moving quick!'

The young man said 'It's a public road.'

The man at the gate turned and went down the path towards the cottage. He stopped at the corner and listened again. The moon made the willow trees splash. Behind him there was the voice of the young man – 'Christ, you'd think they owned this bloody country!' The man by the cottage swore. He bent down and felt on the ground and in some rubble found an iron bar. In the valley, under the willows, there was the scraping again; someone digging. He went round the cottage to where the cinder path went down through nettles; put his hand in his pocket and pulled out a heavy torch. He came to a place in the path where boards had fallen across it. Behind him, in the lane, the car's horn blew; there came a shout of laughter. He crouched in the shadows. The nettles above his head were like arches. He could hear movement in the undergrowth beyond him, moving away, breaking sticks without caution. He stood up and shone his torch; the light was a solid bar; he held it at arm's length to one side; called 'Who's that? Halt!' Soft footsteps ran and became fainter, disappeared. He went on down the path and came to the willows; a new track had been made towards a ditch. He shone his torch; leaves were like rain. The undergrowth had been cut and trampled; there were fresh stones, earth, of someone having been digging. He bent and touched the ground; ducked and swung his torch up suddenly. There was the branch of a tree in the shape of an iron bar. He stood up and brushed at his clothes. He went back up the path to the cottage.

Coming round the corner to the front again there was the laughter and the drawling high-pitched voices and the figure of the young man and girl coming down the path from the gate. The young man, in front, whispered 'Watch for the bogeyman' and the girl behind sang 'Bogey bogey bogeyman!' The man by the cottage stepped to one side in the shadows from the moon, waited till the figures were close to him, then squatted, stretched his torch at arm's length, and switched it on and shone it into the young man's face. The young man put an arm up. The man, crouching, with his other hand swung his iron bar so that it hit into the side of the young man's knees. The young man fell. The man crouching switched his torch off and moved back to the cottage. The young man shouted 'God they've bust my leg!'

The man by the cottage let himself in at the back and went up quietly to the first floor. He stood by the landing window against the wall. The moon cut him into squares like a graph. Out in the garden people were moving heavily; whispers went towards the car. The headlights came on; doors slammed; the girl's voice screeched, thin and lisping, 'Oh you bloody man!' Then the engine started and the car raced backwards up the lane. The man in the cottage pulled out of his pocket his half-smoked cigarette.

Holding the cigarette cupped in his hand so that it slightly burned him he went along to the bedroom where there was the iron bedstead with the striped mattress and the rug. He switched on his torch and shone it at the bed. The shadows moved like crowds. He crossed the room and put his hand flat on the middle of the mattress where there was a hollow, slightly damp. He moved his fingers round a piece of leather like star; pulled at it like skin coming off. He bent down and smelled: a bitter dryness. He sat on the bed and switched his torch off.

The gate creaked in the garden; footsteps came down the path again. He moved to the landing quietly and went down the stairs. When he reached the front door the footsteps had stopped. He held his torch ready: another torch moved outside. He pulled the door open and shone his torch in a man's face. The man shone his torch back; blinding him.

The man outside said 'Who are you?'

He said 'That's what I want to know.'

'I don't know you.'

'Should you?'

'I know most.'

'Well you don't know me.'

The man said 'Herald.'

'Got your card?'

The man moved past into the cottage. Flashing his torch round the downstairs passage he said 'Well well well, I could have done with a bit myself. But I'd'ave found meself a better 'ole.'

The policeman said 'Where're you goin'?'

The reporter said 'Not that I wouldn't mind. Lollita mollita. You're alone? They're getting mean. On such a night as this!'

The policeman said 'My mate's gone to phone.'

The reporter said 'What do Z-cars think? It's all publicity? A fate far better than death?' He put on a Scotch accent. 'Wha's the la'est fu' 'in theory?'

The policeman said 'Search me.'

The reporter said 'As the transvestist said at the customs.' He chanted 'Mary Mary fine and hairy how does your pardon me'. He put a hand to his mouth. 'Well was she with the boy friend or wasn't she, you know what I mean?'

The policeman said 'Dunno.'

The reporter went into the kitchen; said 'This is where they were?'

The policeman said 'Hey hey hey!'

'No arms no pack drill as the thalidomide baby – ' the reporter hit himself on the side of the head. 'Stop it!'

The policeman said 'In the bathroom.'

'You don't say!' The reporter went to the stairs.

'Look I'm going to get into trouble for this.'

'At three o'clock in the morning? Oh you lucky boy!'

The policeman put a hand on his arm. 'I could say I called you in. There've been goings-on this evening. Visitors.'

'What sort of visitors?'

'Dunno.'

'We're not supposed to bribe you nowadays are we? You're supposed to be nut cases aren't you? We've sent you mad!' He put his thumbs in his ears and waggled his fingers.

The policeman said 'You could take a message for me, right?'

The reporter said 'And not so much as a mention of twenty – ' He went up the stairs.

In the bedroom they both switched on their torches and swung them round, coming to rest on the bed.

'Do you know – ' the reporter put his hand on the policeman's sleeve ' -at these deb parties, they have to have a man going round afterwards collecting 'em up, the litter, the frenchmen, in a bucket?'

The policeman laughed.

'Do you know – ' he pulled at his sleeve slightly '–the difference between a lady MFH in the dark and an upper class girl?'

The policeman said 'No.'

'One takes a candle to her hunt – ' the reporter put a hand to his mouth and yodelled 'Sweet Val-ent-ine!'

The policeman said 'What's this about publicity?'

The reporter went to the bed. He said 'Well he needs some doesn't he? The old man. They all do. Poor bastards!' He put his hand on the hollow of the mattress and pressed it. 'I'd sooner be a pimp.' He bent down and smelled.

The policeman said 'Look, I've got to get you out of here.'

The reporter said 'Have you seen these?' He sat on the bed and pulled some photographs out of his pocket.

The policeman came over and shone his torch.

There was one photograph of Mary in riding-breeches on the edge of a polo field holding a stick against her leg: another of Mary climbing into the car at the police station taken from the back, the blanket and her jersey pulled forwards, bare skin showing above her riding-breeches, bent forwards into the dark hole of the car.

The policeman said 'I've seen that.'

The reporter said 'Not this you haven't. It isn't out.'

The policeman said 'I know what I'd do.'

The reporter said 'Oh what is England coming to!'

The policeman handed the photographs back. The

reporter put them in his pocket. He said 'Why did they go when the boy found her?'

'That's all now.'

The reporter said 'Haven't I seen your face? Don't I owe you money?'

The policeman said 'You do. But my mate'll be back.'

The reporter said 'Another?'

'Are you trying to influence me?'

The reporter said 'I'm just counting my bridge score!'

They went down the stairs. By the front door the reporter stopped and looked up at the stars. He put his hand on the policeman's arm. He said 'I've got two daughters at home. I feed 'em; dress 'em; and they're out all night. They're fifteen, sixteen.' He jerked his head back: the moonlight rushed over him. 'And if I lay a hand on 'em I'm up with the courts!'

The policeman said 'Give.'

The reporter said 'Never have children.'

45

In the early morning the green- and blue-painted vans returned to the lodge gates of the country house; edged through the cars at the side of the road, the men in mackintoshes still like fireflies, their cameras appearing at the windows of cars like the flash of guns within embrasures. Men in shirt-sleeves and slippers came out to open the lodge gates; policemen waved the vans through. They crossed the rolling park with the grass covered with a low mist, oak trees rising halfway up as if from water, the battlements of the huge house floating like the backdrop to a stage set. On the terrace the urns swam with the silveriness of swans; one figure still behind the battlements like a ghost. The vans went through to the stable yard behind the laurels and when the engines died there was the insistence of pigeons cooing, the immemorial polishing of the morning air.

Stepping out of the vans and opening doors were men in pullovers carrying wire and equipment out from the back, trailing round the side of the house the façade of which was suddenly lit by the rising sun as if through mica. Men walked backwards spinning the wires out on drums: a man in uniform ran from the terrace and put his fingers to his lips. They were in mime, stepping delicately, with just a faint scraping of shoes on gravel.

Below in the valley the boathouse and the lake etched in small feathery strokes were separated by a mist from the line of oak trees far above which was of a different construction, another cloud-world in the sky. The air rising from the valley brought a blast of cold like that from bricks. The scene seemed vertical, covering areas in time like a Japanese scroll.

Mary, from her bed, heard the noise of footsteps on gravel, put her head under the blankets and drew her knees up. She heard the chink of metal; thought – He was burying the gun. He and she had sat in the upstairs room of the cottage after the man had gone: he had told her of his war, his revolution. He had carried a flag up towards the roof of a government building: single-handed he had taken on enemy tanks. When the driver of one had put his head out he had shot him. She had thought – This is real? He had said, with those dark eyes, that hair that came over his face like feathers – Do you believe me?

Connie heard the noise of a peg being hammered into the ground. When she woke she thought, as always, of what she had not done, of her life stretching back like footsteps in mud. She said, as she always said – Today I will do better: today I will love: it is never too late to love. There were footsteps on gravel outside, and planks banging. She struggled out of bed and went to the bathroom and stood with one foot raised on the lavatory. Her head nodded and she had a vision of a scaffold being built. Cold shivered in her like a waterfall. She felt the hard thing soft inside. She said – This is what it is like: impossible.

Andrew Seymour sat up in bed propped by pillows.

There were soft voices outside; the sound of hammering. A pink-shaded light shone by his bed. He had a book propped on his stomach. He read –

Only what is constant is really good; what changes perpetually cannot claim the characteristics of good: that is why they have declared immutability belongs to the ranks of the Eternal's perfections; but virtue is completely without this quality: there are not, upon the entire globe, two races which are virtuous in the same manner; hence, virtue is not in any sense real, nor in any wise intrinsically good, and in no sort deserves our reverence. How is it to be employed? As a prop, a device: it is politic to adopt the virtue of the country one inhabits . . .

His eyes began to close. He was on eiderdowns and pillows in a Turkish room. There was a noise of water and the smell of incense and a sight of inlaid mother-of-pearl. A shuffling of feet in the ante-room; baggy trousers and pointed leather slippers; dark eyebrows and a mouth like blackberries. The book toppled on to his stomach and he woke with a jerk. His heart thumped. Outside an engine started with a slow popping and speeded into a hum.

Colonel Wedderburn was woken by the telephone ringing. He reached out with his eyes closed; flicked round the light switch, a jug of water, telephone cord, pulled it. He shouted into the receiver 'Yes?' swung his legs over the bed and felt for his slippers. He said 'At the back? Another man?' He reached towards a chair, blinked, a dark blue silk dressing-gown with white piping. He said 'Who were the first lot then?' He slipped an arm into the dressing-gown, became entangled, opened his eyes, wedged the telephone receiver against his ear. 'Might have been the press? Digging? Why the devil!' He got an arm through the sleeve and heaved the dressing-gown round his back. 'How can I help it if a man's digging his garden? Right. Goodbye.' Held his finger on the telephone button for a few seconds; released it and dialled three numbers; said 'Harris? What's the report. Fingerprints. Oak Tree Cottage.' He reached for his cigarettes: opened the case by sliding the two halves parallel. 'Yes. Nothing else? What does that mean?' He got a cigarette out, flipped the case shut, found his lighter, flicked. 'Dear God.' Blew smoke about like camouflage. 'All right, never mind.' He put the receiver down; picked some tobacco off his tongue; examined the end of his finger. He moved to the door with his slippers flapping.

Sir Simon was in bed with a dispatch box and papers and a cup of tea and biscuits. He dipped the biscuits into the tea and lifted them and caught the wet bits in his mouth. From outside came the cooing of pigeons; the sound of wood and quiet voices like a cricket match. They were building a platform; a canvas overhead in case it rained. Once he had been skiing and he had come out of the track in the woods where the earth opened and fell away on a long white wave; a cheering crowd at the bottom and himself crouched with the earth hitting him and he holding on till he shot beneath the banner and turned into spray. Then there had been the band and the speeches and the tiredness that was like love. He pushed the tray away and climbed out of bed and went to the window. There was the white valley with the lines of trees at different levels like a screen. An English autumn with the deer walking between moss. Once in the war he had walked on the tops of mountains like this; the sun coming up on a peak two miles away so clear and close it could cut you. The noise of pigeons was five notes rising and falling; a switchback of wistaria. Men were dragging a canvas screen along the gravel. In the snow, speeding over the white edge of the world, he had come down with the last of his strength, a dying messenger. The noise of tanks had started up in the valley; a crowing of cocks, with his bent cap and field-glasses. He looked out across the pink morning to the world of white mist.

He went back to bed, pushed his papers to one side, picked up a diary, wrote – *I shall resign at the end of this year. I have had a good life. I have done most of the things I have wanted to do.*

In her room with pale painted furniture Mary knelt with

213

her knees on the floor and her top half still under the bedclothes. Dragging herself slowly back as if emerging from a whale's mouth she stood, screwed her face up, hopped, walked to a washbasin with her legs apart, felt down her back and sides, kicked off her pyjama trousers, put a foot on the lever at the bottom of a waste-can, lifted finger and thumb, dropped. She turned on the water in the washbasin, groaned, lifted one knee, was icy. Inside was pain. She went to a drawer in the dressing-table and rummaged among soft things, stockings. On the table was a piece of newspaper with an advertisement of a man grinning with lines going out from his head like sunshine. The paper was torn at the edge where a wire had been through it like a hook in his mouth. It had been taken from the pocket of her riding-breeches. She felt the elastic at the back of her waist. She had been squatting in the heat of nettles, the hard crusted things and flies. She felt where a safety-pin pricked her: she held her thumb up and sucked it. The blood tasted sweet. Cold came over her like water; made her shake.

She thought – I must tell them. There was the long corridor by the back stairs. Peter Ferec would come in, his dark hair scraped to a tuft at the back, his white shirt and hands as if tied behind him, his trousers thin like a bullfighter. Her father would be out in the sun on the terrace. She would try to make herself heard. She could not get the words out. Peter Ferec had an aura of darkness round him; it made her faint; he was climbing over fallen monuments with a banner. She had believed him.

In the drawer of her dressing-table, among the soft white things, was her diary. She picked it up. Going to the window she drew a curtain and looked out over the valley to the line of oak trees which were white in the distant air. When the time came she would climb out on the parapet and they would come to the door and she would hold on with her hands behind her. Then she would fly; a falling thing like a banner. They would gather round her as she lay on the gravel: a small crowd which she could see from

above. Her father was pushing his way through; said –
What's happened? she lay with her eyes open and her
mouth pressed against the ground. They said – it's too late
now. They all stood and stared at her. Peter Ferec was in
a dark corner somewhat apart. Her skin was clear in the
pallor of death. She had fallen from the first floor window.
The man in the mackintosh had put a hand over her mouth.
Her father knelt by her dead body. He put his head down
and wept. They picked her up by the shoulders and carried
her round the side of the house to the courtyard. She was
at the window watching them. She was out on the ledge
again; but she could not go back now. She had already
done it. She wanted to call out –. But it was too late. Peter
Ferec was left in his shiny dark coat, his smile like a singer.
Across the valley was the pale and dark line of oak trees;
in front of it the lake and the boathouse clear of mist.

Holding her diary in her hand she opened it for a
moment, read, then hurled it into a corner.

On the terrace below workmen walked to and fro carrying wooden planks and scaffolding and wires. They seemed
to be building a stage or dance-floor for some entertainment.

46

Inside one of the blue-and green-painted vans a man sat in
front of a line of television screens and below them switches
and dials. On one screen was the front of the house and
terrace; on another the side of the house with the path
going round to the courtyard and the stables; on another a
bald man in a corduroy jacket standing in front of a french
window. The bald man raised his arm. The man in the
television van pressed a switch and there was a picture on
a fourth screen of the man with his arm raised in close-up.
The man in the van held an earphone to his head; murmured into a microphone.

The van was at the side of the house on the grass on wooden boards. Other boards had been taken up and piled at the side of the van: where they had lain had made marks on the grass like a railway track ending on an island.

On one of the screens Andrew Seymour appeared. He wore a dark blue suit and carried a briefcase. He stepped out from the french windows and the sun flashed on his spectacles and made a black halo round his head. The picture changed and he appeared in close-up; his long nose and a rather weak chin as if unshaven.

From the door at the back of the van black wires went round the side of the house to the front by the terrace; through an archway to the drive at the back. There was a camera on top of the van and some fifty yards away another in front of the terrace. The man in the van was saying 'Left' and the bald man on the terrace was moving in front of a small construction like a stage. He was festooned with wires which he flicked out behind him.

On another screen there appeared the drive at the back going away over grassland. By the side of the drive were soldiers in battledress and white-scrubbed equipment. The grassland looked oily with a grey elm tree like a ghost. A Land Rover came over the grass; on another screen, taken from the far side, it appeared to be going in the opposite direction. In the Land Rover was Colonel Wedderburn, wearing a tweed cap and grey suit. The Land Rover on the first screen circled round left towards the back of the house; on the second went right and disappeared behind some laurels. It stopped by the back door and Colonel Wedderburn climbed out of both, turned and walked towards himself, getting smaller and bigger.

The man in the van put his head out of the door. The sun dazzled. He pulled from a pocket a pair of dark glasses the surfaces of which became solid like metal. He held one earphone to his cheek and the other earphone flapped like a wig. He appeared blind.

On one of the screens Andrew Seymour was talking to the man in the corduroy jacket. He pointed along the

terrace; nodded; went off with long strides, his jacket like
a tail at the back and his briefcase shimmering. The man
in the jacket faced the camera and held his arms out;
stepped sideways. Behind him at the french windows Sir
Simon appeared. He was holding the sides of his head
where the wind blew him. The bald man touched his forehead and spoke; his bald head flashed like a sun-spot. Sir
Simon looked along the terrace the way Andrew Seymour
had gone. The bald man took him by the elbow and moved
him forwards; they stepped like a dance-couple halfway
across the gravel. The man in the van spoke into the microphone. Sir Simon stumbled a little. Pigeons swept down
above their heads from above the valley. The bald man
moved Sir Simon this way and that like a tailor.

At the back of the house Colonel Wedderburn stood
holding a walking stick horizontally at the back of his
thighs. Andrew Seymour came into the picture loping with
his low tread. They spoke together; turned and looked into
the back door. A group of soldiers appeared behind them;
an officer saluted. They looked to the far end of the drive
where there was movement by the lodge gates, a screen
showing only the flat curves of grassland, small dark haloes
in the distance like explosions. The camera followed these
so that it was as if bullets were kicking earth up; then there
were the tops of cars in front of the ghostly elm tree, black
lights flashing off their roofs as if they were tanks. They
came up over the brow of the hill and into formation and
were signalled by soldiers into a parking space and stopped.
Out of the cars like a debouching army came the men with
cameras, equipment, flashlights, leather cases; heaving the
straps over their shoulders and moving at a run down the
long hill. There was a slight popping from the generator
for the television van in the courtyard. The men reached
the bottom of the screen with flapping coats and twinkling
trousers, getting larger as if coming to the edge of trenches
and bayonets. Then the man inside the van pressed a switch
and the screen went blank; they were obliterated.

On the terrace Sir Simon had turned with his back to

the camera. Someone beckoned from inside the french windows; he stepped in and disappeared. Round the side of the house, from the direction of the stable courtyard, Colonel Wedderburn and Andrew Seymour appeared. They spoke to the man in the corduroy jacket who pointed to the window where Sir Simon had gone in. Suddenly behind them the men with flapping coats and trousers came into the picture; they had outflanked the camera; they were raising their equipment and wading through the darkness at the bottom of the screen as if it were water. Colonel Wedderburn faced them, raised his stick; men in uniform ran round the side of the house with a rope. The cameramen stopped; were herded back to the edge of the terrace where they formed their group, tight, nudging one another and kneeling and seeming to rest their heads on each other's shoulders. Colonel Wedderburn went on through the french windows. Andrew Seymour stood in front of the group with his hands behind his back; he looked like a child in front of a panel of schoolmasters for an examination.

Sir Simon was walking through the corridor with his head down slightly jerkily past the bronze statuettes and bowls of roses and the pictures of battleships with smoke-puffs like white wool. A voice called behind him and he stopped; Colonel Wedderburn came up to him and said 'Can I have a word with you sir?' Sir Simon said 'What is it?' Colonel Wedderburn said 'I've just had information sir that there's a certain confusion sir exactly what did go on at the cottage apparently – ' Sir Simon said in a flat voice, quick, his hands in his pockets, 'What cottage?' 'The cottage your daughter Mary sir – ' Colonel Wedderburn was out of breath as if he had been running or was embarrassed. He said 'It appears the only fingerprints are of your daughter and this boy Ferec; though some efforts have been made to obliterate – ' Sir Simon said 'Yes' flat again, as if concerned to keep one step ahead of Colonel Wedderburn. 'Also there was a certain activity at the cottage last night sir, someone was digging and another party – ' Sir Simon said ' -What are you trying to tell me?' There was a noise beyond the open space under the stairs; a shouted order and footsteps under the archway. 'I don't like this boy coming here sir.' 'I thought you said you did.' 'Yes sir but – ' 'I've got no time for this Wedderburn.' From outside, beyond the courtyard, there was the noise of tires on gravel. Sir Simon walked to the archway at the back under the stairs and Colonel Wedderburn followed. They stood side by side on the inside of the archway bent slightly like footmen. Colonel Wedderburn said 'They appear to have had a meal together.' There was the noise of car doors slamming outside and people talking in the foreign language; approaching the outside of the archway then fading. Sir Simon said 'Who appeared to have had a meal together?' Colonel Wedderburn said 'Your daughter and Ferec.' Sir Simon put a hand to the side of his head and began pressing his hair back. Andrew Seymour came along the passage from the room with french windows; he looked as if he had been running. He said 'Oh there you are!' Sir Simon said 'Where the devil are they?' Andrew Seymour said 'That wasn't them yet sir, it was Grigoriev.' Sir Simon said 'Goddam.' He began moving back along the corridor. Andrew Seymour said 'I've had a message this morning – ' Sir Simon said 'About Goldilocks and the bears?' Andrew Seymour was walking along beside him. Sir Simon turned to Colonel Wedderburn and said 'That's your job, fix it.' Andrew Seymour said 'The Americans object'. Sir Simon said 'Oh they do do they?' He moved on. Andrew Seymour said 'Apparently they've had their own men on to it and know of Korin's – ' Sir Simon said 'Bugger them'. He came to the large room with french windows on to the terrace; on a table was a pile of newspapers which he glanced at and passed. Andrew Seymour said 'They don't trust Korin.' Sir Simon said 'I don't give a – ' beyond the window was the man with the camera on top of the van, pointing it at him like a machine-gun. Sir Simon said ' -tuppenny fart if they don't trust Korin'. He turned back to the pile of newspapers. On the front of each, the underneath ones repeating it as in an infinite series of mirrors, was an enormous photograph of a girl disappearing like the back of an animal into what appeared to be a cave.

Mary came down the big staircase in the centre of the house with its balustrade and panelling and portraits of men in dark coats and pale hair with their chins up and sad eyes. She wore a grey skirt with dark green stockings and a short black leather jacket. She walked on the uncarpeted wood at the side of the stairs trailing her hand down the banisters as if through weeds; at times drawing her feet so slowly that she seemed to be ceasing, her hand going back as on the handrail of an escalator. Her hair was parted in the middle so that it came down in parallels like a Gothic arch from which her eyes peeped out narrowly; they were encircled with black eye-shadow; her mouth had bright red lipstick. There were two men in dark suits at the bottom of the stairs watching her. She smoothed a hand softly down her hair as if it were a knife. The men looked away.

Connie came along the corridor carrying books. She saw Mary and put the books under one arm and waited at the bottom of the stairs with a hand out. Mary was leaning so far into the banisters that it seemed she might fall over; crash to the stone hallway and die.

Connie said 'Are you all right?'

'Of course.'

Mary moved to the bottom of the stairs and stood in a corner by a bowl of roses. She fingered the petals where there were drops of water like pearls.

Connie said 'What is this?'

'This what?'

Mary looked up the corridor. The black eye-shadow, lipstick, made her face savage.

Connie said 'What have you got on?'

Mary said 'Oh do shut up!'

She stroked a finger down her hair, closing it.

Connie said 'This is a very big day for your father. You must understand.'

Mary said 'I know it is.'

'You must try.'

Mary moved off along the corridor trailing each hip as she walked; trailing hands to pull her jacket down at the back.

Connie said 'You know what to do? When Andrew comes – '

Mary went through the doors of the high room with the oval table and the portraits of ladies in pink and yellow and the french windows on to the terrace. Far away, across the valley, was the line of pale and dark oak trees. Her father was standing by a side-table holding a newspaper. From the door, Mary saw an enormous headline MARY –

Connie said quietly 'Go and talk to him'.

Mary began dragging herself round the large oval table, stopping to press the instep of one shoe against the heel of the other, screwing her face up, seeing past her father's blunt hands the heading MARY HOME *Midnight Drama*: putting her hands carefully up to the sides of her face and pressing them. Below the headline was a picture of herself on the edge of a polo field holding a stick against her leg: on another of the papers on the table a huge picture of what seemed to be an elephant going into a cage. Her father did not look at her. His face was grey with hundreds of pink veins showing on the cheeks like confetti. She went to the table and spread the newspapers round and saw herself with the blanket over her head and her skin at the back showing. She read *Battle In -*. A feeling of darkness overcame her like ether; a fountain. The papers were over the surface of the table in shapes of broken wood. Her father swore. Then he said 'Let's look at you.' She tried to turn. Connie was standing beside him. He held the newspaper with the picture of her in which she was bent like someone tortured. He looked over the top of it with his small grey eyes. He said 'Push your hair back'. She raised a hand and dragged it down the side of her face as if this hurt her. He said 'Take that stuff off'. She began to walk very slowly towards the french windows, drooping each hip, putting fingers out to guide her through the spaces and furniture. She reached the windows and stepped out and there was the sun and her clothes sticky. Connie called after her – 'Mary!' and her father – 'Let her go.' she thought – I was going to tell them.

In front was the balustrade and far beyond it the line of oak trees. The air was still and shadows in the trees black. Small figures moved about by the lake and boathouse. A man in a corduroy jacket sat on the balustrade. Beyond the terrace on the left was a van with a camera on top; a man with dark glasses leaning out of the door. At the end of the terrace was a rope with men in uniform and behind it a crowd of photographers. They began calling, working their cameras like machinery. She went to the balustrade and leaned on it and pointed one toe to the ground. The man in the corduroy jacket stood and said 'Good morning Miss Mary.' Andrew Seymour came out of the house and crossed the gravel holding the palms of his hands out. Mary walked away towards the tennis court. The wistaria was like the linked arms of angels; pigeons cooed; on an urn was a white peacock. Far away by the lodge gates there was the sound of motorcycles: she could see them moving with helmets just above the sweep of grassland; behind were two black cars waving as if in spray; then they were out of sight round the house by the stables. At the tennis court there were roses hanging like bodies from the wire: she put her fingers through, pulled against rust and thorns. Connie had come on to the terrace and was gazing after her. Mary went through the tennis court quickly and past the conservatory and into the bowling alley: crossing this she emerged from a door at the far side and was at the back of the house where the drive came past the laurels and the archway to the stables. She stayed in the shadows watching. Men in dark suits were climbing out of the cars; policemen on the motorcycles kept their engines running. There was the man with the bald head and the beard: the men in brown suits all around them. They went into the house. The motorcycles roared. Across the parkland the grass was bright and the elm trees were like rocks and the saplings sentinels. Once in the park there had been deer which had lain under the trees like statues. She had been able to get close to them by walking carefully, treading over the moss and the crust of twigs. They had had soft lips and noses. There had been the feeling of water, their teeth, her inside falling out.

From the lodge gates, beyond the slope dotted with groups of soldiers, another car appeared and disappeared over grassland. when it reached the laurels at the side of the house it stopped; a soldier had his arm out. It turned down through the archway to the courtyard by the stables. Inside was a young man in the back seat; like a singer, or royalty.

Peter Ferec saw through the windscreen the other cars drawing up in front and the policemen on motorcycles; he sat on the edge of his seat, put a hand to his face, ducked, looked out of the back window. His car had stopped just short of a soldier with his arm out. He felt for the handle off the door: there were soldiers in the fields along the drive. The house had battlements like a castle. The soldier had white-scrubbed equipment and a pistol. The car turned left through an archway into a yard. There was a side door with creepers round it like ropes. Beyond was an opening to the side of a terrace and beyond this the line of oak trees. He stepped out. Some men were running round the side from the terrace with cameras; he put a hand to his face. At the back were stables; doors open halfway and the light in diagonals. A man in a grey suit came out from the house and took him by the arm. He remembered him from the police station. The cameras went off like rockets. The man in the grey suit said 'Follow me.' They went into a long stone corridor.

In the quietness there were footsteps going along just in

223

front of him and at each side. The man in the grey suit carried a walking stick horizontally. There were pipes along the corridor like the boiler room of a ship. The man stood aside at a door and he went in and there was a room with a telephone switchboard and an enormous picture of a dog with a bird in its mouth. The man in the grey suit smiled: said 'Just a formality!' He had a red face with a slight hair-lip. Peter Ferec waited. Some men had come in behind him and they bent and felt under his arms and down his sides and he raised his arms slightly. The man in the grey suit brought out a cigarette case from his hip; slid it open with one hand and said 'Have one?' Peter Ferec shook his head. The switchboard had plugs and wires like a defence work. The picture of the dog had large daisies and grass like blades. The man said 'No one bothered you in London?' When he smoked he picked tobacco off the end of his tongue and looked at his finger. There was a har-monium in the corner with yellow keys. A window had bars over it darkened with ivy and creepers. The electric light was one with an unshaded bulb beneath a green-and-white reflector. A man with spectacles came in and said 'Ready?' The man in the grey suit said 'Come along then.' Peter Ferec followed along the corridor. They went through a green baize door and there was a further corridor with a high roof and dark furniture and bronze statuettes and bowls of roses. There was the man with the round face and small pale eyes waiting in the shadows. Peter Ferec turned to look at the wall; there was a picture of old battleships with puffs of smoke like wool. The tall man with spectacles had gone on ahead. The man in the grey suit said 'Oh Grigoriev – '

The man with pale eyes had a hand in his pocket. In the picture of the battleships the sea was in small pyramids like leaves. The green baize door, behind, had a brass plate brown in the centre from fingermarks. The man in the grey suit said 'Would you mind if Colonel Grigoriev – ' He was being taken by the arm back through the green baize door. The man in the grey suit stayed on the far side. The man with pale eyes was alone with him, bending down, feeling along his sides, under his arms, putting a hand in his pocket, standing up and pressing close to him. He had his back against the wall. The pipes were like a laundry. At the far end of the corridor, where he had come in, was a soldier in uniform. The man with pale eyes had taken something out of his pocket and was pressing it on him. His face was close; smelled through cracked lips. He was holding a pistol. Peter Ferec took it. He put it in his pocket. The man in the grey suit put his head through the door and smiled; said 'Right?' The man with pale eyes stood back: his face had disintegrated slightly, a mask about to be peeled off, darkness showing just underneath the edges. The man in the grey suit said 'Come along then.' Peter Ferec followed him. They went back into the corridor with the bowls of flowers and pictures of sailing ships. There was a bronze Japanese horseman with a spear and a big moustache. Men in dark suits stood in an open space by the stairs. He was led through high doors into a room with a large oval table and portraits of women. The man with pale eyes had not come with them. At the far side of the room were french windows leading on to the terrace. Beyond the valley were the oak trees. The man with spectacles said 'Would you like coffee?' There was an urn with a row of thin and fluted white cups. Ferec's hand was in his pocket and his finger through the guard of the pistol. The handle of the coffee cup was like the handle of the pistol. On the table were newspapers spread out with the pictures taken on the steps of the police station. On the terrace was a group of men standing around a microphone: a tall grey-haired man holding his hair back and talking to a man in a corduroy jacket. Wires trailed out behind them. Peter Ferec looked into the coffee cup; twirled it. From the other end of the terrace a group of men in brown suits emerged, moving close round the short bald man with a beard. Peter Ferec turned his back. He held on to the saucer with both hands; the spoon fell. The carpet was red with a maze of yellow flowers and oak leaves. He bent down

225

to pick up the spoon, the blood in his head, the legs of the
table on rollers like cat's paws. The men in brown suits
had gone past the window. There was a woman standing
just in front of him on the carpet. She had thin legs. He
straightened. The tall man with spectacles said 'Oh Connie
this is – ' The woman had short fair hair and a brown face
with silver lipstick. When she shook hands with him she
held his hand and stared. He put his other hand to feel in
his pocket. The man with spectacles said 'Have you seen
Mary?' The woman said 'No.' the man said 'I thought
you – ' then stepped out through the french windows. The
woman had an odd crouching way of standing like English
women did; as if someone was about to come up and kick
them. She said 'Did you have a good journey down?' He
went to the windows. He saw up the terrace to where the
group of men in brown suits had joined the others by the
microphone. They were in front of an awning and beyond
them were the men with cameras. On a van a television
camera was trained on them like a machine-gun. In the
middle, seen from the back was the short bald man with
the beard: Korin. He was shaking hands with the tall man.
The woman said 'It's too strange, Mary has disappeared.'
She had come and stood beside him. Her mouth closed and
opened like a flower. She said 'Shall I take that?' He was
holding something; the coffee cup; clinging to it as if to a
rock face. He let go and stepped out on to the terrace.
Still behind a french window, the doors of which opened
outwards, he could see through the slightly distorted glass
the group by the microphone. The man with grey hair had
moved forwards and seemed to be making a speech. He
was orating to no one. No one was in front. At one side
the cameramen were kneeling and working their elbows
like machinery; at the other the television van stood on its
island. The speech was made to the air, to the grass slope
and the distant line of oak trees. The tall man held a hand
to his hair and his words blew like confetti: 'gratified . . .
trust . . . momentous . . .' Above, pigeons flew in from
the valley and swooped up towards the roof. Peter Ferec

226

looked the other way along the terrace to where there was the wire netting of a tennis court. He saw a girl in a black jacket and a short grey skirt, fair hair smoothly down each side of her forehead like a candle. The man in spectacles was walking in front of her; he turned and put a finger to his lips; went past and joined the group making speeches by the microphone. Mary was trailing her hand along wistaria; she had dark green stockings and flat shoes. The woman, behind him, whispered 'Have you been told what to do?' Peter Ferec put a hand against the window where there was a hinge; the hinge was in seven pieces with a pin through the middle. Mary had come up and was standing close to him the other side of the open french window. She leaned with her back against the creeper and folded her hands; shook her hair back and looked up at the bright sun. Her lower lip projected slightly; a curve of smudged make-up. Her throat was in small soft lines. Peter Ferec moved his hand up the glass and felt where the paint was peeling. There was a small spider on the glass with a red body. Mary bent one leg up and pressed her back down the wall; her cheek moved in the glass as if beneath water. The spider crawled down the side of her hair. Where he breathed his mouth made a small misted mark on the glass. The woman behind him said 'You two!' At the far side of the valley were the dark trees. By the microphone the words blew about like pollen. Mary suddenly turned and looked at him. Her jacket was drawn back from a white silk shirt with pearl buttons. She had grey eyes. She pushed her lips out. He put a hand to his head. In the heat there was the scent of dust, cobwebs, roses. He could not see her properly because of the mist on the glass. She had moved forwards slightly. He put his hand in his pocket. Looking up, he felt the sun on his face burning him.

Mary had seen him as she came round the corner by the tennis court and he was in a dark suit with a dark tie like a rope and his hair brushed forwards so that it was like the underneath of a wing, something nestling. There was light flashing round him as if from the sun; a black halo. She had taken her place beside him with her back to the wall at the far side of the window; she had looked out across the valley and had put her head back. Her father was making a speech to the trees, to the clouds like seascapes. People were photographing and watching. Korin stepped forwards and spoke into the microphone and there was a man in a brown suit just behind him. Korin was reading from a piece of paper; it blew like sparks. Peter leaned back with his face to the sun as if he had never seen it before, as if the clouds had just opened for him. She could not think what to say. Andrew Seymour was coming back from the group by the microphone and beckoning to her. She tried to smile at Peter; her mouth got the movement wrong and it melted. Andrew Seymour took her by the arm. She was being led into the circle of lights, all the eyes on her, the cameras like a firing squad. There was her father holding on to his hair and the man in the corduroy jacket to one side with a microphone and at the back the short bald man with the beard. Her father put an arm round her shoulder. She was under arclights in a daze, the walls of a white yard, herself no longer but moving bravely and automatically. The man with the beard was being introduced to her. She pushed her hair back. He had small dark eyes; a rubbery face; was trying to say something. He held her hand. He had to hold her hand again while the cameramen worked like pistons. The sun was flashing in her eyes from the line of green trees; from the van. It was as if her eyes were blindfolded. Peter Ferec was coming up from the french windows now, led across the gravel by Connie. He was going up to her father. Her father was tall in a dark suit just in front of the microphone. The man with the beard had stepped back and to one side. She was the far side of the microphone from her father. She was alone, with people always watching her. Peter Ferec had one hand in his pocket. Behind was the row of men in brown and dark suits, their eyes looking nowhere. Colonel Wedderburn was standing with his stick behind his back. Beside him, was his face turned to the gravel as if he would not be seen, she saw the man in a brown suit with small pale eyes. He had been wearing a mackintosh. He had taken her by the arm and led her round the side of the cottage. He had blunt fingers with a ring. They had stood and had watched Peter Ferec come up through the nettles. They were on the terrace, now, with the cameras all around them.

The man in the television van saw on one screen Mary alone for a moment at the far side of the microphone and then suddenly stepping across, as if she had been pushed, and standing in front of her father. Peter Ferec had come forwards and Sir Simon reached round Mary and held his hand out. Mary was brushing her hair back from her face. The man in the television van smoked; his fingers over dials and switches flicking them and the people disappearing and appearing at different distances and angles. Sir Simon shook hands with Peter Ferec. Peter Ferec was seen from the back: his head shone. Then Sir Simon stepped aside and gestured towards Mary. Mary stayed facing Ferec; pushing her hair repeatedly behind her cheeks, her ears. Peter Ferec's head, his long dark hair, obscured her. The man in the van pressed a switch and the whole group was seen from the side in long-shot: Peter Ferec with his hand out, Mary standing stiffly just watching him, her strong face with the bones of a monument or soldier. Peter Ferec let his hand fall then he put it in his pocket. Sir Simon was gesturing down the terrace towards Korin. Korin, his short bald head and beard at the level of men's shoulders which made way for him, came forwards. There was another switch in the television van and Peter Ferec's back appeared in close-up, Korin approaching beyond him, smiling, his hand out. Then Mary stepped between them. She held her hands folded in front of her, leaning forwards, facing Peter Ferec again. She frowned. She was in between him and Korin. She was spoiling the picture. There was a switch again and they were seen from the side, the three of them in a line and Korin motionless and Mary and Peter Ferec over against each other like an archway. There was a curious dark light around them; Mary with her legs apart as if she were balancing, her skirt pulled tight above her knees. Korin was moving to get past her; Mary took a step to keep in front of him. Peter Ferec had taken his hand out of his pocket; he held a pistol. He was looking at Korin. On one screen Sir Simon was frozen with one arm out in the attitude of a wrestler: on another Andrew Seymour and Connie were watching Mary. Mary had her hands out towards the pistol as if she would push at it. Peter Ferec had his mouth open; already seemed shouting. On another screen a man in a blue suit had dropped on one knee and had pulled a gun out. Peter Ferec and Mary were in the centre picture like stained glass. There was an explosion. Peter Ferec swung round with his gun. The men in dark suits from the back were running forwards, knocking people down, as if in a riot. One pushed at Korin and fell on top of him. The man in the grey suit seemed to leap-frog Sir Simon; grabbed at Mary. He swung her by the arm so that she was off her feet; she landed on her hands and knees. Peter Ferec was lying half sideways on the gravel holding an arm as if it were separate from him. The hand with the gun in it was limp. He was looking at it quietly on the ground. A man in a brown suit was walking slowly through the crowds like a doctor among wounded; in close-up, he had small pale eyes. He went past Korin, past Sir Simon, to where Peter Ferec lay on the gravel. He looked at Peter Ferec for a moment as if he might be a horse; bent close; then pulled a gun out and pushed it to his head and shot him. The far side of Peter Ferec's head became involved in a soft white circle of mist and light; a sun spot bursting. He flung back his arm; dissolved. The heads of other people around, about to rise, ducked again on the gravel with the new wave going over them. Then they kneeled and began brushing bits off their clothes. Andrew Seymour found he had blood on his face: Connie was picking at fragments of bone and gristle. Men in dark suits were facing outwards in a semi-circle, guns in their hands, looking round at the battlements and the distant line of oak trees. Pigeons were flying away like spent cartridges. Grigoriev still held his gun; he trod over the gravel past Sir Simon, past Colonel Wedderburn, towards Mary. Sir Simon was sitting in the gravel silver-haired as if on a death bed. Mary was on all fours, her head down, as if she were spitting. Grigoriev stood over her. She was running her hands down her hair, picking bits off it, staring at her hands, screwing her face up. She saw the man above her; saw his gun. She put the palms of her hands down on the gravel and looked up into his eyes. She was at his feet; an animal. His eyes were pale and empty. He began to smile. Peter Ferec was beyond him twitching on the gravel; he had drawn his knees up, then was still. The man's smile was in close-up; and Mary, because she was afraid, smiled back at him.

47

Across the long green curve of grassland there were people running bent and jerked like iron filings, hanging on to the sides and straps of their equipment and struggling up the hill to the line of cars just visible below the horizon. The shimmer of heat off the metal was dark and silver; sometimes a figure would slip on the wet grass and fall with one hand to its side; there were cries on the faint air as if of memories and bugles. When the first line reached the top of the hill they jumped into the cars and the cars turned and backed against one another and bowled off with springs bucking towards the drive and the lodge gates. Parallel with them soldiers were moving from their positions on the grass running with rifles at the trail like trotting cavalry; an officer breaking ahead and with a whistle out charging. The first of the bouncing cars shot past him heading for the gates, these being closed now by a scrum of policemen, their helmets like defence-works. When the car arrived the policemen stood in front of the gates with their arms folded;

a man emerged through the sunshine roof of the car and harangued them like a jack-in-the-box. The officer came up from behind trotting with his whistle and the man in the sunshine roof ducked and the car shot off sideways across the grass again with the man's head appearing and disappearing violently. The soldiers turned off and ran along the inside of the boundary wall where there was a row of trees and undergrowth. Other cars came over the brow of the hill skidding at one side and sinking in and out of the hollows: a voice blew distantly in the wind '. . . stay in your . . . please . . . still . . . no one . . .' and disappeared, under engines roaring, two cars bumper to bumper almost pushing each other on the drive. The car with the sunshine roof had gone fifty yards into the park and then hit a tree stump; smoke rose from it lethargically. Men began climbing out, running, ducking towards the undergrowth and the wall. Soldiers trotted parallel. On the drive by the gates a traffic jam had formed; men leaned out of windows and gesticulated; some jumped out and ran along by the wall in the opposite direction to the soldiers; they reached the undergrowth and went through with their arms up as if through fire; came to the wall and stood with their faces to it while other men bent and made hoops with their hands and lifted them and heaved. Policemen watched them; opened the gates and one or two squeezed through to the road. The men on the wall lay across the top and swung their legs and disappeared. Where the car had hit the tree stump the man appeared through the sunshine roof holding his head. The officer with the whistle spoke to him. The man in the roof looked at his hand and bent down and the officer stood on tip-toe and looked at his head. Men were being turned back from the wall by soldiers with rifles. At the traffic jam the heat was waving off the bonnets and men had climbed out and began lounging against the cars and lighting cigarettes. Then suddenly the cars at the back began reversing and went bucking the way they had come. Immediately everyone followed: leaping into cars and bouncing back over grassland towards the long line of battlements. The voice of the loudspeaker came and went on the wind. The front cars reached the sweep of the drive by the courtyard and stopped; men jumped out holding the straps of their equipment like parachutes. They ran through the archway. A man in uniform appeared from the terrace holding his arms out: the men with cameras swerved and began running by the stables. The man shouted an order. They stopped. A man on the roof pointed a sub-machine-gun. The men with cameras walked slowly back towards the archway. An engine roared on the terrace and there shot into the courtyard the green television van with a man on top clinging on to the camera as if it were a catapult. The men in the yard leaped to one side. The van went straight for the archway and the man on top dived on his face and the television camera hit the top of the archway and was knocked off. Men threw their arms up and shouted. The van stopped. The man on the roof slid head first over the bonnet. The television camera was bent on the gravel like a dead giraffe. the men stood round it. One took his hat off. They began lighting cigarettes. On the terrace, there was a tarpaulin being carried away draped over a stretcher.

48

In the small room with the telephone switchboard and the huge picture of the dog Connie and Andrew Seymour and Colonel Wedderburn stood with their fingers on the round table leaning inwards as if at a seance, a tension between them summoning spirits and ghosts. Andrew Seymour said 'But where did the first shot come from?'

Colonel Wedderburn said 'Harris.'

Connie said 'Not Ferec?'

Andrew Seymour said 'No.'

Colonel Wedderburn said 'Grigoriev – '

Andrew Seymour said 'I was right by her.'

Connie said 'The sound came – '

Colonel Wedderburn said 'You can't tell from the sound.'

Andrew Seymour said 'How did he get the gun then?'

Connie said 'Yes how did he get the gun?'

Colonel Wedderburn said 'Two things. One, I searched him. He hadn't got the gun then. Two, Grigoriev searched him. He hadn't – ' He stopped.

Andrew Seymour said 'Then how did he?'

Colonel Wedderburn looked round as if waiting for someone to come in from outside.

Connie said 'Grigoriev murdered him.'

Colonel Wedderburn said 'That's his job.'

Andrew Seymour said 'Or he'd have got Mary.'

Colonel Wedderburn said 'He was after Korin.'

Connie said 'It was Mary who saved – '

They moved slightly apart; like tigers on stools at a circus.

Andrew Seymour said 'One thing's for certain. There's going to be the most almighty row.'

Colonel Wedderburn said 'Ferec had a gun. Harris shot him. Then Grigoriev finished him. We can say Ferec fired.'

Connie said 'But he didn't.'

Colonel Wedderburn said 'We don't know.'

Andrew Seymour said 'It depends what they want. They can blame us – and there's two years' work gone for some lunatic. Or they can make nothing of it. We can even turn it to our advantage.'

Connie said 'But everyone's seen it on television.'

Andrew Seymour said 'People see what they want on television.'

They moved close to the table; kept an eye towards the door.

Connie said 'How many shots were there?'

Colonel Wedderburn said 'Two.'

Andrew Seymour said 'Three.'

Connie said 'We don't even know!'

The door opened and Sir Simon came in. He looked

feverish, as if he were burning. He said 'You're all here. Good. Now let's get this straight. Korin's with his own people. They're in a huddle. Like at a football match. Now I want this straight. We've got ten minutes. Wedderburn.'

'Yes sir?'

'How did he get the gun?'

'I'll find out sir.'

'I'm not interested in your finding out. You don't know. Right. Andrew?'

'Yes sir?'

'He was out after Korin. Mary stood in front of him. Right?'

'I think so sir.'

'I don't care what you think. That's what happened. Connie?'

'Yes?'

'Where's Mary now?'

'I don't know.'

'Find her. No. Wait. Wedderburn – '

'Yes sir?'

'I thought you said that Ferec was Grigoriev's man.'

'I did sir.'

'Funny way he's got of looking after his men.'

'Yes sir.'

'What are you trying to do; get rid of me?' His eyes glittered.

Then he said 'Andrew, they may drop it. Or not. There's no need for this to alter anything. If they play it.'

Andrew Seymour said 'I've thought of that sir.'

'I don't care what you've thought. Try it. There's been too much talk. I want action. I'm not going to let them get away with this. Right.' He shot out of the room, slamming the door behind him.

Colonel Wedderburn said 'Good.'

Connie said 'Where's Mary?'

Andrew Seymour said 'Let's go.' His spectacles seemed to burn with Sir Simon's reflected fire. They strode to the door.

In the corridor they separated, Connie in one direction and Andrew Seymour and Colonel Wedderburn in another. Connie moved towards the courtyard and the stables; saw through an open window men bending over a tarpaulin on a stretcher, moving it at the ankles like a cricket cover. Andrew Seymour and Colonel Wedderburn went the other way through the green baize door and past the space at the bottom of the stairs where there were men in uniform and in blue and brown suits moving aimlessly like leaves; stopped in the further corridor opposite big doors with velvet linings. Andrew Seymour put an ear to the door; knocked. It was opened quickly by Grigoriev. Inside was a group of men in dark and brown suits round a table; their fingers on the surface leaning in as if plotting some revolution.

Colonel Grigoriev said 'Gentlemen – ' He held the door wide. His face was grey. He said 'I hope I caused you no inconvenience by my – '

Andrew Seymour said quickly 'Not at all.'

The men round the table were watching them carefully. Andrew Seymour and Colonel Wedderburn stepped in and the door was closed behind them. Grigoriev said 'I thought it was a question of action first, questions afterwards.'

Colonel Wedderburn said 'Well done.'

Grigoriev said 'The unfortunate boy – ' Tapped his head.

Andrew Seymour said 'Exactly.'

There was a silence. The men round the table were in a circle, caged, without anything to do.

Andrew Seymour said 'We can agree then?'

Grigoriev pulled out a cigarette case. He said – 'Smoke?'

At the back of the room there were people talking quietly. Andrew Seymour thought – Like doctors after an operation.

The room had pale silk furniture with tapestries of Chinese birds and creepers.

Korin came forwards. He smiled. He faced Andrew Seymour and Colonel Wedderburn. He put his arm round

Grigoriev and seemed to hug him. He spoke in the foreign language.

Andrew Seymour said 'What does he say?'

Grigoriev, his face empty, said 'He is thanking me for saving him.'

Andrew Seymour said 'Good.'

They watched him. His spectacles flashed. It was impossible to see his eyes.

Korin began talking again. He was pulling at Grigoriev's waist and laughing.

Andrew Seymour said 'What does he say?'

Grigoriev said 'It is an old proverb of ours.'

'What?'

Grigoriev said 'Scandal is the destroyer of more than reputations.'

Colonel Wedderburn was slightly behind Andrew Seymour, watching Grigoriev. He thought – He is going to die.

Andrew Seymour said 'Right. The boy was a lunatic. He was shot by the security forces – of both sides?'

The men round the table watched.

Andrew Seymour said 'Miss Mary got in front – helped?'

The man in the striped suit had come up and was talking in the foreign language to Korin.

Korin said, in English, 'Certainly.'

'And beyond that we don't know. How could we know?'

Andrew Seymour watched Korin's face. The eyes went away, dreaming, as if his mind was consuming them.

Andrew Seymour said 'We should like to apologise profusely over the alarm and inconvenience –. I am sure Sir Simon would wish me to say – '

Korin's face was like paper going black.

Korin spoke in the foreign language.

The man in the striped suit said 'Please accept our apologies too for causing – '

From the other side of the door, across the corridor, Sir Simon's voice was suddenly heard shouting into a telephone: 'Nothing! No! There's too much to hide!'

Korin said 'Our two great countries!' He raised his hand as if in a toast.

The men at the back of the room were watching Grigoriev rather than Korin. Their hands in their pockets seemed to follow him.

Connie looked in from the passage. She said 'Has anyone seen Mary?'

Andrew Seymour said 'It's all right.'

Connie said 'What is?'

Sir Simon appeared in the corridor. He saw them through the door, paused, his eyes seemed to spin from one to another for a moment like a dying firework; then he strode in, flung his arms out towards Korin, stood dramatically. Korin went to him. They clasped each other by the shoulders, kissed on both cheeks, pulled their heads to and fro like people plucking blossom, their eyes wandering past each other's necks like knives.

Then Sir Simon, straightening himself, put a hand to his heart and sat down. His face was white as a mushroom.

They gathered round him. Korin still had a hand on his shoulder. Connie, Colonel Wedderburn, Andrew Seymour, leaned forwards. Sir Simon slowly doubled up. The group was like some illustration to a moral story of sickness and death in the family.

49

Mary had wandered out into the courtyard with a man in a blue suit following her. She stopped in the sun and put a hand up to her forehead as if wiping something away there. The man in the blue suit took her by the arm and she went limp and then he let go. She went on across the yard where there were black skid-marks on the gravel. Above their heads was something moving on the roof and the man in the blue suit looked up and saw a young man in leather jacket crawling along the battlements. He shouted at him. The man on the battlements dived head first through a window. The man in the blue suit shouted to Mary 'Stay here!' and ran into the house. Mary went quickly across the yard and into the stables.

Inside was a row of looseboxes in one of which was her horse Silver. She stood opposite Silver with her hands behind her back; the horse put its head over the door to her; Mary backed away. She wiped her forehead again. She went into an empty stable where there was a ladder to a trapdoor to a loft. She climbed up and emerged in a space of beams and hay and cobwebs, one small window on the level of the floor. She closed the trapdoor, crawled to the window and looked out. The man in the blue suit had come back into the yard; he was followed by Connie; they both circled and went back into the house. Mary lay on her back and put her hands up and touched a beam. There was a spider with a reddish body; the strands of its web a silver maze. The web was torn in the middle like a sail flapping above the sea.

There were footsteps in the stable below. Mary crawled into a corner behind hay. The steps came to the bottom of the ladder, began climbing up. The trapdoor opened and a young man's head came through. He crawled in, closed the trap and propped himself in a corner opposite Mary. Mary was hidden. He carried a small leather case which he opened and from which he pulled out wires attached to a microphone. He adjusted knobs and began speaking into it quietly. He said 'I am in the loft of the stables of Hassington Grove. The situation is complex. The boy Peter Ferec is dead. It is not known about others. The shots seemed to come – '

Mary suddenly burst out from the hay like an explosion. The young man ducked. Mary stood and brushed at her clothes violently. She said 'There are rats!'

The young man had fallen on his tape-recorder. Swore.

Mary shouted. 'They never clean this place out!'

The young man stared; said 'You're Mary!' He began blushing.

Mary was tearing bits of straw out of her hair.

The young man said 'What happened?' He adjusted his equipment, shaking.

Mary said 'I don't want them to find me!'

The young man said 'Who?'

Mary said 'There's a man follows me like a dog.'

She backed away. She sat on the edge of the hay and crossed her legs.

The young man held out the microphone to her like a lollipop.

Mary said 'They did nothing to stop it! Honestly! They're cretins!'

She put her wrists to her temples and pressed them: looked out between vertical forearms.

The young man said 'Yes?'

Mary said 'I'd seen it for hours!'

The man said 'Who shot him?'

Mary suddenly screamed. 'I knew it was that man as soon as I saw him! I'd seen him before! He was going to kill me!'

The young man said 'Please. Begin again.'

Mary rocked backwards and forwards with her head in her hands. The young man followed it like a pendulum with the microphone.

Mary began picking bits of stuff off her skirt violently.

She said 'I had to. Honestly. No one else would have.' She screwed up her face and began to cry.

The young man looked towards the trapdoor. He said 'Did you talk to him?'

'Who?'

'Ferec.'

Mary stopped crying. She shouted. 'I was with him two days!' Then – 'Oh I'm always saying things that sound wrong!'

The young man said 'Two days?'

Mary said 'Not really.'

The young man took the microphone back. He fiddled with the equipment. He said 'Well what's happening now?'

'They're talking.'

'What about?'

'They wouldn't be serious! They wouldn't tell me anything! They kept playing jokes all the time!'

The young man said 'Jokes?'

'Lies. Calling me piglet, and that sort of thing.'

The young man said 'Piglet?'

Mary raised her arms as if there were heavy weights on them. She screeched. 'They must have planned it the two of them! Everything! It wasn't my fault!'

The young man said 'Of course it wasn't. You're the heroine!'

Mary lowered her arms. She seemed to be listening for noises outside.

The young man said 'This is my big chance, you've got to tell me the story. How did he have a gun? Who was he after?'

Mary said 'What d'you mean I'm the heroine?'

The young man said 'Well you got in the way, didn't you?'

Mary said 'Yes.'

'Well then.'

Mary picked up a piece of straw and began chewing it. She drew her legs up so that her skirt was above her knees.

The young man said 'Who were you with those two days?'

Mary suddenly put her head down and giggled.

The young man looked quickly out of the window.

Mary said 'Oh sorry!' Wiped her eyes.

'Who took you? Who rescued you?'

Mary said in a high pitched voice. 'I couldn't watch it, honestly. He put the gun right to his forehead. The hole at the back's always bigger than at the front. Did you know that? There were bits of brain all over the terrace. I had some on my hair. I couldn't get it off.' She drew her breath in and widened her eyes and pressed a hand between her teeth. Her eyes remained half smiling.

The man said 'Here, you ought to be – '

Mary shouted 'Leave me alone, What do you want?' She stared. Then she yelled 'Are you one of them?'

The young man put a hand on her leg. 'All right now – '

Mary jerked her leg back. She let her breath out in a wail.

The young man said 'I'm going!' He put a hand over her mouth.

Mary went limp. She gazed up at him. When he took his hand away she wailed again, loudly.

He said 'I haven't seen you. I don't want a story!'

He found himself holding her hands and kneeling over her. He murmured 'Get me out of here.'

He backed away to the trapdoor and opened it with one hand. Mary was lying in the hay with her knees up and her hair spread out. She watched him go. When he had disappeared, and the trapdoor had closed, she rolled over and picked up bunches of straw. She tore at them. She took hold of her hair at the back of her neck and held it in a tuft, and began wiping it with the straw violently.

50

Sir Simon sat in a corner of the terrace by the conservatory with a rug over his knees and a panama hat on his head and beside him the enormous umbrella. He had his writing rest propped in front and on it a letter. He had written 'My dear Malcolm, I am sure you will understand if I say that in the circumstances I feel I can no longer – '. He had laid down the pen and was looking across the valley. The line of oak trees was heavy and gold in the evening air, close above the lake and the boathouse with the slope between them brown and bare. There was a slight rush of wind which took leaves like swallows fast and low above grass. Far away were sounds of dogs barking; traffic in a ring of fire.

Beside him evening papers lay unopened face up. The

headlines of each, above photographs, were so huge that they appeared to be advertisements or announcements for some entertainment.

At the far end of the terrace, near the corner to the courtyard, canvas screens had been erected such as are put around lavatories at fairgrounds.

Sir Simon picked up his pen and continued the letter. He had neat writing with long horizontal strokes. He finished ' – for all the kindness you have shown me during the last three years. Yours sincerely.' He signed his name.

He lay back and looked at the distant wall of green. It rustled with a profusion, softness, that seemed to make an emptiness behind; the edges of some dark explosion.

He felt the pain in his heart and pressed his fingers through thin ribs: his life like paper.

He laid down his pen and looked inwards to his mind for some reassurance. There was the English summer day, the cooing of pigeons.

When he opened his eyes again he saw that Mary had come on to the terrace and was walking towards him dragging her fingers along the balustrade. The stone seemed to crumble; she raised her fingers and flicked it off. She was wearing a loose red dress through which her body showed heavily. She looked suddenly much older. Wondering if it was really she, he noticed that much of her hair had been cut off.

He watched till she was close to him: then patted his knee.

She came up sidling like a cat; squatted down on the grass and put her head against his thigh. She looked away over the valley.

He put out a hand and stroked her head: short rough tufts like grass. He thought – Like someone in an asylum.

She held on to his leg below the knee: took deep breaths and sighed.

He said 'You mustn't mind all these stories you know. Don't believe them. Always, without fail, stories get things wrong. We've just got to live through this. Both of us.'

She squeezed and pressed the bone of her cheek against his bone.

He said 'I'll take you away somewhere. Where would you like to go? Greece? Italy?'

She nodded and made a small noise like a screech.

'You can take a term off from school. Would you like that?'

The pressure again: her mouth making a wet patch on his knee.

He said 'You've got to forget about all this. We may never know what really happened. People don't, you know. We imagine we know what's at the back of things, what makes things happen, but we don't. Often, when we look too closely, there's just darkness and confusion.'

Mary had become still, The short golden hair, which he stroked, was dark at the roots like corn.

He said 'What matters are the effects; the future. There are many things I won't ever know, you won't, we won't even try. But we do know something, what we've achieved. You and I. Together.' He squeezed her.

Mary had gone limp around his leg. She swallowed: a movement like swimming against his body.

He said 'Perhaps it's too early to say. But I think most of what I have worked for in these days has been achieved. Things change very quickly. There'll be a great deal of sympathy after this.' He was parting her hair with his fingers; watching her head carefully.

He said 'It is the small things, the irrelevant things, that alter history. Become symbols.'

He waited for her to speak. She seemed to be sleeping.

He waved his hands at the papers. He said 'Even they help in this. This is a mystery.'

When she still did not speak he took her skull in his bony fingers and pressed it as if with pincers and drew back his own lips from his big teeth. He said 'No one is hurt. No one in danger. All is well.' He chanted. 'And because of you!'

244

He tried to turn her head round. She resisted. He said 'You are pleased? You'd like to come away with me?'

She cried 'Yes!' which came out like a screech again.

He let go of her head. He stuck his chin out and gazed across the valley. He said 'I shan't ask you things. We've all been to blame in this. But I'm sure, I know, you've always had good intentions. And you've behaved – ' he blinked ' – honourably.' He had a catch in his voice.

Mary lifted a hand and pushed some hair at the back of her ear.

He said 'That's what counts. That's the symbol. Behind it there's always chaos. But it's that, ultimately, that wins.' He stroked her neck. He said 'Do you understand me?'

She nodded and clung to him like a child.

He said 'At a certain cost, of course.'

From across the valley, where the line of trees shivered like explosions, he looked down at her head where it lay gold on his knee; and he had a revulsion against it, which was of emptiness and the pain in his heart; then a happiness, of its belonging to him like warmth. For a moment he held these two visions of Mary's head quiet and bursting like a sun; and then there was the scene again, her head like corn, a father and daughter in an English summer.

*Also by Nicholas Mosley
and available in Minerva*

Hopeful Monsters

'Quite simply, the best English novel to have been written since the Second World War'
A. N. Wilson, *Evening Standard*

'This is a major novel by any standard of measurement. Its ambition is lofty, its intelligence startling, and its sympathy profound. It is frequently funny, sometimes painful, sometimes moving. It asks fundamental questions about the nature of experience . . . It is a novel which makes the greater part of contemporary fiction seem pygmy in comparison'
Allan Massie, *The Scotsman*

'A gigantic achievement that glows and grows long after it is put aside'
Jennifer Potter, *Independent on Sunday*

'Enormously ambitious and continuously fascinating . . . There is an intellectual engagement here, a devouring determination to investigate, to refrain from judgement while never abandoning moral conventions, that is rare among British novelists – for that matter, among novelists of any nationality'
Paul Binding, *New Statesman and Society*

'Nicholas Mosley, in a country never generous to experimental writing, is one of the more significant instances we have that it can still, brilliantly, be done'
Malcolm Bradbury

'An expansive and liberating adventure of tests, quests, miracles and coincidences . . . It stands as a well-weathered, very benign, widespreading kind of tree, drawing sustenance from the dark earth of a 20th-century experience, and allowing all kinds of unexpected illuminations to shine through'
Michael Ratcliffe, *Observer*

Imago Bird

'An inventive, wickedly amusing coming-of-age novel
. . .Mosley shapes a narrative the way a nuclear
physicist might track a quantum experiment in
thousands of discrete moments, recording his characters'
immediate sense impressions, the gap between what
they speak and what is churning within'
Publishers Weekly

'Nicholas Mosley gets all of it – psychoanalysis, youth-
ful sex, and politics – exactly and hilariously right. He is
ingenious and cunning . . . Anybody who is serious
about the state of English fiction should applaud
Mosley's audacity – his skill is unquestionable'
Frank Rudman, *Spectator*

'*Imago Bird* is a convincing account of a highly intelli-
gent adolescent confronted by a random and discon-
tinuous world'
Peter Ackroyd, *Sunday Times*

'There is a sharp, elliptical quality about Nicholas
Mosley's writing that constantly checks the flow of
words and prevents you letting the story engulf you.
The plot of *Imago Bird* is simple enough: it's the angular
telling that gives it its piercing, metallic quality'
Martyn Goff, *Daily Telegraph*

'Mosley has a genuinely original view of the world,
making *Imago Bird* the most interesting novel I have
read for some time'
Thomas Hinde, *Sunday Telegraph*

Judith

'Switching perspective from one book to another, from
one character to another, from a watchtower to a three-
eyed sheep, from the Bible to a television flickerswitch,
from the immediate to the eternal and back again,
Nicholas Mosley is in the midst of constructing an
answer as tricky and uneven, as holy, as powerful and
as old-fashioned as prayer'
Craig Brown, *Times Literary Supplement*

'*Judith* is perhaps the kind of book we are asked to see as
"new" and call magic realism, although it comes out of
a long and continuous tradition. In this most demanding
kind of writing Nicholas Mosley scores high. The
present-day setting, his heroine's odd perceptions and
the meeting of myth and reality all join together easily'
Guardian

'Nicholas Mosley is a brilliant novelist who has
received nothing like the recognition he deserves . . .
One can only hope that his reputation will some day be
commensurate with the quality of his fiction'
Robert Scholes, *Saturday Review*

Catastrophe Practice

'Mosley has started one of the very few genuinely experimental projects in modern English writing; while others cling to pessimism as if it is the artist's passport, he strives to communicate the real presence of optimism, its subtlety, its secrecy, its apparent incompatibility with the language'
Craig Brown, *Times Literary Supplement*

'Mosley's sequence of novels aims "to make myths about myths" – or to produce fictions in which legend and archetype are wittily paralleled, parodied, tilted at different angles to display what they contain of psychological or social truths. Part of his purpose is to depict the ambiguity and paradox of much human response – to the conflicting claims of mind, body and emotions, or the differing demands of individual and community'
Peter Kemp, *Listener*

'Mosley is that rare bird: an English writer whose imagination is genuinely inspired by intellectual conundrums'
Robert Nye, *Guardian*

A Selected List of Fiction Available from Minerva

While every effort is made to keep prices low, it is sometimes necessary to increase prices at short notice. Mandarin Paperbacks reserves the right to show new retail prices on covers which may differ from those previously advertised in the text or elsewhere.

The prices shown below were correct at the time of going to press.

☐	7493 9145 6	**Love and Death on Long Island**	Gilbert Adair	£4.99
☐	7493 9130 8	**The War of Don Emmanuel's Nether Parts**	Louis de Bernieres	£5.99
☐	7493 9903 1	**Dirty Faxes**	Andrew Davies	£4.99
☐	7493 9056 5	**Nothing Natural**	Jenny Diski	£4.99
☐	7493 9173 1	**The Trick is to Keep Breathing**	Janice Galloway	£4.99
☐	7493 9124 3	**Honour Thy Father**	Lesley Glaister	£4.99
☐	7493 9918 X	**Richard's Feet**	Carey Harrison	£6.99
☐	7493 9028 X	**Not Not While the Giro**	James Kelman	£4.99
☐	7493 9112 X	**Hopeful Monsters**	Nicholas Mosley	£6.99
☐	7493 9029 8	**Head to Toe**	Joe Orton	£4.99
☐	7493 9117 0	**The Good Republic**	William Palmer	£5.99
☐	7493 9162 6	**Four Bare Legs in a Bed**	Helen Simpson	£4.99
☐	7493 9134 0	**Rebuilding Coventry**	Sue Townsend	£4.99
☐	7493 9151 0	**Boating for Beginners**	Jeanette Winterson	£4.99
☐	7493 9915 5	**Cyrus Cyrus**	Adam Zameenzad	£7.99

All these books are available at your bookshop or newsagent, or can be ordered direct from the publisher. Just tick the titles you want and fill in the form below.

Mandarin Paperbacks, Cash Sales Department, PO Box 11, Falmouth, Cornwall TR10 9EN.

Please send cheque or postal order, no currency, for purchase price quoted and allow the following for postage and packing:

UK including BFPO   £1.00 for the first book, 50p for the second and 30p for each additional book ordered to a maximum charge of £3.00.

Overseas including Eire   £2 for the first book, £1.00 for the second and 50p for each additional book thereafter.

NAME (Block letters) ....

ADDRESS...

....

☐ I enclose my remittance for ....

☐ I wish to pay by Access/Visa Card Number

Expiry Date